Dear Reader,

I had a lot of fun brainstorming ideas for this story! The idea of the fake distress call for a burning boat came from a real piece I heard on the news; I wondered who would do something like that, and why? The obvious answer was to cover up another crime, and I ran with that.

But I knew I also wanted to bring in the Ivy Bay Glass Museum. The glass museum in this story is (very loosely) based on the glass museum in Sandwich, the oldest town on Cape Cod. Several people, including my mom, had told me how interesting it was, so I knew it would be fun to read about too.

To research this book, I went to the museum, and it was fascinating. Sandwich used to be a big glassmaking town, and I'd always assumed it was because of all the sand they had on hand with the beaches, but it turns out the sand in that area is not pure enough to use in glassmaking. What the region did have was woods, which glassmakers used to stoke the ovens used in the glass factories. And I learned all about different processes for producing glass pieces. I even got to see a glassblowing demonstration. I loved learning about the history of glassmaking in Cape Cod. If you're ever in the area, it's worth a visit.

But my favorite part of this story to write was Lizzie's wrestling with whether to go back to work. I have a young daughter and a full-time job, and Lizzie's struggle to decide whether to stay home with her children or to accept her dream job brought out a lot of the angst and hand-wringing I felt as I decided—and continue to evaluate—how to balance doing the job I love with supporting the people I love. As more of my friends have babies, it's something I see them wrestling with as well, and though we sometimes make different choices, we are all trying to do what's best for our families. I loved seeing Lizzie work through what this meant for her family, and I hope it feels real to you.

I hope you enjoy reading this book as much as I enjoyed writing it!

Blessings,
Elizabeth Adams

# Secrets of Mary's Bookshop

# Cover Story

SECRETS *of* MARY'S
BOOKSHOP

# Cover Story

*Elizabeth Adams*

**Guideposts**
New York

*Secrets of Mary's Bookshop* is a trademark of Guideposts.

Published by Guideposts
16 E. 34th St.
New York, NY 10016
Guideposts.org

Acknowledgments

Every attempt has been made to credit the sources of copyrighted material used in this book. If any such acknowledgment has been inadvertently omitted or miscredited, receipt of such information would be appreciated.

"From the Guideposts Archives" originally appeared in *Daily Guideposts, 1979*. Copyright © 1978 by Guideposts. All rights reserved.

Cover and interior design by Müllerhaus
Cover illustration by Ross Jones, represented by Deborah Wolfe, Ltd.
Typeset by Aptara, Inc.

Printed and bound in the United States of America
10 9 8 7 6 5 4 3 2 1

# Acknowledgments

I'd like to thank Jonathan Byar for his help understanding the coast guard and how it responds to distress calls. Thanks also to Joey Ruiter for teaching me how to sink a sailboat, and Melissa Langdon for helping me with some banking details. And thanks to Wayne, my own personal computer nerd, for information about tracking down a stolen laptop.

# ONE

---◆◆◆---

Pale winter light streamed in through the oversize windows of the Ivy Bay Glass Museum. The sun had started to set, and from her spot by the wall, Mary Fisher could see the rays of the waning February day cast a soft glow over the quaint shops and quiet streets of the little town. The angled light also lit up the collection of antique vases lined up against the museum's windows, throwing colorful patches onto the wide pine floors of the historic building.

Mary looked around the room at the party in full swing around her. Waiters in tuxedos passed trays of hors d'oeuvres and distributed fizzy drinks in delicate glasses. Big bunches of exotic flowers filled the air with a sweet scent. A string quartet played in the corner, and the murmur of quiet conversation filled the room.

Mary moved to the middle of the museum's main gallery and studied the cut-glass decanter on the pedestal at the center of tonight's festivities. It was crafted of clear, thin, rose-colored glass, etched with elaborate geometrical patterns. Mary leaned in closer and saw tiny imperfections in the glass's surface. According to the information card affixed to the pedestal, this was evidence that the piece was handmade.

Mary imagined a master craftsman had huddled over a blazing furnace, handcrafting this piece. A security guard stationed by the decanter eyed her warily. Mary leaned back, and his shoulders relaxed.

It truly was a beautiful piece, and—she checked the information card again—it was called the Hamilton Decanter, named after the man who had made it. It was one of the earliest examples of American mold-blown glass in existence today.

Goodness. America was barely even a country when this piece was made, and Cape Cod was still a rugged fishing outpost a day's journey from Boston. There was no electricity, no running water, no real roads, even. This building would have been one of the few in town, and from previous visits to the museum, Mary knew that it had started life as a barn before housing the glassworks and now the Ivy Bay Glass Museum. Looking around at the fancy party here tonight, Mary was reminded how much things had changed since then.

"This is some shindig." Henry Woodrow came up beside Mary. She turned and smiled at her good friend.

"Henry." She leaned in and gave him a quick hug. "I didn't see you come in."

"I just got here," he said, pulling at the knot of his necktie. He had the tie slightly askew, and the sleeves of his shirt were just a little too short. "And I didn't know this was such a fancy affair. I would have worn a sport coat."

"You look wonderful," she said. He really did look handsome in his blue button-down. Even in late February, there was a ruddy glow to his skin.

"Besides, we both know that if you'd realized there would be people in black tie"—she eyed Lincoln King, a quirky documents expert she'd come to know, as he walked by in a full tuxedo—"you would never have come." She reached out and straightened his tie for him.

"You're probably right," Henry said. A group came toward them, looking at the decanter, and Mary and Henry stepped toward the windows to give them space. "Are all of Eleanor's parties like this?"

"Eleanor always likes to do things nicely," Mary said. She looked around the room and found her sister Betty, who was laughing at something Cynthia Jones had just said. She also saw Tabitha Krause, her late mother's best friend, chatting with Eleanor Emerson Blakely, Betty's sister-in-law, who was chair of the glass museum's board of directors. Tabitha's helper Dawn Santiago stood just off to the side, keeping an eye on her. And Mason Willoughby, an artist who owned a gallery in town, was talking to Virginia Livingston, director of the Ivy Bay Glass Museum. All of the town's wealthiest citizens were here tonight, rubbing elbows, and hopefully raising the money needed to repair the glass museum's aging roof.

Mary felt as uncomfortable in this crowd as Henry looked, but she reminded herself she was here for Betty. She knew Eleanor had spent months organizing this fund-raiser and had roped Betty into helping out, and she was grateful Betty had bought tickets for her and Henry. But she knew she stuck out, and she would be much more comfortable at home, reading a good mystery on this frigid February night.

"At least the drinks are free," Mary said wryly as she tucked the small beaded clutch Betty had insisted she carry under her arm and took a glass of sparkling water from a tray of drinks a waiter held out to them. Henry laughed and reached for one as well.

"No plastic cups for this crowd," Henry said, holding a glass in one hand and with the other, reaching for a stuffed mushroom from a tray of passing hors d'oeuvres. He popped it into his mouth and wiped his fingertips on his dark wool pants.

Mary caught her sister's eye from across the room. Betty was now chatting with Taylor O'Connor, a recent college grad whose father owned a manufacturing company in Hyannis. Taylor was interning at the museum this winter—a gig her father's connections had no doubt afforded her. Betty looked away from the young girl and gave Mary an encouraging smile. Betty looked stunning tonight in a pale-lilac beaded dress and a silk shawl. She was always so at ease in crowds, and she knew instinctively how to start up a conversation with anyone.

"This museum is nice," Henry said, looking around the room. "Can you believe I've lived in this town my whole life and I've never been inside?"

"Not once?" Mary shook her head. "Now that's a shame."

Glassmaking had once been a big industry in Ivy Bay, and the glassworks had employed thousands of the town's residents through the decades. The museum chronicled the town's history as a glassmaking center and showcased some of the pieces produced at the glassworks through the years. In addition to the permanent collection of historic glass pieces—vases, pitchers, decorative bowls—there were always new and interesting displays. In one of the smaller galleries at the back of the museum, there was currently an exhibition about modern developments in glassmaking, including fiberglass, optical fibers, and something called Gorilla Glass, which was used to make screens on cell phones. Virginia Livingston did a good job of keeping new and interesting displays rotating through the museum, but Mary preferred the historical collections of molded and handblown glass produced right here in Ivy Bay.

"Misty came here a few times, but…" Henry shrugged. "I'm just a simple fisherman. Pretty glass vases aren't really my thing."

Mary smiled. Henry was so much more than a simple fisherman. He was an entrepreneur and also led tours of the waters around Cape Cod on his boat *Misty Horizon*, named for his late wife. He was also one of the kindest men Mary had ever met. His showing up here tonight was proof of that. She was about to correct him when Eleanor Blakely approached them. She wore a long black crepe gown, and her silver hair was pulled back into an elegant chignon.

"Mary, so good to see you," Eleanor said, leaning in to kiss Mary on one cheek, then the other. She turned to Henry and repeated the gesture. "Henry, always a pleasure. I'm so pleased you both made it tonight."

"This is a beautiful party," Henry said.

"The glass museum is such an important part of this town's history," Eleanor said. "It's our duty to protect it." Her words seemed canned, but she gave Mary a warm smile, and Mary realized that the sentiment was genuine.

When Betty had first married Edward Emerson, Mary had found his sister Eleanor cold, and Mary still struggled to warm up to her, but she often reminded herself that Eleanor was simply proper and believed there was a right way to do things. And for all her faults, Eleanor cared deeply about this town and its history, and much of Ivy Bay's historic charm was no doubt due to Eleanor's care and attention.

"Have you seen the Hamilton glass yet?" Eleanor gestured to the center of the room, where a group of ladies from Betty's book club was examining the decanter. "It's on special loan from a glass museum in upstate New York. Isn't it gorgeous?"

"I did see it," Mary said. "It really is exquisite."

"I haven't taken a careful look yet, but I mean to," Henry added.

"It's so rarely displayed. You really must."

Eleanor's teardrop diamond earrings glinted in the overhead lights as she nodded toward one of the guards, wearing a navy-blue police uniform, who stood close to the decanter. Betty had told Mary that the museum's insurance company had required the guards to be in attendance while the piece was on display, and they had hired several off-duty members of the Ivy Bay police force to patrol the museum tonight. Mary vaguely recognized one of the guards she'd seen wandering the galleries. He was a fortyish man with a brown mustache, from church. Alex something? Or Alan?

"This event must have been a huge amount of work to organize," Mary said. "I'm sure the glass museum is grateful for all the effort you put in."

Eleanor nodded. "I'm glad to be able to help preserve our history. Plus"—she reached out and touched the arm of a young man in a navy-blue suit as he walked past—"I had help. Thomas, come say hello."

The man stopped and turned toward Mary and Henry. He was young, maybe college age, with rosy cheeks and brown hair that came down in a widow's peak.

"Mary, you know my grandson Thomas."

"My goodness, you've grown up a bit since I saw you last," Mary said as she finally recognized him. They'd met a few times over the years at events the Emerson family put on. Thomas had been in high school the last time she'd seen him, at Edward's funeral. Mary knew that he had gone to elite schools his whole life, and, if Mary remembered correctly, was currently at one of the Ivies. Yale, maybe. Or Brown? She'd have to ask Betty. "It's so nice to see you again."

"Thomas has plenty of time on his hands these days while he's staying with me, so he helped me out getting things ready for the fund-raiser," Eleanor said.

Mary paused and replayed the lines back in her head. Yes, it did sound like Eleanor had been making some kind of jab at her grandson, but before Mary could respond, Thomas smiled and held out his hand good-naturedly.

"It's good to see you, Aunt Mary," he said. Mary started to stretch out her hand, but he leaned in and gave her a hug. Mary wasn't technically his aunt, but it was nice of him to call her that. "How is your bookshop?"

"It's going really well. Thank you for asking."

"And how are Lizzie and Jack?"

Mary smiled. It was nice that some young people still had manners these days.

"They're both doing well. Jack is still in Chicago. His daughter Daisy is in high school now, if you can believe it." Thomas widened his eyes as if he couldn't. "And Lizzie and Chad are doing great. They're actually bringing the kids for a visit this week." She'd been looking forward to the visit for weeks, and she felt giddy just saying it. "Lizzie is going to help me in my bookshop while my employee is on vacation."

"That sounds nice."

"And, Thomas, this is Henry," Eleanor said. She gestured for Thomas to extend his hand to Henry, but something about the lines around her eyes and the set of her jaw made it look strained. Mary supposed the stress of putting on an event like this must be getting to Eleanor.

"Your grandmother sure knows how to put on a party," Henry said.

"Henry is a fisherman," Eleanor said. Her pause stretched out just a second too long. "Isn't that charming?"

Mary saw Henry put his glass to his mouth to stifle a response. Eleanor must imagine that Henry sat out on a dock with a fishing pole on sunny summer days. Henry worked hard, getting up extremely early most mornings and heading out to sea in all weather.

"I do enjoy it," Henry said, but he met Mary's eyes, and she saw that he'd found Eleanor's comment highly amusing.

"You must have so many interesting stories."

"I suppose I do."

"Well, I'll leave you all to chat," Eleanor said. Henry met Mary's eyes again and smiled. "But, Mary, Henry, thank you so much for all your support for the museum."

Surely Eleanor knew Betty had paid for their tickets to the event tonight and aside from a few entrance fees, Mary had never given any financial support to the museum. But Eleanor was the consummate hostess. She gave them one last nod and then moved toward a group standing by the gallery entrance.

Beyond Eleanor, Mary saw Chief McArthur walk into the gallery through the double doors that led out to the lobby. Mary had known him when they were children and had worked with the police chief on several mysteries since moving back to Ivy Bay—she had become, much to her own surprise, a bit of an amateur sleuth these days.

The police chief said something to Maureen Rowe, the museum's only other paid employee besides Virginia, who was manning the check-in table by the entrance to the gallery. Maureen was in her early forties, and Mary had met her a few times around town but had never really spoken to her at length.

Maureen turned and gestured toward the center of the room, and the police chief nodded and started walking toward the glass piece. He looked strangely out of place here, hurrying across the floor among the men and women dressed in their finest. He headed straight for the guard standing near the Hamilton glass and then leaned in and said something quietly.

"So, do you fish here in Cape Cod Bay?" Thomas asked Henry.

Henry started to tell Thomas about his fishing business and his boat, but Mary was distracted watching the police chief talk to the guard. The chief's jerky movements and the

way he kept looking around the room made it clear that he
was agitated. She saw the guard look around, spot the other
off-duty officer who'd been wandering the museum, and
gesture for him to come over. He hurried across the floor,
and then Chief McArthur said something to both men.
They both hesitated and then started walking toward the
door. Strange, Mary thought. Eleanor was not going to be
happy they had abandoned their posts.

Henry was explaining about his side business giving
tours of the waters around Ivy Bay when Chief McArthur
started walking across the room. People turned to look as he
clomped across the floor, and Mary watched his long strides as
he came up next to them and stopped next to Henry. Henry
looked up, eyebrows arched.

"Excuse me," the police chief said, gesturing for Henry to
step away from Mary and Thomas. "Henry, can I speak with
you for a moment?"

"Of course." He set his glass down on a table to his left
and turned to Thomas. "If you'll excuse me."

He followed Chief McArthur, and they stopped a few
steps away, just out of Mary's earshot. The chief leaned in
and said something quietly to Henry. Henry's eyes widened.

"I hope everything is okay," Thomas said. Mary continued
to watch Henry, who was now nodding and pulling at his tie
again.

For a moment, Henry stood still, frozen. Then he seemed
to spring into action. He started toward the door but suddenly
stopped and turned back to Mary and Thomas.

"I'm sorry. I have to run," he called out. Then he was
rushing for the door. Chief McArthur stopped to say

something to Eleanor and then followed a few steps behind Henry. They both disappeared out of the gallery.

Mary looked around, trying to make sense of what had just happened. Several people were watching the door nervously, and a few groups were whispering about what they had just seen. Everyone seemed stunned.

What in the world was going on?

# TWO

———◆◆◆———

"Mary?" Betty stepped up next to her sister and placed her hand on her arm. She looked from Mary to Thomas and then back to Mary. "What just happened?"

"I'm not sure," Mary said, playing the scene back in her mind to see if she could make sense of it, but nothing new emerged.

Mary looked around the room and saw that Eleanor had taken up guarding the glass decanter herself. She was talking to a group of people right next to the pedestal. Taylor O'Connor was chatting with some of the waiters on the other side of the pedestal. And Mary could see Virginia Livingston hovering nearby, keeping watch over the piece as well, as she chatted with Evelyn Anders, a glass artist who came into Mary's shop sometimes.

"It looks like Grandma has the situation under control," Thomas said wryly.

Mary realized she was still holding her glass and that her fingers were growing icy. She gently set it down on the table, next to Henry's. The condensation on the glass formed a ring around it on the white linen tablecloth.

"That's probably what we should have done from the beginning," Betty said. "No one would dare touch the piece with Eleanor guarding it. I'd be more afraid of Eleanor than those off-duty cops, anyway."

Thomas snorted, and even as bewildered as she was, Mary cracked a smile. The joking eased the tension in the room a bit, and somehow the air felt lighter.

Just then, Mary's cell phone began to ring, and she pulled it out of her clutch and silenced the ringer. She looked at the screen.

"It's Henry."

"Well, answer it for goodness' sake," Betty said, and gestured for Mary to put the phone to her ear. Thomas urged her to do the same.

"Excuse me. I'll be right back," she said, and she walked as quickly as she could out of the gallery. She ducked into the next room, a smaller gallery with a display about the invention of the Fresnel lens.

"Henry?" she said. "What's going on?" She covered her other ear to block out the noise from the party.

"I'm so sorry to run out like that," Henry said. He seemed to be short of breath, and Mary heard a siren in the background.

"Where are you?" Mary asked. She looked out the gallery windows at the now-dark sky.

"At the marina. Mary, there's a boat in trouble out on the water. There was a—" Henry paused, and she heard the sound of a metal gate clang shut and then footsteps. "There was an explosion on board a large cruiser. There are half a dozen people on board—"

"Oh, Henry!" She sucked in a breath. "Are they okay?"

"We don't know. The coast guard picked up their distress call, and the boater said at least one person was hurt and the boat was taking on water." She could tell Henry was moving as he talked, but she couldn't make sense of the indistinct noises she heard. "The problem is, the explosion knocked out the boat's mechanical system. They don't know where they are on the bay, and the coast guard can't get a location on them, so they put out a call for help searching the water. The police are heading out to search too."

"That's why Chief McArthur needed the security guards?" Mary's mind was whirring, trying to take this all in.

"They're police first," Henry said. "The force is short staffed tonight, and Alan McCaffrey is trained in water rescues, so Chief McArthur pulled them in to search," Henry said.

"Of course. And because you know the waters out there so well, he asked you to go out and search as well," Mary said. She thought about Henry, dressed in his good wool pants and his dress shirt, heading out onto the choppy Cape Cod Bay on this freezing night.

"Most people put their boats up for the winter, so there aren't as many people to help search as there would be if it were summer. And the more boats we get out there, the better our chances of finding them quickly." A motor kicked on.

"Will you be okay? Do you need me to bring you a coat, or better shoes, or—"

"I keep a couple of parkas here on deck," he said. "And there's no time to lose. We need to find those people fast, before..." His voice trailed off. "We need to get out there right away and start searching."

Mary's stomach turned, thinking about the poor people, lost and afraid for their lives out there on the dark water. "Go, then. Keep me posted."

"I will," he said.

"And, Henry? Please be careful," Mary said.

"I'll do my best," Henry said. He hung up.

Mary stood still, staring out the big windows of the museum, trying to wrap her mind around what she'd just heard. Six people trapped on a burning boat, lost on the bay. She shivered and said a prayer that the rescuers would find the disabled boat quickly and the Lord would protect the people on board until help arrived. She looked out at the dark night and prayed for safety for the rescuers, and thanked God for Henry, a man willing to drop everything to search for missing strangers.

Slowly, she walked back into the main gallery and told Thomas and Betty what Henry had said.

"Oh, that's horrible," Betty said, going pale.

"Is there anything we can do to help?" Thomas said, setting down his drink.

"I don't think so." Mary shook her head sadly. "Except pray."

Around them, people were standing in clumps, chattering, and Mary overheard someone say something about a boat and an explosion. Word seemed to have traveled quickly. People all over the room were talking animatedly, looking shaken. If Mary had to guess, she'd say that very few people were thinking about glass at the moment.

Eleanor was still standing guard by the Hamilton Decanter, smiling a little too broadly and trying just a little too hard to pretend the fund-raiser hadn't just taken a dramatic turn. Mary had read that even as the *Titanic* sank, the band played on.

Oh—Mary could have kicked herself. That was not a good comparison right now.

"I'd better go talk to Eleanor," Betty said, and Mary nodded. Betty excused herself and strode over toward her sister-in-law, who was now talking quietly with Virginia Livingston, a smile still plastered on her face.

"I wish I knew what I could do to help," Thomas said again. He seemed agitated, as though he were ready to jump into action. "My parents have a boat. Maybe I could get it out of storage and head out and join the search too."

Mary's first thought was that yes, he should join the search party; the more boats the better. But then she looked at Thomas—the smooth, clear skin; the thick brown hair; the hint of stubble on his chin—and remembered he was only a child, really. He couldn't go out there alone on a pleasure boat on a rough night like tonight, even if he could get the boat out of winter storage at this time of night. It was better to leave this to the men who knew these waters backward and forward.

"Henry said the coast guard was on its way out," Mary said, as much to reassure herself as to make Thomas feel better. "And the police are sending out boats. I'm sure they'll handle it." Around them, people were talking more loudly, and several were moving from group to group, trying to find out if anyone had information about the missing boat. What had been a quiet cocktail party was now a room full of people moving around, speculating about the doomed boat's location.

"Eleanor is asking for everyone to carry on," Betty said, coming up to them again. "She doesn't want this to take people's focus away from the fund-raiser, and she asked me to do my best to get people to focus on the museum again." By the way her eyebrows were raised, Mary could see that even Betty doubted that was possible. "And she wanted me to remind you both there will be baskets by the door for donations to the museum," she said. She wouldn't meet Mary's eyes, and Mary could tell that her sister was trying not to smirk.

"That sounds like Grandma," Thomas said. "In that case, can I refresh your drink?" He nodded at the glass Mary had set down.

"That would be lovely." Mary suddenly felt shaky, and her mouth was dry. A cool glass of water would be perfect.

"So what else did Eleanor say?" Mary asked as soon as Thomas was out of earshot. Mary watched him approach one of the waiters and chat with him as he refilled their glasses.

"Oh, you know," Betty said. "Tonight is extremely important for the museum, we can't let this turn of events ruin the party, the Hamilton glass must be protected at all costs, that kind of thing." She waved her hands in a spot-on imitation of Eleanor. Mary laughed a little, but then a somber silence settled over them.

"How bad do you think it is, Mar?"

"I don't know." Mary let out a breath. She wished there was something she could do to help, but she couldn't think what she could do here on land. Still, it would make her feel better to do something instead of stand around and wait. "It didn't sound good," she finally admitted. "Let's just pray they find them soon."

———————

The party wound down early, despite a valiant effort from Eleanor to get the event back on track. Both Eleanor and Virginia had given impassioned toasts about the importance of the glass industry in Ivy Bay history, but it hadn't taken long for the museum to clear out after that, and now, most of the guests were long gone. The overhead lights were bright, and the waiters were gathering up stray glasses and plates. The string quartet had packed up and left, and Eleanor was standing, ramrod straight, next to the Hamilton glass, guarding it as a professional art handler carefully packed the piece into a padded storage crate.

Mary checked her phone. Henry hadn't called. She supposed he was busy and out of range of a cell phone tower. But still, she wished for news.

"I'll just be a few more minutes," Betty called to Mary from the table by the entrance to the gallery, where she was counting the cash and checks from the donation baskets Eleanor had set by the door. Mary waved to indicate that there was no rush. She was anxious to get home, and the strain on Betty's face showed that her sister was tired and ready to leave as well, but Betty wouldn't leave until she had finished her responsibilities.

"Is there anything I can do to help?" Mary asked. Betty shook her head but kept her eyes on the stack of checks in her hands. Then, as she got to the bottom of the stack, she wrote something on the paper in front of her. "Actually, you could take this to Virginia," Betty said, holding up the paper. "I need to take the money to the safe, but Virginia was anxious to see the total. She's in the office." Betty nodded toward a hallway that branched off at the back of the gallery.

"I think I can handle that."

"Thank you." Betty folded the paper in half and handed it to Mary, and Mary could see that her sister's face was pale and drawn. She'd have to make sure to encourage Betty to sleep in tomorrow. She needed her rest or her rheumatoid arthritis would flare up.

The art handler was wheeling the crate down the hallway as Mary approached the doorway. Thank goodness nothing had happened to that decanter tonight in all the chaos. Once those security guards were gone, who knows what could have happened—

Mary had to laugh at herself. She had read too many mysteries. What exactly did she imagine might have happened to the decanter once the guards had left? That Tabitha Krause and Cynthia Jones might have banded together to steal it, one of them tucking it under her arm and them both running through the middle of a crowded party? It was a funny picture, but an unlikely scenario. The guards had probably been there more to keep partygoers from getting too close than because of any real danger that the piece would disappear.

Mary started down the hallway slowly. She'd never been back this way. All that was down here, as far as she could see, was a door that must lead to the museum office and an exit door at the end of the hallway. The door was propped open to allow the caterers to carry trays out easily. Mary could see the dark edges of cars in the museum's side lot. Cold air was seeping down the hallway, and Mary hurried to the open office door.

As she turned to go in, she ran into Maureen Rowe. She bumped right into the younger woman, who was heading out of the office. Maureen's eyes widened, and they both stepped back quickly.

"I'm so sorry," Maureen said, sucking in her breath. "Are you okay?" Maureen was bundled up in her puffy winter parka and purple knitted scarf and had a large tote bag draped over her shoulder. She was obviously on her way out.

"It was my fault," Mary said, waving away her concern. "I wasn't watching where I was going."

Maureen hitched up the tote bag on her shoulder, the fabric stretched tight. "No, it was my fault. I'm in such a rush I wasn't even paying attention." She looked at her watch and laughed a little, but not like she thought anything was actually funny. "I have to go get my kids." Mary had a vague recollection that Maureen had a couple of small children, but she couldn't picture them.

"Well, then, I'd better let you go," Mary said, and stepped back so Maureen could pass. Maureen smiled gratefully and brushed by Mary as she headed toward the open door. Mary watched her for a moment as she hurried down the hall.

Mary didn't know Maureen well, but she seemed tense, on edge. It had been a long night, and everyone was stressed, Mary realized. Maureen readjusted her bag again as she went out the door and vanished into the side parking lot.

Mary turned and stepped into the small back office and found Virginia Livingston standing in front of a sleek, blonde-wood desk, talking to Taylor, whose back was to Mary.

"I really don't know," Taylor was saying, gesturing at the desk. Virginia saw Mary and held up a finger to ask her to wait, and Mary stopped.

"You didn't see anyone else back here?" Virginia said. A small woman, she still seemed imposing in her skirt suit and low heels. Mary could see Taylor shrink back and shake her head.

"No. Not"—Taylor took a deep breath—"not that I know of."

Mary felt awkward listening in on a private conversation, and she started to step away, but Virginia stopped her.

"I'll be right there, Mary."

Mary nodded and looked around the room, trying to focus on something other than the conversation in front of her. It was a small office, and there were sleek minimalist desks with modern office chairs on each of the two side walls. On one desk, Maureen's no doubt, there was a laptop and a handful of pictures of two small boys. On the one Taylor had been pointing at, there was no laptop. Beyond the small outer office, there was a small glassed-in room with the name Virginia Livingston on the door. The whole office was impeccably neat, and there was not a stray paper or unsorted stack of mail anywhere.

"I'm really sorry," Taylor said. "I really don't know what happened. I'll pay for it, if you need, and my dad will—"

"It's okay, Taylor." Virginia sighed. "It's not your fault." She put her hands on her lower back and leaned back. She shook her head. "And if the police can't spare anyone now, I guess there's not much more we can do tonight anyway. Why don't you go home and get some rest?" She turned to Mary and waved her farther into the office. "We'll follow up with Chief McArthur tomorrow."

Taylor, dismissed, turned and hurried to the door. Her eyes were red, and her cheeks were wet, and Mary gave her what she hoped was an encouraging smile, but the girl looked away and hurried out the door.

"Betty asked me to deliver this," Mary said, holding out the paper. Virginia hesitated, looking at the folded paper in Mary's hand. "It's the grand total."

Virginia took the paper, flipped it open, and lifted her glasses to read the number. She stared at the number for a moment and then shook her head, folded the paper, and tucked it into the pocket of her suit jacket.

"Is Taylor all right?" Mary asked. She didn't want to pry, but the girl was obviously upset, and if there was anything she could do to help—

"She'll be okay." Virginia sighed again and grabbed the back of the desk chair next to her for support. Mary saw purple half moons under her eyes. "Her laptop is gone." She gestured to the desk she stood in front of. All that was on it was a lamp, a stainless-steel penholder containing half a dozen identical black pens, and a photo of a small dog. "It disappeared during the party."

"Oh, I'm so sorry." Mary felt her stomach turn. "It was her work computer?"

Virginia nodded. "It belongs to the museum. But of course, the police are all busy searching for those boaters and can't spare anyone to look for a missing laptop, so they can't take a police report until the morning." She gave Mary a weak smile, and Mary could see she didn't mean to be insensitive, but she was tired, just like everyone else.

"Does she have any idea who might have taken it?"

"If she does, she's not saying." Virginia looked down at the empty spot on the desk where the laptop was supposed to be. "What I can't figure out is, why just one laptop?" She gestured to Maureen's desk on the other side of the office. A sleek silver computer was sitting in plain sight on that desk. "Why not both of them? And compared to some of the other stuff in this museum, the laptops are worth almost nothing."

"A laptop would no doubt be more valuable to some people than historic glass," Mary said.

Virginia considered this for a moment, as if she'd never thought about it that way, and then she cracked a smile. "I suppose you're right," she said.

"It sounds like tonight was kind of a bust for the museum overall," Mary said.

"At least nothing happened to the Hamilton Decanter." Virginia laughed, but it sounded hollow. "But no, I won't be sad to crawl into bed and put an end to this day."

"That makes two of us," Mary said.

She and Virginia stood there, smiling for a moment.

"Well, I should go find Betty," Mary said.

Virginia nodded and turned back toward her office. "I'm going to start locking up." She moved toward the glassed-in office, and the overhead lights turned on automatically. "Thank you for coming, Mary."

Mary nodded her head and hurried back out toward the main gallery.

Betty was waiting for her by the table, wearing her black wool coat. "Ready?" Betty asked, and held out Mary's coat.

"Ready."

Mary slipped on her coat, and together they walked out the double doors of the main gallery toward the lobby and the front door. Mary tried not to worry about what was happening on the water. She would hear something soon. For now, all she could do was go home and get a good night's rest. Things would look better in the morning.

# THREE

———◆◆◆———

Sunday morning dawned clear and cold. Mary pulled on a soft flannel robe, knotted it tightly, and slid her feet into fuzzy slippers, but she still rubbed her hands together as she walked out of her bedroom. Mary hadn't slept well, and she yawned as she padded downstairs. She adjusted the thermostat in the living room, and the heater kicked on softly.

She went into the kitchen and started a pot of coffee, then stood at the doors that led out to the deck while she waited for it to brew. The sun was rising over Ivy Bay, and the sky was streaked with fingers of pink. A few high clouds, cast in a rosy glow, stained the sky. The grasses on the sand dunes that separated the house from the beach twisted in the wind; beyond that, white-capped waves dappled the surface of the bay.

She hadn't heard from Henry since the phone call at the museum last night. She checked the clock on the stove. He was usually up early, but he had been out late last night, and she didn't want to wake him if he had managed to sleep in. She looked back out at the water. She wasn't sure what she hoped to see, but there was nothing, just gray-green water all the way to the horizon.

Mary stepped away from the doors and pulled her robe tighter. All she could do was pray.

And, she reminded herself as she took a mug down from the cabinet, that was something. It was probably the most important thing anyone could do.

She prayed for the boaters; by now, she hoped they had long since been pulled to safety. She prayed that any injuries they had would be healed quickly, and that they would be comforted and calmed after what was surely a traumatic night. She prayed that if the search was still going on, the rescuers would be safe. And she prayed that God would be glorified, no matter what happened.

Mary felt a little better as she poured coffee into her mug. Tiny wisps of steam curled up, and the rich aroma comforted her. She stirred in milk, wrapped her hands around the cup and took a sip. There was nothing like that first sip of coffee in the morning.

There were four hours until church. If it had been summer, she might have gone for a walk along the beach, but it was too cold to head outside this morning. Instead, she'd use this time to finish getting things ready for Lizzie and her family.

Mary felt a little thrill. She would see her grandchildren in only—she checked the clock again—six hours, give or take. She'd already put fresh sheets on the beds in the guest rooms and purchased extra food—including the kids' favorite breakfast cereals—but there were some last-minute things she still wanted to do. She took another sip of her coffee and then headed to the hall closet and took down some board games. Lizzie had said Luke was on a Clue binge recently, and Mary thought he might be old enough to try

Monopoly as well. She set out some toys she'd purchased at garage sales. She knew the kids had plenty of toys at home, but she loved finding things she knew they'd like so there was always something new and fun at Grandma's. The cookie jar was empty, so she pulled out the ingredients for peanut butter cookies, one of Luke's favorites, and started to work.

When Betty came into the kitchen half an hour later, the room was filled with the sweet smell of baking dough, and Mary was loading measuring cups and spoons into the dishwasher.

"Are we having cookies for breakfast?" Betty asked, yawning as she headed for the coffeepot. She wore a cornflower-blue robe over her nightgown, and matching slippers, and her hair was neatly arranged. Mary couldn't understand how Betty always looked put together, even just after she rolled out of bed.

"Only if we promise to save some for Luke," Mary said. "Otherwise, you get to explain that you ate all his cookies."

"Well, I would hate to disappoint him." Betty poured a cup of coffee and inhaled the warm steam that rose from the cup. "How about an omelet instead?"

"That sounds wonderful." Mary finished loading the dishwasher and leaned up against the white tile counters. The sweet smell of baking cookies mixed with the earthy aroma of brewed coffee. It was marvelous.

"Any word on the boaters?" Betty asked as she pulled the carton of eggs out of the fridge. One of the photos Betty had taped to the fridge slipped out of place, and she adjusted it as she looked for more ingredients.

"Not much," Mary said and pushed the morning edition of the *Ivy Bay Bugle* she'd retrieved from the porch across the counter. "The paper has an article about it. Lieutenant Peters is on the case on the coast guard side, and we already knew the police were looking, but there's no update. I guess they hadn't found anything by the time the paper went to press." She tried to keep the edge of disappointment out of her voice. No news was probably good news. "Do you think it's still too early to call Henry?"

She glanced out the kitchen window, which was coated in a fine layer of steam. The sky was a soft blue now, and wispy clouds scudded across the sky.

Betty pulled a tomato and a red onion out of the crisper. "Why don't you text him?" She let the door of the fridge shut softly behind her. "Ask him to call you when he wakes up."

"That's a good idea." Mary dug her cell phone out of her purse and typed a message on the screen.

A moment later, the phone rang. "Hi, Mary," Henry said. He sounded tired. "I wasn't sure if you were up yet, so I didn't want to call, but I'm glad you got in touch."

"Have you been up long? I know you were out late last night—"

"Actually," Henry said, "I was just leaving the marina."

"Just leaving?" Henry spent most mornings out on the water, but he didn't usually work on Sundays.

Mary saw Betty's eyes widen.

"You haven't been out all night, have you?"

Henry was quiet for a moment. She could hear wind whipping around the phone. Then he said, "We didn't find them, Mary."

Mary felt her stomach turn. Betty pulled a chair out from the kitchen table and lowered herself into it.

"Well, that doesn't mean they're not okay." The words sounded hollow to Mary's ears, but maybe they were true. "No one knew where they were, right? They could have drifted..."

Henry sighed. "That's what I want to believe." Mary heard the scream of a seagull. "But I'm exhausted, so I'm going home for now. There's a new police team heading out to relieve the men who've been out there all night. Hopefully, they'll find the boaters. Otherwise, I'll go back out and look this afternoon."

"Good," Mary said. "I'm glad you're going home to get some rest."

"I hate to leave the search, but it doesn't do anyone any good if I'm so tired I'm making mistakes out there."

Mary could hear the disappointment in his voice, so she tried to be encouraging. "You're very smart to play it safe." The timer for the last batch of cookies went off. She shut it off quickly and turned off the oven. "And you're not going to try to come to church, are you?"

Henry hesitated, then said, "I'm afraid I'll probably sleep through it this morning."

"Good. You need your rest."

"Yeah. Hey, I'm at my car now, so I should probably go. But thanks for touching base. After a rough night, it's nice to hear your voice."

"You too." Even when Henry was dead on his feet, he could still say just the right thing. "I'll talk to you later."

"Bye," Henry said, and then he hung up.

"They didn't find them?" Betty said it so softly that at first, Mary wasn't sure she'd said anything.

"No," Mary said simply.

Neither one of them seemed to want to say more. They both knew every moment that passed made it more unlikely the boaters would be found safe and sound.

"Then we'll pray," Betty said. And once again, Mary was so thankful to be living with her older sister, who always knew what to do.

———

"That was a beautiful service," Betty said as she drove down Main Street after church. There were people gathered outside the Black & White Diner, but most of the little shops along Main Street were closed on this cold Sunday morning, and it was calm and peaceful.

Mary nodded, though she couldn't actually remember much of what had happened during church. Between worry for the boaters, concern for Henry, and excitement about Lizzie's arrival this afternoon, she probably hadn't been focusing on the service as much as she should have.

"It was really nice how Pastor Miles prayed for the boaters," Betty said.

Mary did remember that. During the segment of the service where they prayed for the needs of the community, Pastor Miles had lifted up the missing boaters, and he had also prayed for the brave men and women who had spent the night searching and were still out on the water now. There had been reports that at least one of the rescuers had been injured during the long night, and they prayed for protection for those who remained.

"Yes, that was nice," Mary said.

Betty laughed as she slowed for a red light at the intersection with Route 6A. "You weren't paying attention at all, were you?"

Mary felt her cheeks flush. Her sister knew her too well. "It was difficult to focus," she admitted.

"What time are Lizzie and Chad getting here?" The light turned green, and Betty eased her car forward.

"They were leaving after the early service at their church, so they should be here soon."

Betty flipped on her blinker and turned right onto Shore Drive. The Walinski boys were playing football in the street, and they reluctantly moved when they saw the car. As Mary and Betty passed, the kids filed back into the road, and Mary looked down the street toward their house. There was a gray minivan in the driveway. Her heart sped up.

"I think they might be here," Betty said, laughing, as Mary's seven-year-old grandson Luke saw their car and came flying down the grass toward them. He had grown since Mary had seen him last. He was taller and lankier, and his curly hair was longer. Betty pulled into the driveway and stopped behind the van, and Luke ran up to the car, shouting, "Grandma! Grandma!"

"I think he's excited to see you," Betty said, turning the engine off.

"We've been waiting here *forever*," Luke yelled, and as soon as Mary stepped out of the car, he flew into her arms.

Mary pulled her grandson into a hug and took a deep breath, enjoying the little-boy smell. My goodness, she'd missed this.

"You've been waiting *forever*?" Mary laughed.

"More like five minutes," Lizzie said, stepping out of the minivan. She wrapped her arms around her body and walked toward Mary.

"That *is* forever in little-boy time," Betty said, as she started up the path toward the house.

"Luke, let your grandma breathe," Chad, Lizzie's husband, called as he stepped out of the driver's side of the van. Luke pulled back and ran to his dad's side, where he started jumping up and down.

"Luke, why don't you show Grandma how good you are at doing laps around the yard?" Lizzie called, and the little bundle of energy immediately shot out toward the lawn and started running around the perimeter. Lizzie then walked to Mary and wrapped her in a hug.

"It's so good to see you." Mary pulled her daughter in close. "Thank you for coming to help me this week."

Lizzie laughed. "Are you kidding? The alternative is being stuck in the house with *that* all winter break." She nodded toward Luke, who had his arms held straight out on each side and was making airplane noises as he did loops around the yard. "Thank you for having us," Chad said as he approached. Chad was tall with curly blond hair and an easy smile.

"Sorry to ambush you. Church got out a little early and there was no traffic, so we got here quicker than we expected."

"I'm thrilled you're here," Mary said, pulling her son-in-law close. "And where's that granddaughter of mine?"

"Finishing up a chapter of a book she can't bear to put down," Lizzie said. "Emma, come say hi to your grandma."

"I understand that feeling," Mary said, and her heart swelled with pride that she had another little bookworm in the family. And when Emma yanked open the back door of the minivan and stepped out, her heart swelled again. Her granddaughter got prettier every time Mary saw her. Emma was only twelve, but it wouldn't be long before boys would be beating down the door. Chad had better be prepared.

"Hi, Grandma," Emma said.

"How are you, dear?" Mary remembered the first time she'd held Emma, when she was only hours old. She'd been so tiny, so helpless, with her little tuft of dark hair and fists balled up at her side. She missed holding her precious grandbabies but loved seeing the young people they were turning into.

"Cold."

Mary had to laugh. It was in the low thirties today—not bad for February on the Cape, but not exactly the kind of weather to keep you outdoors.

"Then let's go inside," Mary said.

Chad started unloading the luggage, and soon Lizzie had corralled her family into the house. Luke immediately dove for the pile of games, and Emma disappeared into the living room with her book, while Chad lugged the family's suitcases to the spare bedrooms.

"Sorry for the chaos," Lizzie said.

"Oh, honey. I don't mind the chaos." Lizzie was in the thick of parenting and probably had no idea how much she'd miss this all someday. "I'm just glad you're here."

"It's going to be a good week," Lizzie said.

Mary smiled. She couldn't agree more.

———

Henry called just after lunch to tell Mary there was still no news on the boaters and that he was heading back out to search. Henry didn't say it, but if the boat had been on fire last night, Mary knew the chances of good news at this point were slim, and she was thankful again that Henry was willing to go on what was surely not a pleasant mission. Before she hung up, she invited him to dinner, and he gladly accepted. She suspected he hadn't eaten much since the distress call had come in last night.

Mary spent a lovely afternoon playing Monopoly with Emma and Luke. Chad built a fire in the fireplace, and Betty put on a CD of classic hymns. Through the fogged-up windows, she could hear the Walinski children playing football outside, but she and her family stayed inside the cozy house drinking cocoa and eating peanut butter cookies. She couldn't help feeling a little guilty that poor Henry was out on the water while she was here safe and warm enjoying a perfect Sunday afternoon.

Henry showed up a little before six. He had dark circles under his eyes, but he had changed into khakis and a navy-blue sweater, and he brought a selection of cookies from Sweet Susan's Bakery for dessert.

The kids chattered throughout dinner. Luke amused them all with his elaborate plans for a tree house he intended to build this spring, complete with built-in openings to launch his Nerf gun rockets at "enemies" and a slide for easy exits, and Emma shared about how she'd flubbed a line at the audition for the school's spring musical. Her story was punctuated by dramatic eye rolls and giggles. Chad, really just a big kid himself, egged the kids on, making funny faces and adding sound effects to their stories at inopportune times, and at several points during the meal, Mary was laughing so hard she had to swallow her food quickly to avoid choking.

Henry laughed along with the rest of them, but he seemed distracted. Mary could see that he was far away, thinking about something beyond this table. A few times, Mary saw him look out the window toward the beach.

After dinner, as the kids cleared the table and Chad and Lizzie loaded the dishwasher, Mary asked Henry if he'd like to step outside for a minute. Henry nodded and followed her out to the deck.

The air was cold and dry, and the sky was a deep silvery blue, dotted with thousands of tiny stars. Mary handed him a quilt from the stack they kept out here during the winter months, and Henry wrapped the thick handmade blanket around his shoulders and walked to the handrail at the far side of the deck. It was a still night, and the sound of the surf pounding against the hard-packed sand beyond the dunes was peaceful.

"No one found them." Mary intended it as a question, but it didn't come out that way, and she realized she wasn't holding out hope anymore. By the tired, resigned look in his eyes, she suspected that Henry wasn't either.

"Not a trace."

"With all those boats out there searching? No one found anything?"

Henry clasped his hands together and rested his forearms on the railing. "The coast guard thought they had a lead at one point when they found some scraps of wood floating in the waves. But it turned out to be just debris that had fallen over the side of a tanker."

"You must have covered most of Cape Cod Bay with that many boats." Mary shivered and pulled a quilt tighter around her shoulders. She wanted to ask more about how he felt about the search, what he was thinking about on that long night alone on his boat, remind him that it wasn't his fault that he hadn't found the stranded boaters. But she didn't want to push him. Like many men, Henry tended to keep his feelings bottled up inside, and Mary didn't want to make him uncomfortable. He would open up when he was ready.

"You'd think so," Henry said. "It wasn't just people from Ivy Bay looking for them either. Towns all along the coast sent police boats, and there were many volunteers like me." His voice was weary. "We just didn't know where to look."

"Doesn't the coast guard have any way to trace the distress call?"

"Not really." Henry sighed. "It's not like making a phone call, where they can tell which house a phone number is attached to. They rely on a system of radio towers to pinpoint approximately where calls are coming from, but when a lot of people are using the radio waves, it's easy to get them confused."

"And that's what happened last night?"

"Yes. So many people were responding and trying to help, they ended up scrambling the signal and making it hard for the coast guard to pinpoint where the burning boat was."

Light from the kitchen streamed out across the deck, but beyond the deck, the dunes were dark, and all she could see past that was a vast emptiness. The wrought-iron deck furniture, draped in canvas covers for the winter, looked eerie.

"Did the person who made the call have any idea where they were?"

Henry stared out over the waves for a minute.

"According to Lieutenant Peters"—Mary knew the young officer from church and had been glad to hear he was working on the case—"the boater and his family were on a forty-foot cabin cruiser. Basically a small yacht."

Mary knew enough to understand that was a big boat but couldn't say much more than that. "Does a boat like that have sails?"

"Nope. Just a pretty major engine. If the engine were disabled, they would be stuck." He rested his foot against the lower beam of the railing. "They had set off from Provincetown, and the caller said he could see land not far away. They were close enough he thought they might try swimming, if it came to that. He thought he was somewhere near Ivy Bay. He said he could just see the lights of the marina, off to the starboard side, and he could also see the lighthouse, on port."

Mary nodded. If he could see those landmarks, it did sound like he was near Ivy Bay.

"It was getting dark, the caller said, so he couldn't describe much more than that. He was scared, obviously, and confused, and nothing he said was totally clear. I mean, I would be overwhelmed, too, if my family and I were on a burning boat."

Mary heard plates knocking together and silverware clinking inside.

"If that's all you had to go on, it was no wonder you didn't find them." Mary hoped her words would comfort Henry, but his shoulders didn't unhitch, and in the dim light, she could see that his eyes hadn't lost the flat look she'd seen during dinner. Mary reached out and put her hand on Henry's arm. He didn't react.

"How did it end?"

"The man and the coast guard were talking, and it just cut off. That was it. Not even two minutes long, and the last the coast guard heard from them."

She tried to imagine what would have been going through her mind if she were in the boater's situation. Trapped on a burning boat. Scared for his family. Knowing they would only survive for a short time in the ice-cold water. She tried to picture the scene. If she were on a boat looking at the lighthouse and the marina—

"Henry?"

He turned to her.

"He said they were close enough that they might be able to swim to shore?"

"Lieutenant Peters told him to stay out of the water. This time of year, it's cold enough they'd only make it a few minutes before hypothermia set in." He looked down, but not before she saw his eyes start to tear up.

Mary tried again. "But the caller did say the land was not far off?"

Henry thought for a moment. "From what I understand, yes."

Mary closed her eyes, reviewing what she knew of the coastal landscape. The public beach, the one right near the main strip in town, was on a spit of land that jutted out where the bay met the Cape Cod Canal. The marina was on the other side of the spit, around a bend, on the canal side. The lighthouse was down the coast in the other direction, on a narrow stretch of deserted beach several miles east of Ivy Bay.

"I can't picture this. Where on the water would you have to be to see the marina and the lighthouse at the same time?"

Henry looked down at the wooden railing. He was thinking. Mary drew an invisible line on the railing with her finger.

"If this is land," she said. "And the boat is here..." She pointed to a spot a short distance from the line that represented the shore.

Henry nodded; he was following, but he didn't see what she was getting at.

"The marina is here, around this bend. But the lighthouse is over here. He couldn't see both unless he was actually quite far out. Several miles out, probably." She pointed to a spot on her imaginary map far away from the line of the shore. "The only other place I can think of where you could see both the lighthouse and marina at once would be here"— she pointed where the spit of land would be—"standing on the town beach."

A light flipped on in an upstairs window.

"You're right," Henry finally said, shaking his head. He glanced out at the waves again, then back at Mary.

"It probably doesn't mean anything," Mary said quickly. "As you said, he was confused. There was a lot going on, and he probably just said the wrong thing."

"Probably," Henry said quietly. He redrew the diagram Mary had made with his finger and seemed to be running it through his mind. "He probably just got mixed up in the confusion. But..."

Mary looked out to the dunes. The boater had to have been scared and confused. The heat of the fire, the sound of the waves slapping against the boat, the acrid smoke obscuring his vision.... He had to be disoriented and scared. But still, something didn't make sense.

Mary waited for him to go on, but he didn't say anything more for a moment. He curled his fingers around the handrail.

"But what?" she asked.

"But doesn't it seem strange that with all those boats combing through the water, no one saw anything?" Henry said at last. "I was so focused on finding them I didn't stop to think about it until now. But isn't it odd that we saw no smoke, no fire, no scrap of wood or slick of oil or any kind of debris?"

"Couldn't the circumstances have something to do with that? If the boat sank, the fire would have gone out quickly, right? And maybe the smoke was blown away by the wind?"

Henry shook his head. "That's what we originally thought. But still, there should have been *some* sign of them. And now, twenty-four hours after the distress call was received, there is not one scrap of evidence there was ever a boat in distress at all." He ran his hand through his tousled silver-gray hair, his eyes distant.

It did seem strange, when he put it like that, but Mary was not a boating professional, and the men who responded to the call were. Couldn't a boat vanish without a trace?

"Henry, I'm sure he just said the wrong thing. I didn't mean—"

"I know you didn't. But something felt off about it, all along. You just put your finger right on it."

"Henry, what are you saying?"

Henry didn't say anything for a moment.

Finally, Henry spoke. "I'm beginning to wonder if there really were ever any boaters at all."

"You can't decide that based on that one little slipup. There are probably people still out there, waiting for someone to come find them."

"I'm not basing it on one little slipup. That slipup simply pointed out what we all should have realized much earlier."

"Henry, you don't really think that's true, do you?"

But then she felt a thrill of hope. What if there never were any boaters? Maybe no one had perished in the water off Ivy Bay last night. Her heart lightened, and she looked up at Henry, but his face didn't reflect the hope she felt.

He looked angry. "I think it might be. I think whoever made that distress call was standing here on the beach, just like you said. Which means this whole thing was a hoax." He let the quilt slip off his shoulders and started toward the sliding-glass doors. "And I think we need to call Chief McArthur."

# FOUR

◆◆◆

Sun was streaming in through the front window of Mary's Mystery Bookshop when Mary and Lizzie stepped inside Monday morning. Compared to the frigid air outside, the store felt warm and cozy. Mary flipped on the overhead lights and set her purse in the cubby behind the counter. Then she put Gus's carrying case down on the floor. The little cat scuttled out and darted toward the patch of sun by the front window. He flopped down in front of the radiator, stretched out, and closed his eyes. Mary fished her cell phone out of the front pocket of her purse.

"Coats go in the back room," she said as Lizzie started peeling off her wool peacoat. "I'll take both of ours and go get the coffee started." Lizzie held out her jacket, and Mary draped it over her arm and headed for the back of the store. "Rebecca left a sheet of instructions on the counter," Mary said. "Maybe you could start by looking over that while I get a few things set up."

Mary's assistant Rebecca Mason had spent a good part of the previous week preparing for her vacation, and Mary was grateful. After all Rebecca had done, Lizzie should be able to just jump right in.

Lizzie nodded, ducked behind the counter, and placed her purse in one of the little cubbies. Before Mary stepped into the back room, she saw Lizzie sit down and then pick up the sheet of instructions Rebecca had left.

Mary shrugged off her heavy wool coat and hung it, along with Lizzie's, on the coatrack.

Then she checked her phone. No messages. Henry would be out on his boat fishing at this time of day, but if he'd heard anything from Chief McArthur, he would have found a way to let her know. She could call the police chief herself, but he probably wasn't in yet.

She and Henry had gone into the station and talked to Chief McArthur for over an hour last night, and he'd seemed as shocked as Henry was they'd all missed that clue. None of them were certain it meant the call wasn't real, and they couldn't explain why someone would make a false distress call, but it was starting to feel more and more fishy as time passed. The police chief had promised to let them know if he found out anything he could share. She'd try to sit tight for now.

Mary moved to the beverage station and started the coffeepot. It gurgled and hissed, and a few moments later, brown liquid started streaming into the glass carafe. Then she crouched down in front of the fireplace and flipped the switch that turned on the gas-powered flames. She straightened up and looked around the shop. The wide pine floors were polished to a high sheen and gleamed in the morning light. The books on the heavy satinwood shelves were lined up neatly. The children's area behind the white picket gate was neat, and the old pedestal bathtub that served as a reading space for kids was clean and ready to welcome its next customer. The sea-blue and sea-green pillows were arranged perfectly on the ivory twill armchairs—they looked casually tossed, but it had taken Rebecca some time to get them to look so careless. The shop looked good. She'd just get the computer up and running and show Lizzie how to shelve the new shipment of books that had come in on Saturday, and they'd be ready to open.

"I love the way it smells in here."

Mary looked up to see Lizzie standing in front of the display table, taking a deep breath, a wide smile on her face. She picked a book off the table—a hardcover thriller set in nearby Plymouth—and opened it and stuck her nose into the open pages.

Mary laughed. Lizzie looked ridiculous, but Mary had to admit she was right. There was something about the way the paper and ink and glue came together that was intoxicating. And Susan Crosby was already hard at work inside Sweet Susan's Bakery this morning, so the scents of baking bread and cinnamon drifted into Mary's Mystery Bookshop and mingled with the scent of the brewing coffee. It smelled pretty much exactly how she imagined heaven would.

"You looked over all the notes Rebecca left?" That hadn't taken long.

"Mostly." Lizzie closed the book and put it back down on the stack. "The rest I'll figure out as we go along."

Mary hesitated. Rebecca had spent a lot of time leaving detailed instructions for some of the things that were likely to come up this week. Mary had told Rebecca that Lizzie wasn't a mystery reader, so Rebecca had also outlined the basic categories of mysteries they stocked. She'd wanted Lizzie to at least take a look at that. But Lizzie seemed ready to get started, so Mary just nodded and gestured for her to follow her to the back room.

Together, they dragged three heavy cardboard boxes out into the main room. Mary had scanned the books into the inventory system on Saturday, and now she showed Lizzie how to find the category the publisher printed on each book and pointed to where different kinds of books were shelved in her store. Lizzie figured it out quickly, and Mary left her to log on to the computer on the counter. She checked her e-mail and then at ten flipped the sign on the door to Open.

There was no mad rush of customers. In fact, an hour later, not one person had come into the store. For a Monday morning in February, this wasn't totally unexpected, and it did give Mary a chance to catch up on her e-mail. She corresponded with a publicist who was trying to set up an author event in her store and followed up on an order that was supposed to have arrived last week.

Lizzie chattered about the kids as she and Mary worked. She told a story about how, the previous week, Luke had had his little friend Aiden over, and they had tag-teamed her to get at the batch of cookies she had just baked. Aiden asked for her help with a toy, a Lite-Brite that needed a new bulb, and while she was distracted, Luke had grabbed a handful of the warm cookies. Mary laughed, pleased at their ingenuity, if not the way they had applied it, and Mary was more grateful than ever that her daughter was willing to spend the week working with her.

Lizzie had finished shelving one box and was just starting to open another when Betty passed by—or stormed by— the front window of the shop. She was leaning forward, her head down against the February wind, her arms pumping as she hurried down the street. Mary hadn't seen her move so quickly in a long time, and by the firm set of her jaw and the look in her eyes, Mary could tell she was not happy about something.

"Can you hold down the fort for a minute?" Mary called. Lizzie nodded, and Mary scooted off the chair and out the door. As soon as she was outside, a blast of cold air hit her and she realized her mistake, but her coat was in the back room all the way at the far end of the shop, and if she wanted to catch up with Betty, she didn't have time to spare.

"Betty!" Mary called. Her sister slowed and looked around. "Wait up!"

Betty turned, and when she saw Mary, she stopped and waited. Mary hurried to her side.

"What's going on?" Mary asked. Main Street was mostly quiet, with only a few people bustling into Meeting House Grocers. Gems and Antiques was dark, as Jayne and Rich Tucker were in Europe at this time of year. Bare branches, stripped of their leaves, swayed lightly in the chilly wind.

Betty gestured that they should keep walking, and Mary was happy to oblige, as her cable-knit sweater was doing little to keep out the chill. They started walking again, and Betty took a few deep breaths, as if she were trying to calm herself down.

"I was on my way to my nursery committee meeting at church"—Mary had seen the announcement in the bulletin that they needed volunteers to renovate the nursery, but didn't realize Betty had signed up—"and I stopped at Sweet Susan's to get croissants."

So far, this story wasn't going the way Mary had expected. Croissants and the church nursery didn't usually elicit the kind of anger she saw on Betty's face.

"Did something happen in Sweet Susan's?" The charming bakery was one of Mary's favorite places in Ivy Bay, and Susan made the best pastries around.

"I picked out the pastries, and Susan loaded them in the box, but when I went to pay, Susan told me that my debit card was *declined*," Betty said. Mary could see the horror on her sister's face. "So I told her to try it again, and she told me it had been declined again. Can you imagine? I know there's money in that account. I just deposited a check on Friday." She stopped outside the Ivy Bay Bank & Trust and reached for the door.

"Is it possible the check you deposited just hasn't cleared yet?"

They stepped inside the bank. The polished marble floors reflected the soft lighting overhead. The room had high ceilings and brass teller windows.

"Even if it hadn't, I'm not out of money." Betty didn't often talk about it, but her husband, Edward, had been from one of Ivy Bay's wealthiest families, and he had left her quite well-off. She certainly didn't throw money around, but Betty was not hurting for cash, and it would be quite unusual for her to have an empty account. "Susan offered to let me take the croissants and pay her back later, but I told her I needed to get this straightened out first."

"I'm sure it's just a mistake." Their footsteps echoed in the cavernous room as Betty hurried past the small seating area. "We'll figure out what happened."

"We'd better," Betty said, and they stepped toward the teller windows. There were two tellers waiting, and Betty walked up to Sandra Rink.

"Good morning, Betty, Mary. What can I help you with today?" Sandra asked, friendly as always. Her hair was pulled back into a low ponytail, and her blue button-down shirt was neatly pressed. She smiled, revealing the small gap between her front teeth, which Mary always found endearing.

"I need you to tell Susan Crosby that I have money in my account," Betty said and set her purse down on the carved mahogany counter with a little more force than necessary.

Sandra's smile didn't falter, but she looked around the room and then back at Mary when she didn't find Susan.

"There seems to be a problem with my sister's account," Mary said quickly. "She tried her debit card at Sweet Susan's, and it was declined. Can we see what's going on?"

Sandra smiled at Mary. "Let me see what I can find out," she said and started typing on the keyboard in front of her.

Betty was rattled. She was usually so composed that Mary knew this bothered her more than she would have expected. But then, Betty was a widow, Mary reasoned, with health problems and no way to earn a living on her own. Mary had worked in a library most of her life and now owned her own shop, but Betty depended on the money her husband had left her. If it suddenly vanished, she would be in serious trouble. Of course, Mary would take care of her as best she could.

Sandra's brow creased. She narrowed her eyes and leaned in to the computer. She hit a few more buttons, then shook her head and straightened up.

"I'm seeing a checking account and a savings account." She still had that gap-toothed smile on her face, but there was something about it that seemed forced. "Was there another account as well?"

"No, I just have those two accounts here," Betty said. "And I know there's money in them. I just deposited a check on Friday."

Sandra scanned the screen, typed something more in, and pressed her lips together.

Mary was starting to get that jumpy feeling she often got when something was wrong. Sandra was now talking to herself, saying something just quietly enough that Mary couldn't hear it. Betty's spine was ramrod straight, but Mary could see her hand trembling.

"I'm going to call Steve over," Sandra said and stepped away from the counter before either of them could react.

Mary gave Betty what she hoped was an encouraging smile. Betty carefully avoided meeting her eyes. To most people, it would have probably seemed aloof, unfriendly, but Mary knew her sister better than that, and her heart ached. Betty had gone from angry to scared, and she was worried that if she met Mary's eyes, she might cry. Mary put a hand on Betty's back to steady her.

Sandra returned with Steve Althorpe trailing a few feet behind her.

"Good morning," Steve said and then turned his attention to the screen. Steve wore a dark tailored suit and a sharp paisley tie and looked the part of the trustworthy banker he was. "How are you this morning?"

"We're okay. But I'd be better if you could tell me what happened to my account," Betty said.

"It seems that there's a misunderstanding," Mary said, and Sandra flashed her a grateful smile. "And we're hoping you can let us know what's happening."

Sandra pointed something out to Steve on her computer screen, and he nodded, then turned to Mary and Betty. "Mrs. Emerson, do you remember the last time you made a withdrawal from your account?"

"A week ago today," Betty said. "I was headed to lunch at the club and stopped in here first." Her fingers curled around the handle of her purse. "Can you please tell me what is going on?"

Steve let out a long breath. "Why don't we step into my office and talk about it?" he said, gesturing for them to follow him.

"Why don't you just tell me what's going on?" Betty said, her voice hard.

Steve looked at Betty, then at Mary, questioning. Mary nodded slightly, almost imperceptibly. He turned back to Betty.

"Mrs. Emerson, your account has a zero balance."

"What?" Betty leaned forward, twisting so she could see the screen. Sandra angled the screen toward her. "But...no, that's not possible."

"I'm not sure what happened, but it says here that early this morning, the entire amount was withdrawn." He pointed to a line on the screen that showed a great deal of money had indeed been moved out of Betty's accounts just a few hours before.

Goodness. Mary rechecked the number, just to make sure she hadn't added a digit. Mary had no idea her sister had that much cash on hand. It was more than Mary had made in the past year.

"You're saying you didn't make these withdrawals?" Steve asked.

"No. W-what would I do with t-that much cash?" Betty stammered.

"The money was transferred electronically. Are you sure you didn't move it, say, to an account at another bank? Or maybe a brokerage fund of some sort?"

"I think I would remember that, Steve." Betty's voice had that tinge of a teacher scolding a student. "I may be in my sixties, but my memory is not gone yet."

If Steve minded her tone, he didn't show it. "Mrs. Emerson, if you didn't make these withdrawals, then I'm afraid we have a problem."

"I should say so," Betty said. "So the money, it's just"— she hesitated—"gone? You have no idea where it went or who took it?"

"I don't have any more information than that right now," Steve said. "But I can assure you we'll do everything we can to figure this out as soon as possible. Sandra, could you please call the police?"

Sandra nodded and reached for the phone sitting next to her computer.

"Tell them we need to report a theft."

# FIVE

◆◆◆

By the time Deputy Wadell had arrived and talked with Betty, promising to try to find out what happened to her missing money, Betty's meeting had long since passed. It had taken some time for them to ask Betty repeatedly if she'd accidentally given out her account information, or whether she'd lent someone her debit card. She had done none of the above, and when they were finished, she was still so keyed up that Mary drove her home before returning to the shop. They would come back and retrieve Betty's car later. Steve Althorpe had reassured Betty they would try to trace the funds, and the police were also opening a case, but it didn't seem to make Betty feel any better.

Just before noon, Mary stepped back inside the store. Mary was so thankful to feel the warm air of the store wrap around her. She would not be heading outside without a coat again anytime soon.

Lizzie was seated on one of the stools behind the counter and looked up from a paperback she was reading.

"How's Aunt Betty?"

"She's...rattled." Mary settled onto the other stool and stuffed her purse into a cubby behind the counter. She had called Lizzie from the bank and told her what was going on and asked her to cover the shop for a little while.

"Of course she is."

Lizzie flipped the book over, and Mary could see that it was a new paperback that had come from the stack on the best-seller table. She could also see that the spine was now cracked, and because it was resting open, facedown, it would never close quite right again. Well, what good was owning your own store if your family couldn't enjoy the goods?

"So the money is just…gone?" Lizzie asked.

"It was transferred electronically to an external account. They're looking into where the account is and how to get it back." Mary rubbed her hands together. She was starting to thaw, but she still had a chill.

"The bank is going to pay her back, right? If they can't find it, I mean?"

Mary had wondered the same thing. "I don't know. I suppose they are. But I imagine it will be a while if they do, and that would mean the bank is out a great deal of money."

"Let's just hope they find it."

Mary agreed and then sat back and looked around the shop. There were no customers at the moment, and everything looked just like she'd left it. Everything, including the boxes of books Lizzie had started unpacking before Mary had left. They were still in the middle of the floor, between the two upholstered chairs.

"Get distracted?" Mary nodded at the boxes.

Lizzie looked to the back of the store and laughed. "Oh goodness, I forgot about those." She pushed her stool back and headed toward the boxes. "I'm sorry. Some customers came in, and I forgot to go back to them."

Mary didn't like to have the store look messy, and Rebecca didn't usually let boxes sit out like that. Still, it was Lizzie's first day. She was learning.

"Oh? Who came in?"

Mary pushed back her stool and walked over to join Lizzie. The boxes were still full. She couldn't have put away more than a couple of books since Mary left. She reached for a mass-market paperback copy of Agatha Christie's *And Then There Were None* and walked to the section of the shelves where she stocked British mysteries.

Lizzie was staring at the back of a hardcover. From here, Mary could see that it was the new Vince Flynn.

"That's a thriller," Mary said. Lizzie continued to look at the back cover. "The category is sometimes printed on the inside of the front flap on hardcovers."

Lizzie flipped the book open, looked at the front flap, and nodded, then walked toward the rows of thrillers.

"But that one actually belongs on the best-seller tables," Mary said.

Lizzie laughed, lifted the three copies of the book from the cardboard box, and brought them to the front table.

"It was a cute older couple," Lizzie said, picking up the question Mary had asked. "They're just here for a visit and were looking for some good books to read."

"What did they end up with?"

"They asked for a recommendation, but I didn't know what to tell them, so they left with nothing." Lizzie walked back toward the boxes, reaching for another book.

It wasn't really a big deal. One or two books would not make or break the store. But in February, when there weren't many tourists and even locals were scarce, Mary appreciated every sale.

"That's why I was reading when you came in." Lizzie picked up a book and looked at the cover, then trotted over to the cozy section. "I didn't want to have to tell any other customers that I hadn't read many of the books in the shop, so I figured I should get reading."

Her logic was good. Mary could appreciate the thought process. Still, she would have preferred if Lizzie had handled a few things differently this morning. Mary reached into the box and pulled out the last book.

It was only Lizzie's first day, she reminded herself. And she was working for free. You couldn't complain too much when the help was free. She grabbed the invoice out of the box and set the box aside.

They put away the rest of the books quietly. Then Mary asked if Lizzie wanted to take her lunch break. Lizzie smiled gratefully and said she was planning to meet Chad and the kids at the Black & White Diner. She called Chad, who was with the kids at an old-fashioned toy store on Liberty Road. Mary watched through the front window of the store as Lizzie hurried across the street and arrived just as Chad and the kids did. Lizzie gave the kids hugs, and then they stepped inside. It was good for them to have family time, Mary knew. But she couldn't help feeling a teensy bit left out anyway.

Well, this was a good time for Mary to get some work done. She broke down the boxes, carried them to the back room to set out with the recycling, and then straightened a few books on their shelves. There wasn't actually a whole lot to do. It wasn't as if they'd had a stampede of customers this morning. Mary looked around the shop. Everything was in order, and the shop was empty.

That meant Mary could turn to another kind of work. She settled down behind the counter and shook the computer mouse to wake the screen.

Mary's fingers hovered above the keyboard. Somehow, someone had gotten hold of Betty's bank account information and used that to clean out her account. She had to find out how.

She wasn't sure what exactly to search for, so she typed in the words *identity theft*. She got pages and pages of results, but she sorted through them and found a few that looked relevant. Identity theft occurred when someone used another person's personal information, often for financial reasons. That sure sounded like what had happened with Betty. Mary read on and discovered that there were several common methods of obtaining personal information.

There were, of course, the attempts everyone knew were scams—e-mails from African princes who asked to borrow money temporarily and would pay you back with interest; foreign investors who wanted to use your bank account information to reward you for helping them with some small task. But there were many more sophisticated scams out there as well. Sometimes, a thief would send a fake e-mail designed to look like it came from your bank, asking you to log on to your account online through a link included in the e-mail. Once you entered your information, it was captured by the scammer, who would then use it to log on to the bank's real site himself and move your money to his own account. She learned that sometimes a similar scam worked by phone, where someone pretending to be from your bank would call and ask you to verify your account information and would then use it to steal from your account. Scams like these were often successful on seniors, Mary read. Seniors were less likely to be comfortable with technology and less likely to recognize when something hadn't come from a legitimate company.

Mary sat back on her stool. Could Betty have fallen prey to such a scam? She hated the thought of people out there specifically trying to trick older Americans into giving away their bank account information, but it appeared to be common. Some of the scams were quite sophisticated. Could Betty have accidentally given out her information? Steve Althorpe and Sandra Rink had hinted at that this morning, and Betty had been huffy, saying she knew better than that, but Mary wondered if she might have given her account information away without realizing it.

Another Web page Mary found talked about ways personal financial information could be stolen from corporations. Sometimes internal computer systems were accessed, and, in a few cases, computers containing customer information had been stolen. Or sometimes hackers got past a company's security system and were able to access a company's customer records while the computers sat exactly where they belonged.

It was enough to make you afraid to buy anything at all. It seemed no matter what you did, your financial information could be put at risk. Several of the sources Mary read reminded readers that credit card companies offered the greatest protection against identity theft, and that most would not hold users accountable for false purchases made on their cards. Well, that was something.

Mary had just clicked on a new link when the phone rang.

"Mary's Mystery Bookshop," Mary said, holding the phone to her ear.

"Oh good, you're there."

"Hello, Henry." She could hear wind whistling past the phone. Henry was standing outside somewhere.

"Hi, Mary. I just ran into Chief McArthur at the diner," Henry said.

"Oh, Lizzie is there with the kids now." Mary craned her neck and looked out the front window of the shop toward the diner but didn't see either Henry or her daughter's family outside. In fact, she didn't see many people at all outside on this gray, raw day.

"Yes, I saw them. The kids were having a great time sword fighting with their french fries." Henry laughed. He had two grandsons and was used to their antics.

"That sounds about right." She heard the wind whipping around the phone again. "Where are you?"

"I'm headed back to the marina. I went through a lot of gas the last few days, and I need to refuel and fix a couple of things."

"Fix things? Like what?"

"The waves were pretty rough out there this weekend. Some salt water got into the electronics of my boat, and I just need to adjust a few things."

"Henry!" Mary shook her head. "Is it all right?"

Henry sighed. "It's going to be fine. I just discovered it this morning."

"You didn't go out on the water with your boat not up to snuff, did you?"

"No. I didn't." Mary heard the disappointment in his voice. He wouldn't say it, but she knew that he depended on the income he received from his mornings on the water. "But that's not why I called. Listen, Chief McArthur told me you were right."

"I'm glad to hear it." She laughed. "About what?"

"The call that came in? It was a hoax, after all. The coast guard looked into all the transmissions that came in on Saturday night. It was a bit scrambled, but based on their best guess of where the radio signals were coming from, they suspect it came from that spit of land right at the edge of the town beach, not way out on the bay. It's just like you thought."

"A hoax." Mary's mind reeled. She had begun to suspect as much, but it was still shocking to have it confirmed. She knew she should be relieved to find out there never had been any boaters' lives in danger, and she was, but... "Who would have done something like that?"

"They would really like to know, that's for sure. So would I."

Mary thought about all the people who had dropped everything to go out on the water to search for the missing boaters. All those hours spent searching. All those lives put in danger on a cold February night. There had been at least one rescuer injured, she'd heard in church. And now Henry's boat needed repairs and was keeping him from his livelihood. And Eleanor's fund-raiser would have no doubt brought in more money for the museum without the interruption. The damage was incalculable.

"The chief was spitting mad. He was talking about thousands of dollars being wasted, dozens of volunteers put at risk." She heard a clang, and then Henry's footsteps got louder. "He is going to find out who did it and punish them to the full extent of the law."

"I should think so."

"Anyway, I just wanted to let you know. I know you've been worried." There was a thud, and the wind whipping around the phone intensified. "Hey, I'm here at the marina now, so I should go, but nice work."

"Thank you for telling me. I appreciate it."

"I'll talk to you soon."

Mary set the phone down gently and tried to make sense of what Henry had told her. Someone had purposefully made a false distress call, causing the police, the coast guard, and dozens of volunteers to head to the water and waste many hours and thousands of dollars on the search. But who would do such a thing, and... Mary shook her head. And why?

Was it just some kids, playing what they thought was a funny joke? Someone bored, looking for some excitement on a wintry night? Mary shook her head. There had to be a reason. Someone had put real thought into their story, creating an elaborate and vivid picture of a family in danger.

Mary thought back to that night—the party, Chief McArthur coming in, Henry and the guards leaving, Eleanor and Virginia guarding the Hamilton Decanter. Everything had been chaotic for a while. No one had been paying attention to who was where. For a while, Mary had been worried something would happen to the antique glass, but the only thing that had gone missing that night had been the museum's laptop.

The phone rang, jarring Mary out of her memories of Saturday night, and it took her a moment to realize what the sound was.

"Mary's Mystery Bookshop," she said, hoping she sounded more composed than she felt.

"Mary, it's Betty."

"Betty, how are you do—"

"Can you come pick me up? My car is still downtown."

Betty was clearly upset. She was never rude and must still be distraught to cut Mary off like that.

"Betty, what's going on? Where do you need to go?" She tried to make her voice calm and soothing.

"Eleanor just called."

Well, a talk with Eleanor was enough to make anyone agitated, as far as Mary was concerned, but she didn't think that was what had Betty so rattled.

"Is everything okay with Eleanor? Did something happen to one of her children?"

"No. She just found out her bank account was emptied this morning too."

# SIX

———◆◆———

Mary sat back on her stool, absorbing the news that Eleanor Blakely's bank account had been emptied, just as Betty's had.

"Are you sure?" she asked Betty.

"Of course I'm sure."

"My goodness." Mary didn't know the specifics of Eleanor's finances, but Betty's husband, Edward, had left Betty well-off, and Eleanor, Edward's sister, had inherited the rest of the Emerson family money. She certainly never lacked for nice clothes as far as Mary could tell. She was quite sure there had been a sizable amount of money in Eleanor's bank account. "I'm so sorry to hear that."

"She's pretty upset," Betty said. "I need to go see her."

Mary could understand why Betty would want to see her sister-in-law, but she couldn't leave the store just yet.

"Sure thing. Lizzie's on her lunch break right now, but she should be back soon. As soon as she gets back, I'll come pick you up. Why don't you get ready to go? I'll be there shortly."

There was a pause, and for a moment, Mary was afraid Betty was going to argue, but she simply sighed.

"Thanks, Mar. I'll see you soon."

It couldn't be a coincidence that both accounts had been cleaned out in the same day. Mary was sure there had to be a connection between the two thefts.

An idea started to form in her mind. Was there a chance there had been a connection between these thefts and the other theft?

The night of the party, everyone had been so worried about protecting the Hamilton Decanter after the guards had been called away. But what if the antique glass hadn't been the most valuable thing in the museum that night? What if someone had wanted everyone to be focused on protecting the glass so he or she could get access to the most important thing the museum owned?

Suddenly, Mary had a pretty good idea why someone might have taken the laptop. Why someone might have even created a chaotic situation at the museum so there would be an opportunity to take it.

Mary shook her head. She hoped she was wrong. But if she was right, what was on that laptop was worth far more than anyone had realized that night.

It was almost an hour later before Lizzie returned to the shop. Mary tried to use the time well, but she was anxious, and if she was honest, a bit frustrated. It wasn't as if she were paying Lizzie, and they hadn't exactly had a busy day at the shop, but still, a two-hour lunch break seemed excessive. While she waited, she called the Ivy Bay police and told Chief McArthur her suspicion, and he promised to look into it.

Betty was still quite upset when Mary picked her up. In the hour since she'd called Mary, she'd found out that Lincoln King and Cynthia Jones had also had their bank accounts hacked. Mary worried about Betty driving in her agitated state, but Betty promised she'd be careful. Mary could see that it gave Betty some measure of peace to be able to comfort Eleanor, and she hoped spending some time with her sister-in-law would be good for both of them.

Mary dropped Betty off by her car, but before she headed back to the shop, she decided to make one quick stop. After hearing about Cynthia and Lincoln, she was even more sure she was on the right track.

The Ivy Bay Glass Museum was just off the main road, on a small street that snaked its way toward the shore, wandering past beach bungalows—now shuttered for the winter—and a small park, ending at the town beach. Mary had read that the spot was carefully chosen when the glassworks opened centuries ago, because it was close enough to the beach to utilize the fine sand in glassmaking and close enough to the water to allow for the glass to be easily loaded on boats and shipped out. Back then, there had also been ample timber to fuel the ovens used to heat the molten glass. The white clapboard building looked bright and cheerful, and Mary stepped inside gratefully.

Taylor O'Connor was sitting at the admissions desk. That was odd. The museum had only two full-time employees—Virginia and Maureen—and Taylor, the unpaid intern, but they were all usually working in the back office. The admissions desk was generally manned by one of the volunteers Virginia and Eleanor recruited. Every time Mary had been in here, one of the ladies from their book club or one of their friends from the yacht club had been here selling admission tickets and handing out gallery maps.

Taylor looked up and gave Mary a bright smile. She was wearing a stylish wool turtleneck, and her blonde hair hung long over her shoulders.

"You look like a popsicle," Taylor said. She gave Mary a genuine smile and stood up and came around the desk.

"I feel like one too." Mary pulled off her hat and unbuttoned her coat. Taylor took Mary's coat and hung it on one of the hangers at the small rack by the door.

"Not too many brave souls ventured down this way today." Taylor walked back around the counter and sat down. She was tall and thin, and she moved gracefully, effortlessly. She picked up a cell phone lying on her desk and typed something on the screen almost without even looking.

"That's how it's been at my shop as well," Mary said, smiling. "I guess that's February on Cape Cod for you."

"I cannot wait until summer." Taylor nodded, and Mary noticed the girl's earrings caught the light, sparkling and dancing. Diamonds. Mary only owned one pair of small diamond earrings she'd inherited from her mother, and she only broke them out on the most special occasions.

"You don't usually sit up here at admissions, do you?" Mary hoped she didn't sound too nosy, but she wanted to understand who did what—and who had access to what—at the museum.

"Nope." Taylor's phone buzzed, and she glanced at it and typed with well-practiced fingers as she continued. "Madeline Dinsdale was supposed to come in, but she's sick today, so I'm covering the front desk."

"I hope she's all right." Mary knew that Madeline was a member of Betty's book club.

"She says it's just a cold, but in weather like this, better to rest up, right?" Taylor sent her message, set her phone down, and looked up at Mary.

"I hope she feels better soon," Mary said.

Taylor nodded and looked at her phone, waiting for a reply.

"I imagine it must be quite a task, keeping track of all the volunteers that come through here."

"Probably." Taylor shrugged. "Virginia handles that, though, so I don't really know." A message popped up on her phone's screen, and Mary saw that someone had sent Taylor a picture of a small brown dog. "And it's not that complicated a schedule, really. We just have one each morning and another in the afternoon. It's hardly rocket science."

"So if I wanted to get a list of all the volunteers, Virginia is who I'd talk to?"

Taylor narrowed her eyes.

"I'm interested in that laptop that went missing Saturday night," Mary said. Taylor froze, for just a fraction of a second, and then smiled. For a moment, Mary wasn't positive the young woman had actually frozen after all. "And I'm trying to figure out who might have had access to different parts of the museum."

Taylor started to say something, but then she stopped.

"So Virginia would be the person to talk to?" Mary said.

Taylor waited a moment and then shrugged as if she couldn't be bothered to ask why Mary would want such a thing. "Yeah. Or anyone on the board of directors. They sometimes help with the volunteers." Taylor was typing something on her phone again.

"Ah. Can you tell me who is on the board of directors?"

She thought for a moment. "I don't see why not." She finished typing her message and set the phone down. "There's Mrs. Blakely, of course." Mary nodded. "Mason Willoughby. He owns that gallery downtown. Madeline Dinsdale, actually. And Tabitha Krause." She counted them off on her fingers.

"And what do they do?"

Taylor tapped her fingers on the phone screen. "I don't know. They keep an eye on things, I guess. They make decisions about how to spend money, that sort of thing. Virginia reports to them."

"Interesting." Mary watched as Taylor picked up her phone again and navigated to a social-media site while she apparently waited for whoever she was texting with to reply to her last message. Whoever it was, Taylor seemed to be much more interested in her virtual conversation than the one she was having with Mary. Kids today always seemed to be split between the real world and the virtual one. But Mary still had a few questions. "Do you like interning here?" She leaned over the counter, as if this were just a casual, friendly chat.

"Sure," Taylor said. "The people are nice."

That wasn't a resounding endorsement. "What did you do before this?"

"I just graduated in June, and I traveled around over the summer. I started here in November." Taylor touched something on the screen, and up popped a picture of Taylor and her father in front of the Eiffel Tower. "Here I am in Paris with my dad." She swiped her finger across the screen, and Mary saw another photo, this one of Taylor drinking tea in a china teacup, her pinkie finger cocked. "London."

"It sounds like fun," Mary said as Taylor showed her another photo, this one of Taylor on the Great Wall of China. "What sorts of things do you do here at the museum?"

"Oh, you know." The awaited message came through, and Taylor abandoned photos of her world tour to type a response. "Data entry, mailings, filing, photocopies. Whatever Virginia needs me to do. Maureen is in charge of the artistic side of the galleries, like arranging the displays, so they mostly use me to handle office details."

"I'm sure there's a lot you can learn by doing the day-to-day stuff of running an office."

"Yeah, it's not the most thrilling work, but whatever." She set the phone down.

Mary laughed. "Sounds like there's something else you'd rather be doing."

Taylor sighed. "I wanted to start a dance company, but I can't really afford that, and my parents didn't want me to just sit around, so"—she gestured around the foyer—"here I am."

"You're a dancer?"

"Trying to be. That's what I majored in at college. That's what I want to do."

Mary had met Taylor's father at Eleanor's Christmas party last year. A hardworking, self-made businessman, he didn't seem to have much of a sense of humor and didn't seem likely, based on Mary's short acquaintance with him, to think his daughter's career ambitions were admirable. Mary wasn't surprised he had steered her toward learning some practical skills.

Mary shifted her weight forward. "That sounds like a tough career to break into."

"If you want to dance for one of the big companies, yeah, it is." She spun the phone around in a circle on the desk. "But I don't want to move to New York and go through all that. That's why I want to open something here on the Cape. Then I could be the creative director and not have to answer to anyone else about what we do and when and why."

Interesting. "How would you go about starting your own company?"

"Well..." Taylor tapped at the screen. She seemed to not know what to do with herself without her phone in her hands. "You have to find investors, normally. But..." She trailed off. "I don't know. I might not. We'll see." Taylor gave up and picked up the phone and slid her finger across the screen.

"Oh." Mary tried not to show her surprise. "You may not have to raise the money?"

"I don't know. I've been thinking about other ways to make it happen." She went back to the social-media page and tapped an icon under a photo. "Anyway, if you want to know about what's happening with the laptop, you should talk to Virginia."

"I hoped to, if she has time. But before I do, can you think of any reason someone might have taken it?" A light hiss of steam came from the radiators under the windows. "With all the valuable artifacts here, why would someone take a computer?"

Taylor shrugged. "It was probably easier, I would guess. The glass is all pretty much locked up in display cases. And a computer is probably easier to unload. I don't know many people who'd know how to sell off a piece of antique glass, but a laptop, sure. That wouldn't be hard to find a buyer for."

Mary knew she was right, about both points, but it didn't explain why Taylor's computer was the one taken. Maureen's laptop had been out on her desk as well.

"I thought about that too. But then I wondered if there was anything on the computer that might have been valuable to someone. Was there anything on the computer you know of that someone might have been after?"

Taylor's phone buzzed, and she grabbed for it. "I don't think so. It was just boring museum stuff. I can't imagine who would have wanted that."

Mary smiled conspiratorially. "What about things like the museum's donor records? Is there any chance those might have been on the laptop?"

Taylor stopped her frantic typing. She looked up at Mary for just a beat too long and then shook her head. "I was working on some databases, but I don't know why there would have been donor records. But like I said, I've only been interning here for a few months. Someone else was probably using that laptop before I was." Taylor looked at something just past Mary. "It's possible there might have been something like that on it before I started."

There was something Taylor wasn't telling her; she was sure of it. Something about the set of her jaw and the way she wouldn't meet Mary's eyes.

"But even if there was something on the computer someone was after," Taylor said quickly, "the laptop was password protected. The thief wouldn't be able to get into it, anyway."

Mary considered that. It was likely true. But surely there were people who could get around such things. She knew that computer hackers could get into just about any system these days. And, more important, there was something about the sure, final way Taylor relayed the information that raised a red flag for Mary. It was almost as if she had rehearsed it.

"When did you see it last?"

"I went back there during the party, maybe around seven or so, to grab something. It was on my desk then. I went back later to get a pen, and that's when I noticed it was gone."

"Do you know what time you went back?"

Taylor sent her message and looked back at Mary. "It was after all that craziness with the guards had started to die down. I don't know, maybe a quarter to eight or so?"

Mary ran back through the evening in her mind. Chief McArthur had shown up around seven thirty. If the thief had made the false distress call to create an opportunity to steal the laptop, that allowed about fifteen minutes for the theft to take place.

"Well, if you do think of anything more about what was on that computer, would you let me know?"

"Sure thing." The lines around Taylor's mouth were tight, and she still wouldn't meet Mary's eyes.

"Thanks so much. I appreciate it."

"No problem. It was great chatting with you." Taylor was staring at her phone.

"Is Virginia available, by any chance?"

Taylor nodded. "She's in the office in the back."

"Do you know if she's busy?"

"If I had the laptop, I'd be able to check the schedule, but since I can't do that…" She laughed nervously. "Why don't you just go on back? I'm sure she'll have time to see you."

"Thanks so much." Mary smiled at Taylor once again, but the girl was talking to someone online and had already forgotten her.

Mary walked through the open door into the main gallery, where the party had been the other night. From somewhere back in one of the smaller galleries, she heard low voices, but the main gallery was quiet, and her footsteps echoed against the polished wooden floor. It looked so different in here today. The spot where the Hamilton Decanter had stood was now filled with a padded bench, and the overhead lights were bright, illuminating the colored glass that lined the walls. It was hard to believe that just days ago, this room had been filled with dozens of people dressed in their finest, drinking, chatting, listening to a string quartet. Mary liked it better this way; but then, as a career librarian, she'd always enjoyed the hush that fell over spaces meant for learning.

She crossed the room and ducked down the hallway that led off toward the office. At the end of the hallway was the side exit where the caterers had been loading their vans Saturday night after the party. Mary ducked into the outer room of the office. Maureen's chair was empty, but the light was on inside Virginia's office, and she could see Virginia seated behind her desk through the glass panel.

Virginia looked up as Mary stepped in, and she waved for Mary to come in. Mary stepped inside the office, which, like the outer office, was clean and sparse, with modern furniture and big windows that looked out toward the bay.

"Hello, Mary." Virginia shifted her glasses and pushed them back so they rested on the top of her head and laid down the papers in her hand. "Couldn't get enough of us, huh?" The skin around her eyes crinkled, and Mary was reminded that Virginia had always been genuinely warm with Mary. She associated Virginia with Eleanor, and so she often assumed Virginia had the same prickly personality, but she had always been kind. "Please, sit."

"It is a beautiful museum," Mary said, playing along. She lowered herself into a metal chair with a thin green cushion. "But I'm afraid that's not why I'm here. I have...I have a bit of a strange question for you."

"I raised three boys. I guarantee I've heard stranger."

Mary laughed. She did remember Betty saying something about Virginia's children being a handful. "Point taken. I have a son as well, and boys are...well, they're a different breed, aren't they?"

"Indeed." Virginia took the glasses off and folded them, and then laid them on the desk.

"Virginia..." Mary tried to choose her words carefully. "Is there any chance any of your donors' financial information was on that laptop that disappeared Saturday night?"

"Our donor information?" She lifted her glasses and then lowered them again. "Goodness. I should hope not. That's classified information. We protect it very carefully."

"I'm sure you do. It's just that, well, this morning we found out that all the money in Betty's bank account had been cleaned out."

Virginia's eyes widened, and she reared her head back. "I'm so sorry to hear that. Will the bank reimburse—"

"They're still sorting that out," Mary said. "But then this afternoon, we found out that the same thing had happened to Eleanor's account, and Lincoln King's and Cynthia Jones's as well."

"Oh my goodness." She opened her glasses again and sat up straighter in her chair. "That's..." She faltered.

"When we thought it was just Betty, I considered the possibility someone had tricked her into giving out her personal information somehow. But then when I heard about the others, I started to wonder."

"Wonder what?"

"Well, I know Betty has donated money to the museum. And I assume Eleanor has too. And both Cynthia and Lincoln were at the party on Saturday. I have no idea if they're regular supporters, but I assume they must have bought tickets to the fund-raiser. So there seems to be a point of connection there."

"Betty, Eleanor, and Cynthia are three of the most involved women in Ivy Bay. They have their fingers in so many pots in this town. You could find a point of connection between them and just about anything else in Ivy Bay."

Mary had to acknowledge she had a point, but that didn't change the fact that the money had started disappearing Monday morning, after the laptop was stolen Saturday night. And banks were closed on Sundays. That couldn't be simply coincidence.

"Did you hear that the distress call that came in during the party was fake?" Mary watched Virginia's reaction carefully.

"I did. It's atrocious, isn't it?" Perhaps Mary should be more surprised Virginia had already heard, considering Mary had just learned about it herself. But she'd lived in a small town long enough to understand news traveled quickly, and bad news traveled even faster. "Who would do something like that?"

"I'm not sure," Mary said. "But it seems to be quite a coincidence that the fake distress call came in, and the guards left to go search for the missing boaters, and while everyone was distracted, the laptop disappeared. Then, money starts disappearing from the accounts of the people who support the museum."

Virginia held up her hand. "Slow down. We don't know exactly when the laptop disappeared. It could have been before the call came in."

"Fair enough." Mary had to acknowledge she was right; however, it simply meant she would need to find a way to nail down the timing more precisely.

"And we don't know that the laptop had any of the donor information. It shouldn't have. The list of our donors' names is used for a number of purposes, like creating mailing lists, so anyone here could have gotten access to that. But the donors' financial information itself? That's top secret. It's kept in a database on my computer. The only people who have access to it are me and our IT specialist."

"May I ask who your IT person is?" Mary had heard the term before and knew it referred to an information technology specialist—basically, the person who set up and maintained the computers.

"We hire Megan Lee on an hourly basis."

"Megan?" Mary smiled. Megan was the teenage grand-daughter of Bea Winslow, who ran the county clerk's office. Megan was only in high school, but she was a computer whiz.

"She's great. For being so young, she sure knows what she's doing. And her rates are reasonable. If you ever need someone to help you out in the shop, you should give her a call."

"She's quite talented." Mary was still trying to understand the database Virginia had mentioned. "So what kind of information would be in that top secret database with the financial records?"

"Well…" Virginia paused. "Addresses and phone numbers. Bank account numbers. Bank routing numbers." She shook her head, realizing, as Mary was, that this didn't look good.

"Is it normal to keep information like that on your donors?"

Virginia shrugged. "A lot of places these days are using services that allow you to donate online and mask your information, so the charity you're donating to never sees your bank account information." Mary nodded. She'd used services like that to buy used books online. The service stored her credit card number, but the vendors never saw it themselves. "But our major donors are—how can I say this— more *traditional* than most."

Mary understood. The idea of Betty going to a generic Web site and entering her credit card information was laughable. She always wrote checks or used cash whenever possible.

"But at the same time, a lot of our donors are sustaining members, meaning they make a preset donation each month."

"And they tend to use direct transfers from their bank accounts instead of, say, a credit card?"

"It depends on the person, but yes, a lot of them do have their accounts set up to transfer money directly from their bank accounts."

"That doesn't seem as safe, does it? With a credit card, if a strange charge shows up on your account, you can dispute it, and the card company waives the charge. But once money disappears from your bank account, it's gone, unless the bank decides to refund the money."

Virginia nodded. "I agree. But not all our donors see it that way. Many of them prefer to donate directly from their bank accounts. It can make things easier come tax time."

Mary mulled this over. She knew Betty often found it easier to budget if she stuck to her debit card and cash. Well, as much as Betty budgeted. She could see that maybe others felt the same way.

Virginia sighed. "And, confidentially, I can tell you the people you mentioned do indeed all donate regularly directly from their bank accounts."

"Is there a way to find out if someone else might have gained access to that database?"

Virginia snapped the glasses shut. "I'm not sure..." She let her voice trail off.

"Of course, if I'm right about this, you'll want to bring Chief McArthur in on this as soon as possible," Mary said, and that seemed to appease some of Virginia's hesitations.

"I suppose I can ask Megan if there's a way to find that out," Virginia said.

"Thank you." Mary tried to phrase this next part carefully. "And what about the security system here? Do you have security cameras?"

"We may be a small-town museum, Mary, but we're not rubes." Mary was surprised, but she could see that Virginia was grinning. "Yes, we have security cameras here," Virginia said. "I've already reviewed the footage and sent a copy to Chief McArthur, and I can assure you, there's no sign of anyone walking out with a laptop."

Mary gave her a gentle smile.

"You want to see it for yourself, don't you?"

Mary nodded sheepishly. "If it would be possible, I would love to take a look. It might help to narrow down the timeline so we can figure out who might have had access to the office and when." And, Mary thought, it might help establish who was where and when at that party. The museum wasn't very far from that spit of land where the call had likely come from. That didn't necessarily mean someone at the party had snuck out and made the call, but taking a look at the footage couldn't hurt.

"As I said, the police are looking at it, but what can it hurt? I'll make you a copy." Virginia sounded defeated, but she looked at Mary with something like admiration. Virginia stood and opened a cabinet door behind her desk. Mary glimpsed stacks of envelopes, reams of paper laid in precise piles, and neatly labeled boxes of supplies before Virginia pulled out a CD and shut the door. "The security footage is all digital," she said as she slid the disk into the tray on her computer tower and pressed a few buttons on her keyboard. "It's stored on the server." A moment later, she pulled the CD out, labeled it with a permanent pen, and handed it to Mary.

"Thank you. I'll let you know if I notice anything suspicious."

"I hope you won't, but if there's any chance it was our database that led to these thefts, we obviously want to figure it out and fix the problem."

"I thought you would say that." Mary slipped the disk into her purse and stood. "Aside from the main entrance and the door that leads to the side lot, are there any other doors out of the museum?"

"The door to the side lot is generally used only by the staff. Aside from that, there's just the emergency exit in the Samuelson Room." Mary recognized the name of one of the early families in Ivy Bay, one that had been influential at the glassworks two hundred years ago. "But if that's opened, an alarm goes off, and that never happened that night. I checked this morning, and the alarm is in working order, so you can cross that door off your list."

"That's good to know. So I'll just focus on those two doors, then." She moved toward the outer office. "And if you think of anything more about that laptop, no matter how insignificant, please let me know." Mary hitched her purse up over her shoulder and turned to go. "And thank you for your help."

"I just hope we can find it, especially if your suspicion about those records is true."

Mary stepped out into the outer office. The two desks were still empty. Taylor was sitting at the admissions desk, Mary knew, but Maureen didn't seem to be here.

"Virginia, is there any way I could talk to Maureen, just to see if she saw anything that night?"

"Sorry, she called in sick today." Something flickered across Virginia's face. Mary couldn't read it, but Virginia wasn't saying something about Maureen.

"Oh. I'm sorry to hear that."

"Yes, I hope she'll be back soon."

Mary watched Virginia, but she didn't give away anything more.

"I'll be in touch if I find anything on the video," Mary said breezily and headed for the door.

Virginia knew something about Maureen. Now, Mary just had to find out what.

# SEVEN

———◆◆———

M ary made a phone call, and then, instead of heading straight back to the shop, she turned right and headed toward the waterfront. She felt a little bad about leaving Lizzie alone for so long on her first day, but Mary was sure she could hold down the fort for just a little while longer.

The Ivy Bay Marina was quiet on this chilly afternoon, and she bypassed the warrens of fishermen's shanties and headed toward the coast guard building that stood on a small rise overlooking Cape Cod Canal. She had to show ID to get onto the government-owned property, but then she was ushered inside and shown up the stairs to the office of Lieutenant Peters.

"Hello, there, Mary," he said, standing up as she walked into the office. Mary knew that Lieutenant Peters's first name was Rusty, but she had only ever heard anyone call him Lieutenant.

He shook her hand and then sat down in his wooden desk chair. He gestured for Mary to sit in the chair across the desk. The office was decorated with framed certificates and some large-scale nautical charts, and there was a large picture window behind his desk that looked out over the canal. Mary saw a large tanker chugging along down the canal toward the Atlantic.

"What can I help you with today?"

"Thanks for letting me stop by. I wondered if you had time for a couple of questions." Lieutenant Peters had helped her with mysteries in the past, and she hoped he could illuminate a few things for her now.

"I have a meeting in twenty minutes, but I can talk to you until then," he said. "What's up?"

"I wanted to ask you about the distress call that came in on Saturday night."

"Ah. Yes." He blew out a breath and leaned back against his chair. "The false distress call. If you're here from the press, I have no comment."

Mary laughed. No doubt Johanna Montgomery had been all over this story for the *Ivy Bay Bugle*, and the coast guard was probably not thrilled to talk about it.

"I promise to leave my sources anonymous," she said, smiling.

Lieutenant Peters sighed. "What happened Saturday night was one of the more frustrating and embarrassing things that's happened around here in a long time."

"So you know for sure that the call was phony?"

"We're fairly sure. I heard you figured that out just about the same time we did?"

Mary wasn't sure when they'd discovered it, but she nodded. She explained her theory that whoever made the false distress call had been trying to create a distraction so they could steal the museum's laptop once the guards were gone.

"I may recruit you yet, Mary Fisher," Lieutenant Peters said. "So what can I help you understand?"

"Well..." Mary wasn't even sure what to ask, exactly. "Who first heard the distress signal? How does that even work?"

"Ah." He reached into his desk and pulled out what looked like an oversize walkie-talkie. "Have you ever seen a marine radio before?" He set it down on the desk, and Mary picked it up. It had a small screen and a number of dials and knobs.

"I've seen one in Henry's boat, but that was built right into the dashboard."

Lieutenant Peters nodded. "This is a handheld version. Portable. This is likely the kind of thing that was used to make the call, if it was truly made on land."

"And how does that work, exactly?"

He gestured for her to hand the radio back to him. He flipped a switch, and a crackle and a low hum came out of the speaker. He twisted one of the knobs, and a number on the small screen changed.

"Boaters use radios like these for a lot of purposes, but channel sixteen is the station designated 'hailing and distress.' When boaters are in trouble, they tune to channel sixteen and state the name of their vessel and their location, and they use the word *Mayday* three times to indicate there is a serious problem."

"Wow. I thought that was something people only said in movies."

"I'm afraid not." His tone was serious, but Mary could see the hint of a smile on his face.

"So who would hear a call like that?"

"We have radio watch standers on duty at all hours monitoring that station, and all vessels of a certain size are required to monitor it as well. Generally, when a distress call is made, we'll then confirm that we heard it and ask them to switch to another channel to keep channel sixteen clear for other emergencies." He turned the dial, and the number on the screen went down again. "And then we'll talk to the boater to try to determine their location and what kind of trouble they're in."

"And if they don't know their location? Henry Woodrow said something about radio towers to help determine that."

"Yes. The coast guard has a system called Rescue 21. It uses a network of towers along the coast to pinpoint where distress calls are coming from."

"Henry told me about that. But he also said that when too many people respond, it can end up scrambling the signal."

Lieutenant Peters nodded. "Thereby rendering the Rescue 21 system close to useless."

The tanker was now in the middle of the picture window, trudging slowly across the wind-whipped waves. Mary briefly wondered what the boat was carrying and where it was headed.

"And that's what happened here."

He nodded sheepishly. "The watch stander on duty received the call about seven fifteen. He followed protocol, but he's young, and it was his first emergency call. Probably didn't ask enough questions. Our boats went out, and we alerted other boats in the area. Maybe if we'd taken a few more minutes to think about it, we would have seen what you saw, but in the coast guard, we rotate posts so often that none of us have been here in Ivy Bay all that long. The fact that you can't see the lighthouse and the marina at the same time?" He shook his head. "Most of these guys don't know the area well enough to understand something like that."

Mary understood. Even the experienced fishermen who knew these waters well had missed it.

"Did anything about the call seem unusual?"

Lieutenant Peters shook his head. "Nothing that stood out to the watch stander." He paused. "Except, of course, the idea that there was a yacht out there on a winter night at all."

"So it is unusual for a pleasure boat to be out this time of year?"

"Some people do go out. It's rare, though, because it can be unpleasant and even dangerous out on the water in the winter."

"But lots of boats go out on the water all year, right?"

"Well, commercial operations do, like Henry's fishing boat, but that's a different story. He knows what he's doing and is equipped for all kinds of weather. But small pleasure boaters? You can mess your boat up big-time if you don't take proper precautions in the winter."

"How so?"

"There's the obvious fact that the elements can lead to exposure quickly, and if God forbid someone falls over the side, it takes only minutes for hypothermia to set in." Mary nodded, and he continued. "But there's also the problem that pipes and tubing can freeze. Your engine can freeze. Water can get into all kinds of cracks and freeze. When water freezes, it expands, and you can end up with gaps where water can get in. A boat can sink out there, easy, if you're not careful."

"My goodness."

"That's another reason we probably should have asked more questions."

"Do you have any idea who could have made the call?"

"We're investigating, of course." He picked up the radio and started fiddling with the dial, and strange, almost otherworldly noises came out of it. "But as long as you promise you're not in cahoots with Johanna Montgomery..."

Mary used her index finger to cross her heart.

"In that case, I can tell you that we don't have any real leads. No idea why someone would do something like that. Thousands of dollars were wasted, and hundreds of man-hours. At least one rescuer was injured. It just doesn't make any sense." He turned the radio off and set it down on the desk. "The police are working on this, and the coast guard is doing its own investigation. But the truth is, aside from confirming that the call was made on that spit of land by the town beach, we've got nothing. I encourage you to keep investigating. We need all hands on deck."

# EIGHT

◆◆◆

Mary headed back to her shop, and the rest of the afternoon passed quickly. They only had a few customers, and Mary was glad when it was time to close up shop. Lizzie helped Mary straighten up the store. Then they put on their coats, shut off the lights, and headed for Mary's car.

"That's a long day," Lizzie said as Mary pulled away from the curb. Lizzie yawned and leaned her head back against the headrest. "And you do that every day."

"Sometimes it's even worse. Sometimes we have customers. Then we really have to work." Mary laughed, but Lizzie just nodded. The store was open from ten until six. It was a long day, but it usually didn't feel like it, and there were plenty of people who worked longer hours. "Besides, I don't do it all by myself. Usually, I have Rebecca and her daughter Ashley, and now you. That helps."

"But you don't get home until after six. What do you do about dinner?"

Mary stopped at the red light at the corner and saw that Bailey's Ice Cream Shop was closed, the lights dark. It was one of the many shops that had shorter hours in the winter months. Mary had considered shortening her hours too but always decided against it. Jimmy Shepard was just locking the front door of his hardware store. Mary waved, and he waved back, then pulled his coat tighter and buried his face in his scarf and headed toward his car.

"Often, Betty will get things started, but if she doesn't have a chance, then I just start cooking when I get home." The light changed, and Mary crossed Route 6A and headed toward Shore Drive. "We don't eat until a bit later, but it's not a big deal."

"I don't think Chad would be happy if I asked him to start cooking before I got home," Lizzie said, looking out the window. "And if we ate later, that would probably push back the kids' bedtime."

"I guess I have a more flexible schedule." They crossed over the small bridge that led across the cranberry bog, and Mary turned on the blinker as they neared her street. "That's one of the perks of getting old, I guess."

"Oh, Mom, you're not old and you know it." Mary looked over and saw that Lizzie laughed, but she was still gazing out the window like she was looking for something. They drove in silence for a few minutes, and Mary turned right onto her street.

"Everything okay?"

Lizzie turned and smiled, but it was a little too wide, a little too big. "Just fine." Lizzie looked like she might say more, but as they neared the house, she just shook her head and smiled. "I'm so glad I'm able to help you this week, Mom."

"I'm really glad too."

Mary wanted to ask more, but as soon as they pulled into the driveway, Lizzie hopped out of the car and headed inside.

Mary watched her disappear inside and then slowly followed her daughter into the house.

———

By the time Lizzie and Chad got the kids into bed and dinner cleaned up, they were both yawning. According to Emma and Luke, they'd had an awesome day with their dad, who had taken them out for hot chocolate after their lunch and then let them watch TV for several hours as he checked his work e-mail. Lizzie had given Chad a stern look, but he pretended he didn't see and kicked Luke under the table, which had caused Luke to snort milk out of his nose and started a round of uproarious laughter around the table. But as soon as the house was quiet, Lizzie and Chad said good night and headed upstairs too.

"I don't know how you do that every day," Chad mumbled, and Lizzie laughed and told him to just wait.

Mary set the teakettle on and smiled, watching them go upstairs. It was nice to see Lizzie and Chad interact. It seemed like just yesterday that she and John had met Chad for the first time. They had gone to visit Lizzie for parents' weekend at college, and Lizzie had nervously asked if she could invite a boy to come to dinner with them. John had flown into protective-dad mode, asking probing questions about how well Lizzie knew this boy and what his intentions were, but as soon as Chad showed up at the restaurant that night, Mary had known he was the one for Lizzie. She had been praying for the person Lizzie would marry since the day she was born, and her heart recognized him when she saw the way he looked at Lizzie that night. It took a bit longer for John to start trusting Chad, but he grew to love him as a son, and on Lizzie's wedding day, he had carefully placed his daughter's hand in Chad's and asked him to take care of his little girl.

As she watched Lizzie and Chad disappear up the stairs now, she felt a pang of loneliness. She missed John.

"She turned out all right."

Mary was thankful to see Betty come up beside her. Betty wrapped her arm around Mary's waist and pulled her in for a side hug. Once again, Mary was reminded how lucky she was to have a sister like Betty, who understood things Mary hadn't even said.

"She did, didn't she?" Mary agreed.

"Not every daughter would drop everything to come help her mom run her business for a week."

Mary laughed. "True, but I'm beginning to think she sees it as a vacation. Chad looked positively worn out tonight. It must be nice for her to have a change of pace."

"I'm sure it is. And it's good for Chad to see what it's like being home with kids all day," Betty said. "It's not as easy as a lot of people think."

The teakettle whistled.

"Cup of tea?" Mary moved to the cabinet by the sink and took down a mug. Betty had been jumpy all day, and her face was drawn, and Mary suspected a cup of herbal tea might help calm her nerves.

"Yes, please."

Mary grabbed another mug and set them both on the counter while Betty pulled the basket of tea out of the pantry. They both selected an herbal blend, and a moment later, they were holding steaming mugs.

"So how are you doing?" Mary asked.

Betty shrugged. "Eleanor says the bank has to reimburse us for the money, so that's comforting. But it's still pretty scary."

"I can't even imagine."

Mary took a sip of her tea, and a pleasant, quiet hush fell over the house.

"So what's your plan for the rest of the evening?" Betty asked.

Mary looked down at the wisps of steam coming up off her tea. She had intended to work on her new flavor for Bailey's Ice Cream Shop this evening. She was working on a frozen hot-chocolate flavor. It was unusual, but Mary thought it had promise. But that could wait. She had something else in mind tonight.

"Actually, I was thinking I might watch a video."

Betty looked toward the living room, where they kept a handful of DVDs next to the television. "Which one?"

A sly smile spread across Mary's face. "I went by the museum today, and Virginia Livingston gave me footage from their security cameras."

Betty cocked an eyebrow. Mary explained why she thought the missing laptop had likely held financial information for the museum's donors, and Betty's skepticism seemed to ease.

"So you think that if you figure out who stole the laptop, you'll know who stole my money?"

"That's what I'm hoping." Mary lowered her nose over her cup and inhaled deeply, and warm peppermint steam filled her lungs. "And I know it's a long shot, but I'll be looking for anything that might indicate if someone from the party placed the distress call."

She filled Betty in on her theory the call might have come from someone at the party, because of the museum's proximity to the spit of land where the call had originated, and because, if she was right, the call had been made specifically to create chaos to allow for the laptop to be stolen.

"Well, in that case, let's get this video rolling," Betty said. Mary agreed. She wasn't sure if the video's file format would play on the TV, so she grabbed her laptop from her room and took the video out of her purse. They sat at the kitchen table, and Mary loaded the disk into her laptop. A moment later, a grainy still image appeared on the screen. Mary enlarged it to full screen, looked at Betty, who nodded, and then pushed Play.

The footage came from a camera mounted near the ceiling in the main gallery. There, in the middle of the room, was the Hamilton Decanter, and a security guard stood nearby. The double doors that led to the museum entrance were at the top of the screen, and the hallway that branched off toward the office, where the laptop had been, was on the right. Virginia had told Mary there was a security camera in each gallery of the museum, but the private areas, such as the office, where none of the museum's collection was kept, were not monitored except by the roving guards. The time stamp in the lower right-hand corner said this video started at just before seven.

Mary found herself quickly, at the side of the room talking to Henry. She watched as the video image of her took a glass of water from a passing waiter. Henry was pulling at the sleeves of his shirt.

"It really was a lovely party, wasn't it?" Betty sighed. "Eleanor did such a nice job pulling the whole thing together."

"It was nice," Mary said, but her attention was focused on the screen. There was Taylor, talking with one of the waiters, and Mason Willoughby, the gallery owner, chatting with Virginia. Betty was talking with Evelyn Anders, the glass artist, and even though Betty was the picture of grace, Mary knew her sister well enough to recognize the small movements that indicated she was trying to extricate herself from that conversation.

"It was nice of Tabitha to come out, wasn't it?" Betty said. "She doesn't get to a lot of events, but she knows how important the glass museum is to this town's history."

Mary nodded, but she kept her focus on that hallway. One of the waitresses from the catering company took a tray loaded with dirty glasses down the hallway and returned about thirty seconds later with a full tray. That was not nearly long enough to do anything other than refill the tray, so Mary didn't think she was worth studying too carefully. She knew Betty was nervous, and chatting was her way of covering that up, so Mary tried her best to listen and respond while she stayed focused. Upstairs, they could hear Lizzie and Chad moving around, getting ready for bed.

The first real motion at the end of the hallway came just after seven, when Taylor walked through the gallery and down the hallway toward the back, just as she'd told Mary. According to what she'd said earlier, this was the last time she'd seen the laptop. Mary stopped the footage and played it back again. What Taylor hadn't told Mary, however, was that she wasn't alone when she went into the office. On the footage, Mary could plainly see that the waiter Taylor had been chatting with a few minutes earlier had followed her down the hallway.

Mary paused the footage and studied the frozen image of the waiter. The shot was blurry, but she could make out blond hair, cut close to his head. He was tall, and he had strong cheekbones, and he looked quite handsome in his tuxedo. He seemed vaguely familiar. Mary remembered seeing him at the party.

"What do we think about him?" Mary used the arrow keys to zoom in on the man.

"I don't know him."

"I don't either. We'll keep an eye on him." Mary shook her head and resumed the video. Taylor and the waiter disappeared down the hallway and vanished out of sight.

"Besides the office, what is down that hallway?" Betty asked. On the screen, Mary and Henry were talking, and Mary guessed this was when he had told her he'd never been to the museum before.

"Just the exit to the side parking lot. I checked while I was there today."

Three minutes had passed on the screen when Taylor and the waiter came back out into the main gallery. Neither one had anything in their hands. If they had anything to do with the laptop's disappearance, they hadn't been brazen enough to carry it out of the office and through the main gallery. But Mary remembered Taylor's furious texting while she had been talking with her today. Was there any chance she was chatting with this waiter, letting him know Mary was asking questions?

"Could they have grabbed the laptop and carried it out the back door and made it back in that amount of time?"

"Yes, they probably could." She considered. "But why would Taylor do that? It's her work computer. Why do it at the party? Why not just take it some other time? And why would she have done it before Chief McArthur came in?"

Betty shook her head. "It doesn't make a lot of sense."

Still, Mary wasn't going to discount either one of them. Taylor had been hiding something today, and she didn't know anything about this waiter. She grabbed a piece of scrap paper—the back of the envelope from their electricity bill—and wrote *Suspects* at the top. Taylor and the mysterious waiter were at the top of the list.

"I'll handle this," Betty said and took the pen and paper from Mary. "You focus on that video."

Mary watched as the party replayed itself in front of her. Now it was seven fifteen, right about the time, according to Lieutenant Peters, the distress call had been picked up by the coast guard. Mary scanned the room to see if anyone notable was missing, but she couldn't see anyone who should have been there but wasn't. There was Betty, talking with Cynthia Jones, and Eleanor was chatting with Bernice Foster. Mary hadn't noticed those conversations when she had been at the party. Taylor was talking with Tabitha Krause at the door by the front of the room, and the mysterious waiter was serving a drink to Virginia Livingston. They were both definitely accounted for while the call came in.

Mary sighed. There was no guarantee that the person who had placed the call had been at the party, but she realized she had come to believe it was true. Why else would someone orchestrate the whole charade, if not to create the opportunity to steal the laptop?

The video had no sound, and the noises upstairs had stopped. A quiet hush settled over the kitchen. It was strange to relive the party, frame by frame. She remembered what she was feeling and thinking as she saw it all unfold again in front of her. And she saw many things she hadn't seen while she was there, including how close Mason Willoughby leaned in to Dorothy Johnson when she talked, and how Dorothy didn't seem to mind. A few people came in through the double doors that led to the admission area, late to the party, but no one went down the hallway.

On the screen, Eleanor came up to talk with Mary and Henry. Then, a few moments later, she grabbed her grandson Thomas as he walked by and introduced him. And just a few minutes later, after Eleanor had moved off, Chief McArthur came in through the double doors and headed straight for the guards on either side of the decanter. Mary knew what had happened in the middle of the room because she'd seen it all unfold, so she kept her attention focused on the hallway.

Just a moment later, the same waiter Taylor had been talking to had gone down the hallway, loaded down with a tray of empty glasses. Mary watched as, not more than a minute later, he returned, carrying a dishwashing tray loaded with clean glasses. He'd barely had time to swap out his dirty dishes for the clean ones, let alone steal the computer. Still, that was his second appearance in the hallway that evening. He was different from the other caterers in that way. Mary would definitely be looking into that guy.

And then, while people were scurrying around the decanter, just about when Chief McArthur pulled Henry aside to explain about the missing boaters, she saw it.

Maureen Rowe, ducking down the hallway, disappearing into the shadows. Mary backed the video up and played it again, pointing to Maureen's figure so Betty would see it too. It was quick, just a couple of seconds. One minute she was in the main gallery, and the next, she was scurrying down the hallway, shoulders hunched, bent forward.

"She almost looks like she doesn't want to be seen," Betty said.

Mary had to agree. And she recalled seeing Maureen leave the party that night with a large tote bag. Could that have had the laptop inside?

"But Maureen has the same excuse Taylor did," Mary said. Mary watched the screen and waited, but Maureen didn't come back. "If she'd wanted the laptop, or the information on the laptop, why not just take it some other time, during work hours? She wouldn't need to arrange the whole distress-call hoax."

Betty shrugged. "Maybe she wanted to throw everyone off the trail. It's possible she thought no one would ever suspect her if there was a big hoax, for the very reasons you said." They watched the screen, waiting for her to come back. Mary realized she was rooting for Maureen to show up again. She had always been nice to Mary, and Mary didn't want to think that this mother of two could have something to do with the laptop's disappearance.

"I always thought there was something fishy about her." Betty added Maureen's name to the list of suspects.

"You did not." Mary laughed. "What could you possibly have against her?"

"She doesn't look you in the eye when she's talking to you." Betty held two fingers in front of her eyes and moved them forward and backward, toward Mary.

Well, that much was true. Maureen was a bit socially awkward. She had a tendency to cut conversations short in clumsy ways and never seemed to know what to do with her hands. But that didn't make her a thief. And even if she had taken the laptop, why wait until the party to walk out with it? It didn't add up.

Still, though, she had been one of the few people who had access to the office that night. And why had she gone down the hallway, and why was she gone so long? On the screen, Maureen had already been gone long enough to have taken the laptop out to her car and come back. And Mary remembered Maureen hadn't shown up for work today and Virginia's strange look when Mary asked her about it. There were still enough questions about Maureen that Mary would look into her.

Betty pointed at the screen. Another woman was ducking down the hallway.

"Is that Evelyn Anders?" Mary paused the video and backed it up a few frames. The woman was facing away from the camera, but she was wearing a floor-length turquoise dress with a contrasting orange scarf wrapped around her shoulders, and very high heels. Her blonde hair was loose around her shoulders.

"Indeed. Who else would wear summer colors in February?" Betty said, shaking her head.

Mary paused the video and stared at her sister. That was as close as Betty ever came to criticism.

"Oh, come on, you're supposed to be the one who notices everything," Betty said, but Mary could see in her eyes she was delighted to have picked up on something Mary missed.

"Fashion is more your purview."

Betty shook her head. "I'm just saying, she stood out. And yes, that was Evelyn."

Mary had only met Evelyn a few times, but she had been eager to tell Mary about the glass pieces she was working on. She had pulled her phone out and shown Mary pictures and had told her all about how she had transformed part of her garage into a glass-blowing studio.

"Exactly."

"That's right. And there she is, disappearing down the hallway toward the computer."

Mary played the video again, and sure enough, Evelyn ducked down the hallway, just minutes after the guards had disappeared, while most people were still focused on the drama unfolding in the center of the room.

"What do you know about Evelyn?" Mary asked, but she kept her eyes focused on the screen.

"I talked to her for a bit at the party. She talked a lot about her glass. I think she just wants to be taken seriously as an artist, but she's trying too hard, if you ask me."

"Anything else?"

"She and her husband moved here from California fairly recently. *Nouveau riche.* They live in one of those ghastly new developments of mass-manufactured mansions."

"So you liked her a lot?" Mary joked.

"She was perfectly nice," Betty allowed. "We just didn't have a lot in common."

It was almost eight minutes later, Mary saw by the time stamp on the bottom of the footage, when Evelyn and Maureen came back into view of the camera, slipping smoothly out of the hallway and into the main gallery at the same time. Maureen said something to Evelyn just before they entered the gallery, and then the two women went separate ways.

"Curiouser and curiouser," Mary whispered.

"Well, I don't know what Maureen was doing down there, but Evelyn is definitely a suspect. That dress was polyester." Betty picked up the pen and started to add Evelyn's name to the list.

Mary tilted her head. "How does that matter?" It wasn't Mary's favorite dress either, but bad fashion choices did not automatically make her guilty.

Betty used the pen to point at the screen. "There are two options for where she could have gone when she stepped down this hallway, right? The office, where the laptop was, and outside through the side door?"

Mary nodded hesitantly.

"She doesn't have a coat with her, and if she'd gone outside in that dress, she would have been freezing." She tapped the screen with the end of the pen to make her point. "If it had been made of a natural fiber, like silk, it would have offered some measure of warmth, but the wind would go right through a dress made of a synthetic fiber like that."

Mary looked again at Evelyn's turquoise dress. It was long, but it seemed to be made of some light material. Betty had a point. "She's wearing a scarf though."

Betty was undaunted. "Decorative. If it had been a cashmere blend, maybe it would have kept her warm, but that's a knockoff. It's just cotton washed thin."

Mary had to trust Betty on that one. But she did have a point. If Evelyn had gone down the hall to the door and gone outside, she would have been frozen solid. Could she have stood out there all this time wearing that outfit? A native New Englander might have been able to stand it, but surely a recent transplant from California would have come inside right away. And if she wasn't outside, there was only one other option for where she could have gone.

Betty added her name to the list triumphantly. Maureen's name was already there, but here was one more thing to ask her about.

Mary looked at the time stamp. It was now almost seven forty-five, and in the main gallery, people were starting to carry on with the party.

Not more than a minute later, Taylor crossed back through the gallery and went down the hallway again. That matched what she had told Mary. This must have been when she discovered the laptop was missing.

Mary saw she was still talking with Betty and Thomas on-screen. Mary felt relief to see that. At least Eleanor's grandson had an ironclad excuse. They would not have to tell Eleanor that her grandson was a thief. She would not have reacted to that well, to say the least.

They watched the recording for a few more minutes and saw Taylor come out of the hallway, her face down, her movements quick and jerky. She was upset. As Mary had suspected, she had just discovered the laptop was gone.

Mary paused the video. Virginia had been right. There was no footage of anyone walking out with the laptop. But since no one had been seen taking the laptop out into the main gallery, the only option was that someone had taken it out through the side door. And they now had a list of everyone who had had access to that side door throughout the window of time when the computer had disappeared.

"So one of these people did it," Betty said, holding out the list. "My money is on Evelyn."

"Because you don't like her dress?"

"Among other things," Betty said. Mary could see she was mostly joking, but there was an element of seriousness behind it.

Mary would talk with Evelyn and see if she could find out why she'd gone down the hallway that night. But she would also check in with Maureen, whose actions seemed just as suspicious. She had some more questions for Taylor too—such as what had happened when she and the handsome waiter had been in the back room? Why had she brought him there? And why had she left that fact out when she'd talked to Mary earlier? And Mary would also need to track down this waiter. It was a good list. A solid place to start.

But Mary wasn't satisfied. Something was teasing at the corner of her mind. She backed the video up.

"What's going on?"

Mary pointed at the screen. The time stamp showed 7:12, just a few minutes before the distress call came in. There was Maureen, talking to Dawn Santiago. Evelyn wasn't hard to spot in her bright dress. She was hanging around at the edge of a group from church. Taylor was at her post by the front double doors. And—Mary scanned the room—there was that waiter, holding out a tray of hors d'oeuvres to Mary. She watched the video play for the next few minutes. All four of her suspects moved around, but none of them left the room. And they were all still in the room when Chief McArthur burst through the door a few minutes later. Mary paused the recording.

"None of them made the call."

Betty tapped her pen against the envelope. "Well, there's no guarantee that the caller was the one who stole the laptop, right? It could have been just a coincidence? Someone taking advantage of a good opportunity?"

It was possible, Mary had to concede, but it didn't feel right. It was too perfect to be coincidence.

"I think there has to be a connection," Mary said. There was something she was missing; she was sure of it.

"Well, at least you have a place to start." Betty handed her the list of suspects.

That was true. Tomorrow morning, she would start to investigate the four people on her list. Hopefully, whatever she was missing would become clear in the process.

# NINE

❖

Mary shivered as she pulled back the covers Tuesday morning. She drew the curtains and saw that dark clouds hung low and heavy over the sand dunes. Mary dressed warmly in a thick sweater and lined wool pants. She heard a chair scraping across the kitchen floor below and then a crash and a thud as a dish landed in the sink, and she smiled. It may be a miserably cold, gray day, but her grandkids were here. That made any day brighter.

"Grandma! It's going to snow!" Luke yelled as Mary descended the stairs. "Snow day! Woo!" He was taking his bowl out of the sink and loading it into the dishwasher, and Lizzie was standing over him, making sure he did it correctly. Lizzie was still in a bathrobe and flannel pajamas, and her hair hadn't been brushed.

"You don't get a snow day if you're already on vacation, dummy." Emma looked up from her book long enough to stick her tongue out at her brother, then returned to the page in front of her. She was eating colorful cereal at the table, and little splashes of pink-tinged milk surrounded her bowl.

"What's this about snow?"

Lizzie pointed to the newspaper, which was open on the counter. "They're calling for two to three inches tonight. It's supposed to start sometime this afternoon."

Mary looked at the paper, and sure enough, snow was in the forecast. On the front page, she also saw an article about the huge expense the search for the missing boaters had cost the Ivy Bay police and the coast guard, and an article about the boater who had been injured in the search. She sighed. She would read it all later.

Luke closed the dishwasher and went to the French doors and peered out, as if he were expecting to see flakes start falling. He was wearing Spider-Man pajamas and a pair of black dress socks.

"Luke helped me pack his clothes for this trip," Lizzie said, noticing where Mary's eyes went. "He told me he'd packed socks. I neglected to ask what kind of socks."

Mary laughed and looked at Luke, bouncing in anticipation of the snow. "Well, if it's going to be cold like this, we might as well get some snow out of it," Mary said as Lizzie poured coffee into a mug, added cream, and handed it to her.

Though snow meant shoveling and spreading sand and clomping through icy slush, it also transformed everything into something beautiful, and she considered it one of God's better inventions.

"So does the impending snow put a damper on the day's activities?" Mary asked.

"Nah. We're just going to some dumb old fishing museum anyway. It's all inside." Emma didn't even look up. "We'll probably be stuck inside tomorrow, though. Thank goodness I brought another book."

"And thank goodness your father will have to be the one to figure out some way to entertain you." Lizzie laughed and took a sip out of her own mug. "I'm a working girl now."

"You've had a job for *one day*." Emma got up and loaded her bowl straight into the dishwasher. "And it's just for Grandma's bookshop. It's not like it's hard. No offense, Grandma."

"None taken."

"Well, even if it is just one day and 'just for Grandma,'" Lizzie caught Mary's eye and smiled, "I'm grateful for it. It's so nice to have some real work to do for a change. I think I could get used to this career-girl thing."

Emma got down a mug and started to pour herself some coffee, but Lizzie halted her and asked her what she thought she was doing. Emma shrugged, picked up her book, and wandered out of the room.

"I'm glad you're enjoying the shop, but don't sell yourself short." Mary pulled down a bowl and got out the carton of milk and sat down at the table. "What you just did there looked like real work to me." There was a box of Cheerios and a box of whatever fluorescent cereal Emma had been eating. Mary decided to give the kids' cereal a try.

"Mom, can I turn on the TV?" Luke whirled around and stared at Lizzie.

"If you only watch PBS," Lizzie said.

"Cool." Luke ran out of the room and slid on his socks toward the living room.

"I know Emma's right, that it's only been one day, but I really am enjoying the job thing. Actually, I've been thinking about—"

Noise blared from the living room, some fast music with a deep rhythmic beat. Mary wasn't sure how Betty was sleeping through this, and she hoped her sister wasn't being disturbed. Moisture in the air sometimes made her rheumatoid arthritis flare up, and Mary hoped a little extra rest would keep her feeling well.

"That doesn't sound like *Sesame Street*." Lizzie sighed and set her mug down on the counter. The noise didn't stop. "I'd better go check that out."

Mary laughed and turned to her cereal. It was some sort of puffy, air-filled thing, shaped to look like sea creatures and dyed colors not found in nature. Mary poured on some milk and scooped up a spoonful dubiously. Not bad, she decided. Not good, for sure—it was too sweet, and as she chewed, it scraped up the roof of her mouth—but she could see why the kids liked it.

The television turned off, and she heard Lizzie and Luke clomping up the stairs. Mary, suddenly alone, shrugged and reached for the Bible she kept on the sideboard and read one of her favorite passages.

"So do not worry, saying, 'What shall we eat?' or 'What shall we drink?' or 'What shall we wear?' For the pagans run after all these things, and your heavenly Father knows that you need them. But seek first his kingdom and his righteousness, and all these things will be given to you as well" (Matthew 6:31–33).

It felt especially reassuring to read that today, with so many questions still swirling about what had happened to Betty's money. No matter what happened, the Lord would take care of her needs.

But that didn't mean she wasn't going to keep looking for the thief, Mary thought as she tipped up her bowl and drank the sweet pink milk left in the bottom.

She pushed her chair back and loaded her bowl into the dishwasher, swallowed the dregs of her coffee, and went upstairs to brush her teeth and finish getting ready. She got Gus into his carrier and put her coat on.

A few minutes later, she was downstairs, waiting for Lizzie. There were lots of footsteps upstairs, and Mary heard a shower turn on. The numbers on the digital clock on the stove kept advancing. Finally, Mary took off her coat and her shoes and ventured upstairs to see what was taking Lizzie so long. She found her kneeling in Luke's room, trying to cajole him into changing into jeans. She was still in her robe, and she hadn't started her hair or makeup.

"Lizzie, do you…" Mary cleared her throat. "Do you think you'll need much time to finish getting ready? I was about to leave."

Lizzie gasped. "Is it that late already? I had no idea." She stood up and combed her fingers through her hair. "I'm so sorry. I got so distracted trying to get Luke dressed. I haven't even taken a shower, and Chad's in there now." She looked down at what she was wearing. "I'll skip it. Give me fifteen minutes, and I'll be ready to go."

In fifteen minutes, it would be past time to open the store.

"Tell you what," Mary said. "I'll just go on ahead. You get there as soon as you can."

"I'm so sorry, Mom. I'll be quick."

"It's okay. I'll see you soon."

Mary hurried down the stairs and drove to the shop. She flipped on the lights, started coffee brewing, started the gas fireplace, flipped the sign on the door to Open, and sat down behind the counter just before ten. Gus climbed out of his carrier, stretched, yawned, and curled up just in front of the radiator by the bay windows, which Betty had decorated with intricately cut paper snowflakes she'd cut from Victorian valentines.

A few minutes later, her first customer of the day, Todd Milton, came in for a birthday gift for his wife, Bev.

"It's so cheerful in here," he said, looking at the blazing fire.

"It sure makes winter mornings more bearable to have that fireplace going," Mary said, steering him toward the British mysteries she knew Bev enjoyed. A few minutes later, she'd rung Todd up, and he stepped outside and rushed to his car, leaving Mary alone.

It wasn't like they had a flood of customers, Mary reminded herself. Still, if Mary hadn't left Lizzie behind and gone to the store when she did, she'd have missed out on a sale.

Mary tried to shake off her frustration. She'd made it. She was having a wonderful visit with her grandchildren. And Rebecca would be back in five days.

Since the shop was quiet, Mary decided to use this time well. First, she scanned through her e-mail. She answered a few e-mails about book orders, deleted some spam, and replied to a message her granddaughter Daisy had sent her.

She also saw a message from her prayer group. Recently, they had started sending out an e-mail with the list of requests after their meeting so they could continue to pray over them throughout the week. Mary had missed the meeting yesterday morning, and she opened the list and began to pray over the requests.

*Lord, please be with AS, because her husband goes to surgery this week. Take care of TO as she travels to visit her mother this week. Please be with JR, still in the hospital after his accident. Please help DJ as she tries to save for new windows on her house.*

They used initials because everything said in prayer meeting was supposed to be private; in case this e-mail got forwarded on or printed out, it wouldn't become fodder for gossip. Mary prayed over the requests and then closed the e-mail. She would continue to pray for these people, whoever they were, all week.

Next, she pulled the envelope with her suspect list out of her purse and smoothed it down on the counter.

She decided to start with the easiest target first. She called the glass museum. An older woman answered, and Mary recognized Hazel Pritchard's voice. Hazel must be one of the museum volunteers.

"Hi, Hazel. This is Mary Fisher."

"Oh, hi, Mary. How are you? How's Betty?" Hazel was older, and she used a cane to get around, but she liked to get out when she could. She had long been a member of Grace Church, and she had always been friendly and liked to chat.

"We're all just fine. My daughter Lizzie is here with her kids this week, so we're all having a good time."

"Oh, that's nice. So what can I help you with today? We're having a special at the gift shop. Two for one Christmas ornaments."

"Well, that does sound nice. Maybe I'll stop in sometime and check them out. But today, I was just calling to talk to Maureen."

"I'm sorry, but Maureen's out sick today."

"Oh." Mary made a note of that by Maureen's name on the back of the envelope. "She was out sick yesterday too. I hope she's all right."

"I wouldn't know," Hazel said. "Though she has been out more than usual these days."

"Oh?"

"Well, just between you and me"—she lowered her voice—"I think she's job hunting."

"Really?" Mary wrote *job hunting?* on the back of the envelope. "Is she unhappy at the museum?"

"Oh, I don't think so, but the museum has been having some financial trouble, you know."

"Really?" Mary knew they had been raising money for a new roof—that was what the fund-raiser had been about, after all—but she suspected if she encouraged Hazel a bit, she might find out more. "How bad is it?"

"Well, you didn't hear it from me, but the rumor is that they might have to let some staff go."

She let the words sit there, and Mary absorbed their impact. Virginia and Maureen were the only two paid employees, and they wouldn't be getting rid of Virginia. If Hazel was right, and if Maureen knew about it, as the fact that she was job hunting would indicate, she suddenly had an excellent motive for finding a new source of income.

"I'm so sorry to hear that. Maureen must be so worried."

"Well, it doesn't help that her husband's grant is about to run out. And they have that big house over on Colonial, right by the school. That thing can't have been cheap."

"Oh?" Hazel had always been a talker, and Mary suspected it must be quiet at the museum today, so she would just try to keep her talking. "What grant?"

"Well, her husband is a marine biologist, and he's been studying some sort of sea anemone or some such thing, from some grant he got from a fancy university. Maureen was telling me about it a few weeks ago. But apparently, the grant is about to run out, and right at the same time that her job is in jeopardy. It's just terrible."

"It certainly is," Mary agreed.

"Well, I can leave her a message that you called," Hazel said.

"That would be great. Thank you so much, Hazel."

"You tell Lizzie hi for me, will you?"

"I sure will."

Mary hung up. Well, that was interesting. She had known the museum was trying to raise money. But she hadn't realized how dire the situation was. No wonder Eleanor and Virginia had been so upset about the fund-raiser being interrupted.

Mary now needed to talk to Maureen more than ever. It was possible she really was sick, Mary thought. But it did look mighty strange that Maureen, who stood to be laid off from the museum, had vanished just at the same time the laptop had. And if her husband was a marine biologist, she no doubt had access to a boat—and a marine radio. But again, why would she arrange such a huge hoax to steal a laptop with information she could access at work anyway?

Mary made a note to look into that, and then she pulled the phone book off the shelf behind the counter. Maybe she could catch Maureen at home. If she really was sick, that was where she would be.

Mary found the number and dialed, then waited as it rang and rang. Finally, the Rowes' voice mail picked up. Mary left a message, asking Maureen to give her a call, and then she set the phone down gently. If Maureen was home sick, why wasn't she picking up the phone? And if she wasn't home sick...where was she?

Mary would try to find out more about Maureen later. Now, while she still had a few minutes of peace, she flipped the pages in the phone book and found the number for Evelyn Anders, the glass artist who had gone down the hallway after Maureen on the night of the party. Evelyn picked up on the third ring.

"Hello?"

"Hi, Evelyn. This is Mary Fisher. We've met at—"

"Of course! Mary Fisher. You have that adorable shop on Main Street!"

"That's right. And I'm sorry to bother you, but I know you were at the fund-raiser for the glass museum on Saturday night, and I was wondering if I could ask you a few questions."

"Oh, wasn't that such a beautiful event? They do such a nice job there. It's so nice to see the glass arts appreciated like that."

"It's true. Not enough people appreciate the glass arts these days." Mary wasn't sure that was a real phrase, but Evelyn seemed to know what she was talking about.

"Oh, it's so good to meet a fellow glass appreciator."

Mary's head was spinning a little. She wasn't sure how Evelyn had leapt to the conclusion she was into glass, but Mary supposed she liked it as much as the next person.

"Yes, it sure is." She hoped that was the right thing to say. "In fact, I wanted to ask you about something to do with other people who love glass as much as you do."

"Well, why don't you come on by the house, and we can talk in person? I'll show you some of the pieces I'm working on."

"That sounds great." Mary hadn't been anticipating a visit to her home, but you could always learn more about someone by seeing them in their natural habitat. "What time would be good for you?"

"I'm free now."

Mary paused. Evelyn was sure enthusiastic. That was a good sign, she supposed. If she had something to hide, would she be so willing to talk about the fund-raiser? But Mary couldn't leave the store until Lizzie arrived.

"Maybe around eleven thirty?"

"That would be perfect."

"Great. I'm looking forward to it." Evelyn gave Mary her address, and Mary said she'd see her soon.

She hung up, and a few moments later, Sherry Walinski walked in. Gus protested at the blast of cold air that accompanied her inside the store, but then he rolled over and went back to sleep.

"Hello, Sherry," Mary said. Sherry unwound a thick wool scarf from her neck and took off her knit cap. Sherry was Mary's next-door neighbor, and as a single mother of two teenage boys, she didn't have a lot of free time to read. Mary didn't see her in the shop very often.

Sherry was looking at the fireplace longingly. "How do you avoid just curling up in front of that fire and reading all day?"

"Sometimes I succumb to temptation." Mary laughed. "Can I help you find anything in particular?"

"I'm actually here to place an order, if that's okay."

"Sure thing. I can order just about anything. What do you need?"

"Mr. Hanson wants to do a special project with his honors history class, and the students have to buy their own copies of these books." She handed Mary a list of three classic British mysteries. "Apparently, they're studying British history this unit, and he thought this would be an interesting way to get into it. So I need fifteen copies of each. The students will come by and purchase the books themselves."

"No problem at all. When do you need them by?"

Sherry grimaced. "Friday, if at all possible."

"That's no problem. I'll ask for expedited shipping. We should get them tomorrow." Overnight shipping would cost extra, but she would make up for it with guaranteed sales for such a large number of books.

"Thank you so much, Mary." Sherry slipped her hat back on and settled her scarf around her neck.

"No problem. Stay warm."

Sherry laughed and stepped outside. Gus squawked but didn't lift his head.

"If you don't like it, move away from the door," Mary said sternly, but he ignored her.

A few minutes later, Lizzie rushed in. She had taken a shower and straightened her hair, and her makeup was subtle but flattering. She looked nice and would represent the store well to the customers, but...

"I'm so sorry, Mom." Lizzie took off her jacket and her hat and set her purse behind the counter. "Emma had a meltdown, and then Luke couldn't find his shoe, and I had to make Chad's breakfast, and—"

Mary held up her hand. "It's okay. I understand. I've had a young family before." She winked at Lizzie. "Let's just get started."

Lizzie nodded and walked toward the back room to hang up her coat. Mary wrestled with whether to say anything more. Mary had been there. She had had young children and a husband who was loving but mostly clueless when it came to the kids. But Mary had also had a job for most of her children's childhoods. She'd had to. Before John's practice started bringing in a steady income, she'd had to show up on time, ready to do her job.

Mary watched Lizzie hang up her coat and smooth out her hair. All of a sudden, she looked like a little girl again. Lizzie used to spend hours straightening out the gorgeous natural waves in her hair when she was in junior high. Mary had always thought of it as Lizzie preparing for battle, doing all she could to defend herself against the mean girls and immature boys who populated middle schools. Kids always found something to pick on, and with Lizzie, it had been her curly hair. Watching her now, Mary felt a pang, remembering that vulnerable girl she'd fought so hard to raise with a healthy self-esteem, but who, she knew, still struggled sometimes.

Lizzie started back toward her, and Mary didn't have the stomach to say something about being on time tomorrow. So what if she'd taken a few extra minutes to put on eyeliner? Lizzie knew she'd messed up. Mary felt sure things would be better tomorrow.

"Ready to get to work?" Mary said, and Lizzie nodded, poured herself a cup of coffee from the beverage station, and then joined Mary behind the desk.

"I'm ready. What would you like me to do today?"

"We just got a special order we need to place," Mary said, opening up the computer program she used to order books. "I'll show you how to do that, and then I need to run out for a little while."

"No problem. I have it under control."

Mary showed Lizzie how to search the program by title, author, or publisher, and then watched as Lizzie ordered fifteen copies of Dorothy Sayers's *Gaudy Night*. She had Lizzie run through the steps for ringing up a sale, and then, satisfied she could handle the store, Mary got her coat, grabbed her purse, patted Gus on the head, and stepped outside.

It was bitterly cold today, and she pulled the zipper on her heavy coat a little higher and ducked her head. As she walked to her car, she reached into her purse, pulled out her phone, and scrolled to find Megan Lee's number. It rang a few times, and then voice mail picked up. Mary left a message telling Megan she had a computer question and asking Megan to give her a call or come by the shop. She hung up just as she got to her car, and she fumbled with her keys and then settled gratefully behind the steering wheel. She started the engine and breathed a sigh of relief as warm air began flowing out of the vents a couple of minutes later. Then she checked the address Evelyn had given her and started off.

There were several people heading into Meeting House Grocers, Mary noted. No doubt people stocking up on basic supplies in case the snow made it hard to get around for a few days. But aside from that, the sidewalks were mostly deserted. She drove past the gristmill and through the charming streets of her small town, enjoying, as she always did, the beautiful colonial homes and smart shops that lined the streets. Even in the pale winter light, the tree branches bare and exposed, it was a beautiful little place, and Mary was proud to call it home.

As she got farther from the center of town, the houses became newer and were set wide apart, and by the time she got to the neighborhood where Evelyn's house was, she could almost be anywhere in America. She found Sand Dollar Lane easily and drove through a development of very large custom-built homes on big lots.

Mary passed a house designed to look like a Tudor manor, and one meant to look like a French chalet, and several faux-colonial homes, and then pulled up in front of the address Evelyn had given her. It was a large home set on a hill, and it was built to look like a Tuscan villa, with stone archways and a terra-cotta tiled roof and a large second-floor balcony. Mary preferred houses with a bit less—well, with just a bit less—but she could see the appeal of a new, large home. Mary followed the driveway around to the back of the house and parked in front of what looked like a four-car garage. There was a kidney-shaped pool, covered for the winter, off to her right, and a wide yard with a tiled patio. She turned around and tried to decide if she was supposed to walk back around to the front of the house or go up to the back door when Evelyn stepped out of the French doors that led to the deck.

"Mary!" She hurried over to Mary and gave her a hug as if they were old friends. "You made it."

Evelyn was wearing fitted black pants and a shirt with sequins under a long wrap. Her hair was carefully arranged in a messy twist that didn't hide the fact her highlights were starting to grow out, and she somehow had a tan in the middle of February.

"I did. It wasn't hard to find, and traffic wasn't bad."

"I'm so glad you could come. I thought I could show you my studio."

"Oh. Well, sure." She'd never been inside a glass artist's studio before, and it might be interesting to see what it was like. "Let's start there."

"Right this way, then." Evelyn led Mary across the driveway to the side of the garage and ushered her inside, then closed the door hard against the wind. Mary looked around and gasped.

"Oh, Evelyn, it's beautiful."

Two bays of the garage had been walled off, and Evelyn had insulated and painted the space a soft white. There was a small propane tank attached to a blowtorch, which Mary assumed she used to heat the glass, and a variety of steel rods and tools arranged carefully in one corner. Evelyn's pieces were stored on the shelves along the walls. The overhead lamp hit the pieces and made them glow in the warm light. There were several large vases, done with alternating strips of primary colors, and paperweights with colored swirls mixed into the clear glass. She'd tried her hand at several smaller, incredibly intricate pieces that looked like miniature animals—cats and dogs and butterflies. And there were a number of Christmas ornaments, including pinecones shaped out of brown-tinted glass, clear angel figurines, and glass balls with streaks of red and green. It was all very contemporary, and while it wasn't Mary's taste, she recognized that there was a lot of skill and a lot of time put into each piece.

She studied a ball-shaped ornament done in clear glass, with swirls of red. "May I?"

"Please." Evelyn nodded and urged her to pick up the piece.

It was made of fine, thin glass, and the piece was perfectly round and smooth.

"How long have you been blowing glass?" Mary asked as she laid the piece back down gently.

"A couple of years now. I'd always wanted to get into it, and then when my husband retired and we moved here, it seemed like the right time, so we had this studio built. I've been working here pretty steadily since then."

"I think I heard you moved here from California. Is that right?" It wasn't unusual for people to retire to Cape Cod, and Mary had met people who had moved here from all over the country to enjoy the slower pace of life and small-town feel.

"That's right. The Bay Area." She handed Mary another ornament, this one done in swirls of blue and green. "My husband was a software developer, and that's the place to be if you want that job."

"I imagine." A gust of wind blew against the garage, and the little building shook. The wind was definitely picking up. "Cape Cod must be a big change in other ways as well."

"Oh, sure. Lower taxes, less traffic, and more space." Evelyn laughed. "And a slower pace of life. Albert created software for banking, so in addition to the crazy hours everyone puts in in Silicon Valley, he had the bankers in New York and London calling at all hours. And believe me, banks are not happy when their software isn't working right. We were happy to leave it all behind." She pointed to the ornament in Mary's hand. "Now look at that. This is one of my more recent pieces. I've been trying to make layers of color in these ornaments, and this is one of my more successful attempts."

Mary nodded, admiring the piece, but her mind was racing. Evelyn's husband designed banking software.

"That is nice." Mary turned it over in her hands. "It's amazing how perfectly round it is. Isn't it difficult to get it so exact?"

"It sure is. I have to get the molten glass to the exact right temperature, and I have to keep twirling the rod it's on so it doesn't settle unevenly, and I have to keep blowing into the rod to expand the glass from the inside. It's a very delicate process." She picked up a rod and demonstrated how the molten glass would be gathered at the end of the rod, and how she heated it up with the blowtorch and twirled it on the stick, and how she blew into the hollow rod—literally blowing glass. It was pretty amazing, but Mary wanted to find out more about her husband's line of work.

"It's nice you finally have the time to pursue your passion," Mary said as she set the ornament down gently. "What did you do before you moved here?" Mary wasn't expecting Evelyn to reveal a secret life of crime, but she was hoping to get a grasp on who she was. That distress call hadn't been a spur-of-the-moment idea, and she wanted to know if Evelyn had any history with boats or any suspicious activities in her past.

"Oh, you know, a little of this, a little of that." She laughed.

"I understand that," Mary said, though she wasn't sure she did. "Did you have a job?"

"Nah, I left making money to Albert. I just like spending it." She laughed again.

"A lot of people come here to indulge their hobbies—fishing, boating, what have you."

"Glassmaking has always been my hobby," Evelyn said. "Well, that and shopping."

Okay, well, that hadn't worked quite the way Mary had hoped it would. She would try a different tack.

"I bet your husband is glad for a change of pace. But it sounds like he was in an interesting line of work," Mary said. "I imagine he must know a lot about online security."

"Oh, sure." Evelyn waved her hand dismissively. "But that feels like a lifetime ago." She held out a paperweight made with what looked like crushed glass at the center. "Do you see that? That's from a piece that broke as I was working on it. I was able to reuse the glass to make a nice design here."

Mary nodded and turned the piece over in her hands. She tried again. "I imagine he must have dealt a lot with preventing identity theft and that sort of thing. You know, just yesterday, I was reading an article about how thieves sometimes capture bank account numbers using different scams and then route the money to their own accounts. But

I don't really understand how they could do that without it being traced. Do you think he'd be able to talk to me about that?"

"I'm not sure." She took the piece out of Mary's hand and set it down gently on the shelf.

Evelyn looked at Mary. Mary saw something pass across her face, but she couldn't read the look. One thing was clear, though. Evelyn didn't want to talk about her husband's work. What Mary couldn't figure out was why. Did she genuinely not know? Not care? Or was there something about it she didn't want to talk about? Mary decided it was time to change tack.

"This piece is beautiful." Mary pointed to a tall vase with a long, thin neck. It was decorated with drips of red and yellow color.

"Oh yes, that's one of my favorites," Evelyn said, brightening.

"I can see why. It is gorgeous. I love how the colors run together so beautifully." Mary picked the vase up and turned it over in her hands. "You know, it reminds me of a piece I saw at the museum on Saturday night. It was a vase shaped much like this one, but it was done in horizontal stripes all the way up the sides."

"I know exactly which one you mean." Evelyn touched the vase gently. "It does look a bit like that, doesn't it?"

"They have so many interesting pieces there. I just loved seeing the Hamilton Decanter." She set the vase down gently. "Did you enjoy the party on Saturday?"

"Oh yes. It was so nice to see so many fellow glass enthusiasts there."

"That's for sure." Mary examined a row of the glass animals and tried to figure out how to phrase this next part. "So many great people. And I was particularly fond of Maureen Rowe. It's interesting to talk to someone who loves glass so much she's made a career out of it. Did you enjoy talking to her too?"

"Maureen?" Evelyn cocked her head. "I don't think I met her."

Mary tried to read Evelyn's face, but she was looking away from Mary. "Actually, I saw you talking with Maureen Rowe at the party, and I wondered if—"

Evelyn shook her head. "I'm afraid you're mistaken about that. I didn't talk to Maureen."

Mary paused. She'd watched the video several times, and she knew she was remembering this correctly. The two women had gone down the hallway at different times, but they'd walked out of the hallway together. Maureen had said something to Evelyn before they walked back out into the main gallery space.

Evelyn was lying to her. But why? What was she trying to hide? Mary wanted to push her, but she also sensed that Evelyn wasn't going to recant her story, even if she found out about the security-camera footage. If she wanted to find out more, she needed to keep Evelyn happy, to keep her talking.

"Oh, I'm sorry," Mary said. "I must have remembered that wrong."

"That's quite all right. There was so much going on at that party it was hard to make sense of it all."

Mary nodded. "I really like this one." Mary pointed to a clear glass ornament shaped like a Christmas tree.

Evelyn beamed.

"Do you sell your pieces in any of the stores downtown? These would look perfect in the museum gift shop. I could also see one of the galleries taking some, and I bet Jayne Tucker could sell a few at Gems and Antiques."

"I would love to get my pieces into the downtown shops," Evelyn said. "Actually, I've been trying to get some of the people you mentioned to come out and take a look for a while, but so far, you're the first shop owner who has come to see them."

Mary was unsure how to respond. It was true she had a shop downtown, but that wasn't why . . . She didn't sell . . .

Her heart sank. Was that why Evelyn had seemed so excited to talk with her today? Because she wanted Mary to stock her pieces in her store?

"They really are beautiful," she said, studying some of the wide bowls on the highest shelf. "I can tell how much care and craftsmanship you put into each piece. But I'm really not sure these would fit in at my bookshop."

"Oh, I wasn't thinking any of those larger pieces would work, for sure," Evelyn said. "But I've noticed that you sometimes stock small items up near the register. Bookmarks and such. And I thought maybe a small basket of paperweights, like this one, might look nice up by the register." She held out a clear paperweight shaped like a book. "I have a bunch more of these in storage."

Mary nodded hesitantly. Evelyn had done her research. She had to give her that. She was watching Mary, her eyes wide, her face hopeful.

Mary wasn't sure how well these would sell, but... She hesitated to think it, but she had to admit that if she agreed to stock a few of Evelyn's pieces, it might give her an opportunity to probe more into her husband's Internet-banking knowledge.

"How much would you charge for a piece like this?" Mary asked. "The cash/wrap area is usually reserved for small, inexpensive items that customers may want to add on to their purchase."

"Oh, not as much as you might think." Evelyn named a number that sounded quite reasonable to Mary.

Mary studied the glass paperweight. She would like an excuse to talk to Evelyn more. It did seem to be quite a peculiar coincidence that her husband happened to be an expert on the very technology that had allowed someone to drain so many bank accounts. And Evelyn had lied about talking to Maureen. Yes, Mary would be grateful for the opportunity to talk to Evelyn further.

"Okay. I'll take half a dozen of these paperweights," she said. "And we'll see how it goes."

"Wonderful. I'll get them all ready to go and bring them by your store tomorrow," Evelyn said, clapping her hands. "I guarantee you won't regret it."

"I'm sure I won't."

"Oh, this is wonderful." Evelyn seemed almost giddy at the idea. "You have absolutely made my week."

Mary nodded, unsure how else to respond. Maybe the pieces really would sell. But even if they didn't, she would get a chance to find out more about Evelyn, and hopefully, she could find out why she was lying.

# TEN

———◆◆◆———

Mary was walking back to her car when her phone rang. She pulled it out of her purse and saw it was Betty calling, and she answered it as she settled in behind the steering wheel.

"Hi, Mary. What are you up to at the moment?"

"Right now? Buckling my seat belt. Why?" She turned the key in the ignition and held her hands up to the heater vents, willing them to start pumping out hot air.

"I didn't mean this very moment. I meant generally."

"I just went to see Evelyn Anders, and now I'm headed back to the shop. Why?"

"Ooh, what did Evelyn have to say for herself?"

Mary was still trying to wrap her mind around what she had learned in her conversation with Evelyn. "I'll tell you all about it later. What's up?"

Betty hesitated. "Well, I got a call from Eleanor."

Mary waited. Betty knew Mary's feelings about her sister-in-law, and she could tell that Betty was reluctant to make this call.

"She wants to talk to you."

"About what?" Mary turned the vents so they were pointed directly at her.

"Well, I mentioned to her that you were looking into the stolen money, and I told her you think the missing laptop is the key to finding the thief. And, well, I guess she has some ideas she wants to run by you."

"Some ideas?"

"She thinks she knows who stole the laptop."

Warm air was starting to come out of the vents, and Mary held her hands in front of them gratefully.

"Who does she think it is?"

Betty sighed. "I'll let her tell you that."

"You didn't tell her I'd call her, did you?"

"No." Mary's shoulders relaxed a little bit. "She wanted you to come by the club and talk to her."

Mary groaned. "And you told her I would."

"The club" was the Highbourne Yacht and Golf Club Eleanor and her friends all belonged to. Mary couldn't say the name without a smirk.

"She had money stolen too. It's probably worth talking to her anyway, isn't it?" Betty asked. "Maybe there's something she can tell you."

Mary watched as the wind tossed a single leaf, which was somehow still clinging to a branch on an elm tree next to the curb. She sighed. Well, she needed to ask Eleanor which catering company she had used so she could track down that waiter anyway. She might as well take advantage of the opportunity. "All right. When does she want me to come over?"

"She said she'll be there until one."

"In other words, now."

"I think that was the idea. She's having lunch."

"Oh dear." She put the car into gear. "Okay. I'll head over there now."

"Thanks, Mary. Let me know how it goes."

Mary hung up and then dialed the number for the shop. Lizzie answered on the third ring. "Mary's Mystery Bookshop," she said cheerfully.

"Hi, Lizzie. How's it going?"

"Hey, Mom. It's great. I placed that order, and I just sold a Nancy Drew to a grandma who was looking for a gift for her eight-year-old granddaughter. I told her Emma had loved those books at that age, and she was thankful."

"I'm so glad. So you've got things under control?"

"Totally. How's your day so far?"

"It's going well. But I need to make another stop before I head back to the shop."

"No problem. It's pretty dead here anyway, and I can hold down the fort until you get back."

"Thank you. I'll be there as soon as I can."

She hung up, slipped her phone back in her purse, and pulled out into the street.

The Highbourne Club was on a small inlet on the bay, not far from the glass museum. Mary drove back through the quiet streets of Ivy Bay and turned onto the private road that threaded past a cranberry bog and over a marsh and ended at the long driveway lined with rosebushes that led to the entrance to the club. Mary found a spot in the lot and walked toward the entrance. The club was housed in an old hotel, and its brick facade was tastefully aged. Ribbons of ivy snaked up the front walls, and the front entrance was flanked by doormen who nodded at Mary and directed her toward the restaurant, where Betty had said she would find Eleanor.

The wide-planked floor was polished to a high sheen, and the air was perfumed with the scent of flowers that bloomed from vases positioned throughout the entrance area. Mary walked through the lobby and into the restaurant, which looked out over the private marina through floor-to-ceiling windows. The maître d' led her to Eleanor, who was seated at a table in the corner, overlooking the docks.

"Mary, I'm so glad you could make it." Eleanor nodded as the maître d' pulled out Mary's chair. She scooted in, and he laid her napkin in her lap and then retreated.

Mary wasn't sure how to answer, since she hadn't exactly been given a choice.

On the table, there was a tray of small sandwiches cut into wedges, crusts removed, and a teapot. There was also a tea cozy with a few scones and a handful of delicate cookies.

"This looks lovely," Mary said. Eleanor nodded and started pouring out tea into fine-china teacups. She handed one to Mary and gestured for her to help herself to sandwiches. Mary took one that looked like some kind of cream cheese and olive concoction. Mary wondered how to start the conversation.

"It was so nice to see your grandson the other night," Mary said. There. Every grandmother in the world loved to talk about her grandchildren. "He seems like such a nice boy."

Eleanor gave her a tight smile. "Yes, he is."

"It must be wonderful to have him around regularly. He's living with you now, is that right? I wish my grandchildren were around more often."

"Oh yes." Eleanor dropped two sugar cubes precisely into her teacup. "It has been nice." She stirred her tea, keeping her eyes on the table.

Mary waited for her to go on, but she didn't. Mary tried to figure out what else to ask. She wasn't exactly sure why Eleanor had called her here and couldn't figure out what else to say. Luckily, Eleanor continued.

"Betty tells me you're looking into the matter of the missing money."

"The authorities are doing the official investigation, but I—"

"The police are practically useless," Eleanor said. "Did you hear Madeline Dinsdale is a victim too? And Tabitha Krause as well. They both just realized it today," she said. Mary's heart ached to hear that her dear friend Tabitha had become a victim as well. "I already talked to Chief McArthur and told him who took the laptop, and he gave me the runaround." She poured cream from a little silver pitcher into her tea and stirred more vigorously.

"We don't know for sure that the stolen money is related to the missing laptop."

"But it's clear it was. It's too much of a coincidence to not be related."

Mary couldn't disagree, but she didn't say anything. Out the window, she saw the marina was mostly empty. There were only a few boats tied up at the dock, and most of them were wrapped tightly in some sort of plastic wrap.

"Anyway, I told Benjamin what I know"—Mary knew she was talking about Chief McArthur, though few in town had the guts to call him by his first name—"and he didn't even take any notes about what I told him, and I just know he's not going to do anything about it." Eleanor laid the spoon down and took a sip of the tea. "But everyone knows you are the one who solves all the crimes around here anyway, so when Betty told me you were looking into it, I knew I had to talk to you about Taylor."

"Taylor?"

Eleanor nodded, took another sip, and then set her teacup down.

"It was Taylor O'Connor. I know it was."

"What makes you think that?" Mary took a sip of tea to cover the fact that her hand was shaking. It was hot and very strong. She set the cup down and added a sugar cube. Betty wouldn't have told Eleanor who was on Mary's list of suspects, so Eleanor must have come up with this on her own. Mary hoped that meant she had actually seen something. She leaned forward and waited for Eleanor to go on.

"Well, she was there that night, for one thing. And it was her laptop. You know what they say, when a woman is murdered, the husband is always the first suspect."

Mary's spoon clattered against her saucer. She stared at Eleanor.

"It's the same thing here. The person closest to the crime is the most likely suspect."

"But if it was the computer she used every day, why wait until the party to steal it?" Mary decided to play the devil's advocate. "And if she wanted it for the financial records on it, why would she need to steal the computer at all?"

"I don't know about all that technical stuff." Eleanor waved her hand dismissively. "But I do know this: Not two months ago, Taylor contacted me and every member of the glass museum board and asked us for money. And now every one of us has had money taken."

Mary had taken a bite of a cucumber and cream cheese sandwich, and she swallowed it quickly. "She asked you for money?"

"She wants to start some sort of dance company."

Mary nodded. "She mentioned that to me. She also said she needed to raise funds, but she said there might be another way...."

"Well, apparently, since no one would give her the money she was begging for." Eleanor took a sandwich and set it gently onto her plate and nodded at Mary knowingly. "But she used the glass museum's list of donors to solicit fund-raising for her company. Meanwhile, she's always taking classes in 'modern dance'"—she shook her head—"and it's not even as if she's studying ballet or something respectable. This is all people wearing sheets walking around on stage moaning and whatnot. She honestly thinks she can get people to pay her to flit around in next to nothing and call it deep."

There was a lot to sort through there, but Mary tried to focus on the information she was after.

"How do you know she used the museum's list?"

"She told me so. Bold as brass, she just called me up and asked that since my support of the museum showed how much I liked the arts, maybe I would want to support her new dance company. I told her I like dance as much as anyone else, but that is not how these things are done." Eleanor's back was ramrod straight, and she nibbled on a sandwich daintily.

"How are they usually done?"

"Fund-raisers." Eleanor said it like it was obvious, and Mary supposed maybe it was, in Eleanor's world. But Mary was more interested in something else Eleanor had said.

"Do you know for sure she was using the museum's donor list?"

Eleanor nodded. "Virginia caught her and called her on it. She wanted to fire her, and it took a hefty donation from Walter O'Connor to keep her on as an intern."

Mary processed this. So Taylor had had access to the list of museum's donors. That didn't look good. But did that necessarily mean she had access to their financial information? Virginia had said that the list of names wasn't guarded as closely as the database with the donors' actual financial information.

"And that's not all." Eleanor set the sandwich down and wiped her fingertips on a floral napkin. "Betty told me about how the false distress call was all a ruse to create the chaos to allow for the laptop to be stolen."

"That's not proven at this point."

"But that's what it was. What else could it have been?"

Mary agreed, but she didn't want to tell Eleanor that just yet. She just let Eleanor continue.

"The distress call was made on a marine radio, right?"

Mary nodded warily.

"Taylor's family are members here. They have a boat, this big gaudy thing with sundecks and a hot tub and who knows what else. It's over the top. Trying too hard to prove something, if you ask me. Anyway, she would definitely have access to a marine radio."

That was an interesting point, but Mary wasn't about to concede that to Eleanor.

"Again, though, it was her computer," Mary said. "Why would she set up such an elaborate hoax when she could have taken the information at any time?"

"What better way to throw suspicion off yourself?" Eleanor said, squaring her shoulders as she took a sip of tea.

"But the call was made by a man. I've seen the security-camera footage from the party, and when the call came in, Taylor was in the gallery. She wasn't outside using a radio."

Eleanor leveled her gaze at Mary. "So she was working with someone. She procured the radio; he made the call. Easy as pie."

It seemed a bit far-fetched. But then, Mary had thought Taylor was hiding something when she saw her at the museum yesterday. And if she really had made use of the museum's donor information recently, there was a chance she'd done so again. And she had been seen with that waiter. . . .

"I'll look into it," Mary promised.

"Why does everyone keep saying they'll look into it? It's obvious who is at fault here. Just tell the police to arrest her and get us our money back."

Mary picked up her teacup and took a long sip to give herself time to formulate a polite response.

"I want to get that money back as much as you do," Mary said carefully. Eleanor stared at her a moment too long, and Mary shrank back. Okay, Eleanor probably did have reason to want the money back a teeny bit more than Mary. But that didn't mean Mary wasn't earnest. She tried a different tack.

"You said Taylor must have been working with someone, since the call came from a man. Do you have any ideas who that might have been?"

"The police can figure that out. Or when they arrest her, they can just ask her."

Mary took another finger sandwich from the tray. This one appeared to be some sort of spreadable meat substance between dry dark bread. If Eleanor's suspicions were at all true—and that was still a big *if*—Mary had a good idea where to start looking for the man Taylor might have been working with.

"When I looked at the security-camera footage of the event, I actually did see Taylor talking to one of the waiters for a while." Mary decided to leave out the bit about them going down the hallway together. "I actually want to look into that anyway, and I wondered if you could tell me the name of the catering company you used."

Eleanor set her cup down a little too suddenly. "It's a very reputable company. I've used them for events for years." She blotted at her mouth with her napkin, and Mary could see her jaw was set. She obviously did not like the suggestion that someone she had hired might have been involved.

"I'm sure they are," Mary said. "But I want to make sure to look into every possible lead. And since Taylor would have needed help if she had been the one to steal the laptop, I'd like to track down that waiter."

Eleanor uncrossed her ankles and crossed them over the other way. She cleared her throat and looked at her hands. Mary waited.

"I really do want to find that money as quickly as possible," Mary said gently.

"It was Charter House Caterers," Eleanor said at last. "Here in town."

"Perfect." Mary said the name over a few times in her head to make sure it stuck. "I'll check in with them and see if I can find out anything about that waiter."

Mary took a bite of the meat sandwich. It was a bit chalky, but the flavor wasn't bad.

"I trust you'll be discreet, Mary Fisher. I intend to work with this company again."

"I will be the picture of discretion," Mary said.

Eleanor cleared her throat, took a sip of tea, and then pushed herself up. "Well. I have to get back." She set her napkin on the table.

Mary realized she was being dismissed. It felt abrupt, but Eleanor had a smile pasted on her face.

Mary set down her half-eaten sandwich and saw that it was one o'clock on the dot. Mary wasn't sure what Eleanor needed to get back to, but she reluctantly pushed herself up as well.

"Thank you for having me," Mary said. "This was lovely."

"Anytime," Eleanor said as she walked Mary to the door of the restaurant. They both knew it was a lie.

Mary made her way back through the lobby and walked to her car. Her stomach grumbled—three tiny sandwiches weren't exactly her idea of a satisfying lunch—and her head was spinning. Mary wasn't sure why Eleanor was so insistent that Taylor was guilty, but she had presented some new information Mary was going to look into. She would get to the bottom of this.

She got in her car and started to drive back toward the shop. But halfway there, she had an idea.

# ELEVEN

———◆◆◆———

Hazel Pritchard had said that Maureen lived on Colonial Road, behind the elementary school, and Mary decided to swing by and see if she could find the house. She drove down Route 6A and turned onto Liberty Road. She drove past small shingled cottages and newer tract-style homes and turned onto Colonial. The bare tree branches swayed overhead, and the clouds were getting darker. It wouldn't be long before the snow started.

As Mary drove down the block behind the school, she slowed and looked for clues as to which house was Maureen's. The third house from the end had Rowe spelled out in capital letters on the side of the plain black mailbox. Bingo. Mary pulled up at the curb in front of the blue two-story. There was a partially deflated soccer ball on the yellow front lawn, and Mary could see two children's bicycles tucked away on the side of the house. There was a minivan in the driveway, and—

Mary couldn't believe her luck. Maureen Rowe was stepping out of the house, trailed by two small boys. Maureen pushed the button on her key chain. The minivan's lights turned on, and a beep announced it had unlocked. Maureen opened the sliding door on the side of the van, and the two boys climbed in.

Mary jumped out of her car and walked toward them. "Maureen?"

Maureen turned, looked at Mary, and froze.

"I'm so glad to catch you. I tried calling the other day, but you must not have—"

"I'm sorry. I don't have time to talk right now," Maureen said as she buckled the younger boy into a car seat. Through the smoky glass of the window, Mary could see the other boy strapping himself in as well.

"I know you're very busy, but I just need a moment of your time. I'm trying to find out about—"

"I really have to go." Maureen closed the van door and started walking around toward the driver's side.

Mary followed her around the car. "I wouldn't bug you, but it's pretty important—"

"I'm sorry, Mary." Maureen got into the driver's seat, turned on the engine, and closed the door. A moment later, Maureen was backing out of the driveway, and she disappeared down the street.

Mary stood on the front lawn, watching her go, trying to figure out what had just happened. Maureen had called in sick to work, but she certainly wasn't laid up in bed, that was for sure. And whatever she was up to, she definitely did not want to talk to Mary about it. What was going on?

———

It was one thirty by the time Mary got back to the shop. It was getting colder outside, and she was chilled to the bone. The sight of the fire dancing in the fireplace and the smell of fresh coffee had never been so welcome. She hung up her coat, sat down behind the counter, and unwrapped the sandwich she'd bought at the Tea Shoppe.

"I thought you were having lunch with Aunt Eleanor." Lizzie walked over and nodded at the sandwich.

"So did I." Mary had to admit the turkey and brie sandwich did look good, and it was a lot more substantial than the sandwiches Eleanor had offered. "I'm sorry. I should have called to see if I could get you anything."

Gus stirred from his spot by the heater, hopped up on the counter, and sniffed at Mary's sandwich. Mary lifted him up and set him down on the floor.

Lizzie nodded. "Oh, I'm okay. I had such a late breakfast, and I brought some snacks, so I'm not even hungry yet."

"Well, let me know when you want to take your lunch break. I think I can handle the crowd." Mary gestured to the empty bookstore.

"We did have a few customers this morning," Lizzie said. "I sold two from the best-seller table and that Nancy Drew I mentioned earlier. And I got those books you wanted ordered."

"Nice work." Mary took a bite of her sandwich. It was delicious—the baguette fresh, the turkey cut thick, the cheese salty, the country-style mustard tangy.

The bell over the door rang, and Mary looked up, expecting to see her first customer of the afternoon. She was excited to see Henry instead.

"Henry."

"Hello, Mary. Hello, Lizzie." He looked at her sandwich. "I'm interrupting your lunch."

"No, no. Just an afternoon snack."

"That's quite a snack."

"It's been a strange day." Mary set the sandwich aside. "So what can I help you with?"

"I was in town and just thought I'd come say hello."

"I'm so glad you did. How are you doing? Have you recovered from your weekend?"

"I suppose." Henry crouched down and reached out his hand toward Gus. The cat lifted his head and stuck his nose out, sniffing Henry's finger. "I still haven't really caught up on sleep, but I did get the boat up and running again, so that's a start."

"I'd say that's more than a start."

Gus pushed himself up, and Henry patted him gently on the head.

"Any luck on that missing laptop?" Mary had told him about the connection between the distress call and the missing laptop yesterday, and now she filled him in on what she had learned today.

"My goodness. You're going to put Chief McArthur out of a job." Henry laughed, straightening up.

"I guess you could say I'm motivated," Mary said, laughing too.

The bell over the door dinged, and Mary turned to see Megan, Bea Winslow's granddaughter, walk in.

"Looks like you've got company. I should get going anyway."

Mary hated to see him go, but she did want to talk to Megan. "I'm so glad you stopped in," she said, smiling.

"So am I. I'll give you a call later." Henry waved and then disappeared out the door.

"Hey, Mrs. Fisher. I got your message. What's up?" Megan was a slight girl with an almost boyish figure. The blue streak in her bangs had faded to an almost turquoise color, and she wore tight jeans and a T-shirt that read No, I Will Not Fix Your Computer under a zippered hoodie and a heavy winter coat that flapped open. Megan dropped her backpack on the floor and walked toward the counter. The rubber soles of her canvas shoes squeaked on the floor. The grandmother in Mary grimaced at the shoes she knew would be soaked as soon as the snow started, but she held her tongue. Megan had her own grandmother to fuss over her, and she didn't need another.

"Thanks for coming by. Are you enjoying your winter break?"

"I'd enjoy it more if I didn't have mountains of homework to do this week. What kind of break is it if you're writing essays the whole time?"

Mary moved her sandwich aside and turned to Megan. "I'm sure the hard work will pay off."

"We'll see." She leaned her forearms on the counter. "So what's up?"

Lizzie drifted off toward the back of the store and disappeared into the office.

"I'm told you do the IT work for the glass museum," Mary said.

"Yep. That and several other places in town."

"It must be so interesting to work with so many different businesses. And the glass museum is a wonderful place."

"Sure. I mean, if you like glass." Megan grimaced. "My grandma loves that place."

Mary laughed. Yes, she supposed a museum about the history of glassmaking wasn't a typical teenager's idea of a good time.

"Did you hear that one of the museum's laptops disappeared at a party Saturday night?"

"Yeah, Mrs. Livingston called and told me Monday morning. She asked when I could help them get the new computer set up."

"She was talking about replacing it, not asking you to help her find the old one?"

Megan shook her head. "Stolen laptops are famously difficult to get back. They're easy to unload, and there's a big market for parts, so by Monday morning, it was probably wiped clean and resold on the black market. I think she's smart to be thinking ahead, because that baby is long gone."

Mary considered that. She hadn't even thought about the idea that the laptop had been sold for parts. She'd been so sure someone had stolen it for the information on it. And in this case, that did seem to make sense. Someone had wanted that financial information badly enough to have gone through quite a bit of trouble to create the opportunity to access it. And not only that, if Mary was right, someone had used the information on the laptop to steal from the museum's donors. That wasn't a coincidence.

"What if I told you I thought someone had stolen the laptop because they wanted access to the information on it?" Mary asked.

"I'm listening."

Mary told her the theory about the laptop containing donor information.

"Well, that shouldn't be hard to find out. I set up the database program for them on the server. I'll just check on the server and see if it was ever downloaded onto the laptop. Piece of cake."

Mary only had a vague idea what a server was, so she just nodded.

"That would be great." Gus rubbed against her legs, trying to convince her to share her turkey, and she batted him away. "Is there any way to track down the actual laptop itself?"

"Do you mean, Is there some secret hacker microchip that tells me where the laptop is?"

Mary nodded. Yes, that was exactly what she was hoping for.

"Nope. 'Fraid not."

"Oh." Mary felt her shoulders deflate.

Megan laughed. "Come on, Mrs. Fisher. You give up too easily. I thought you were supposed to be some kind of detective."

Mary stared at Megan.

"There's no secret chip to track it down, but I'll find the laptop's MAC address."

"The...what address?"

Megan sighed and walked around the counter and shook the mouse on Mary's computer. The screen came to life. Megan clicked on a symbol at the top of Mary's screen, and a box opened up. She clicked on an icon and then pointed to a string of numbers that popped up.

"That's your MAC address. That stands for Media Access Control. Every computer has a unique MAC address. It's like its social security number or DNA or something." She looked up to see if Mary was following. Mary nodded. "Every time a computer accesses the Internet, it leaves a fingerprint, so to speak."

"And if you can find that fingerprint, it can lead you to the laptop itself?" Mary's mind was swirling. Where were these fingerprints computers were leaving all over the place? Was everything she did online out there for the world to see?

"That's the idea."

Mary didn't totally understand it, but Megan seemed confident, so she nodded. "So you'll get the information about the server and the MAC address?"

"Sure thing. I'll find out what I can and be back in touch soon."

"Thank you so much."

"Yep." Megan waved, then turned and stalked out of the shop. Mary turned to her computer and checked her e-mail as she ate her sandwich. Lizzie was still in the back office; Mary could hear her talking on the phone. While it was still quiet, she pulled out the phone book and looked up the number for Charter House Caterers, the company Eleanor had used to cater the party on Saturday. She found it easily and dialed the number quickly.

"Charter House. How can I help you?" A young woman said.

"I've got kind of a strange question," Mary said. She was getting used to starting conversations that way these days.

"Okay…"

"I was at a party catered by your company on Saturday night, and I'm trying to get in touch with one of the waiters who was there that night."

"Okay…" She heard the woman typing something on a keyboard on her end of the line. "May I ask why?"

Mary considered how to answer. "I'd like to ask him about something," she said carefully. That was so vague she couldn't imagine the woman letting her get away with it, but she appeared to be distracted by something on her computer.

The woman typed something more and then answered. "If you can describe him, I'll take down your information and ask my supervisor about it."

"Of course." Mary thought back to what she'd seen on the video and what she remembered about him from the party. "He was tall, lanky, with blond hair in a buzz cut." She tried to figure out what else she knew about him.

"Oh, you mean that guy Max. He's the only one like that." More typing. "Okay, I'll pass this along to my supervisor and see if I'm allowed to pass his info along."

"Thank you so much. I appreciate it." Mary gave the woman her contact info, then thanked her and hung up.

Max. His name was Max. That wasn't much to go on, but it was more than she had a few minutes ago, and hopefully, she would find out more soon.

Mary picked up her sandwich again just as Lizzie came out of the back room.

"Everything okay?" Mary asked.

"Oh yeah. I was just talking to Chad." Lizzie came around the counter and sat down on the stool next to Mary. "He took the kids to the whaling museum, and now they're back and on their way to Bailey's. He promised them ice cream if they behaved."

"Ah, nothing like ice cream on a freezing day."

"I hear there's a great butterscotch special this month."

"Oh, that one is good." Mary smiled. Every month, she created an original flavor for Bailey's Ice Cream Shop, and this month's was one of her favorite flavors yet.

"Oh, check out this picture Chad sent me." Lizzie pulled her phone from her pocket and held it out to Mary. It showed a picture of Emma and Jack in a set of old-fashioned stocks outside the Chadwick Inn.

"I could almost believe they were being punished if it weren't for that goofy grin on Luke's face," Mary said, laughing. "It looks like they're having a good day."

"Yeah," Lizzie said. She bent over and picked up Gus and put him on her lap. "I think they are."

Mary set down her sandwich and turned to her daughter. There was a wistful look on Lizzie's face. "What's wrong, honey?"

Lizzie petted Gus for a moment, looking across the room, but her gaze was far off.

"Mom, can I ask you a question?"

"Of course. You can ask me anything."

"You raised two kids, and you also managed to be a career woman."

"A career woman?" Mary laughed. "I wouldn't say that." Mary had been a librarian at a local branch of the Boston Public Library system until she retired and moved to Cape Cod to open this bookshop.

"You were there for more than thirty years. You worked your way up to head librarian. They threw you a retirement party, and people you'd taught to read as children brought their own children to say good-bye. Most people would call that a career."

"I had fun." Mary took a bite of her sandwich. She'd been lucky. She had truly enjoyed her work at the library, and it had prepared her perfectly for this new stage of her life.

"How did you decide when to go back to work?"

"Back to work?" Mary took another bite of her sandwich and considered. "You mean, after you were born?"

Lizzie nodded. "I know you worked at least part-time when I was a kid, but how did you decide to do that?"

Mary swallowed and took a sip from the bottle of water she'd bought. "It wasn't so much a decision as a necessity. Your father's law practice took a while to really get going, and when you kids were young, we needed the income to pay the bills."

"What about child-care costs? Didn't those eat into your take-home pay?" She was scratching Gus's ears absent-mindedly. Gus looked like he was in heaven.

"Oh, I suppose so, but things were different then. It wasn't like you were in some fancy day-care center or anything. Vivian Snyder from church watched you and Jack a few days a week. Since she had her own kids at home anyway, you played there while I was at work. I didn't pay her much. She mostly did it as a favor."

"I remember that. Her house smelled like cats—no offense, Gus." She brushed her hand along his back. "And her son Justin picked his nose."

Mary laughed. "I don't remember that, but I do know she took good care of you."

"I suppose she did." Lizzie nodded. "What about when we were older? Dad's business was doing fine by then. Did you ever consider just quitting and staying home?"

Mary was beginning to suspect that these were more than idle questions.

"Of course I did. A part of me wanted to be with you both more than anything," she said carefully. "But then, I also loved what I was doing. I loved books, and I loved helping people, and I loved the community at the library." Gus edged closer to Mary's sandwich, and she batted him away again. She looked at Lizzie, who was still staring at something far away. "And, if I'm totally honest, it was nice to have something that was mine."

"What do you mean?" Lizzie wrinkled her brow and turned to her.

"I guess just that, when I was home, you and Jack and your father came first." Lizzie started to open her mouth, but Mary kept talking. "That was the way it should be." Lizzie closed her mouth and waited. "But at the library, I got to be a part of something I loved, something I chose. It filled me up in a way that nothing else did. And probably some people thought it was selfish, but to me, it just felt…"

She tried to choose her words carefully.

"It felt like God had given me these desires and talents, and I wanted to use them. And working there made me happy, which I think made life better for all of us. And so I tried my best to balance my work with time with you all."

Lizzie nodded. "Did you ever feel like you were missing out on our lives?"

Mary felt her stomach drop. "Do you feel like I missed out on—"

"No. I didn't mean it like that. You did an amazing job being there for us. I just meant..." Gus was kneading her lap, and she grimaced as his tiny claws dug into her legs. "I see all these moms at Emma's school who are trying to juggle work and their families, and they never seem to make it to the kids' games or assemblies or volunteer to help at the special events, and I just, I don't know, I wonder if they'll regret it someday."

"Every parent has regrets," Mary said. "That's just a part of being human. None of us ever gets it right all the time." She unscrewed the lid on her water bottle and then screwed it back on. "I suppose, in some ways, I did miss out on things like games and assemblies," Mary said. "I was lucky that my work was flexible, and I was there as much as I could, and I tried to be there for the big events. But I couldn't be at everything. And, I don't know... I didn't really think of it like that. I guess I figured that even though I missed some games, I was able to help create a life for my family that looked more or less how I wanted it to look, and I was grateful for that."

Lizzie rubbed her fingers along Gus's cheek, but she was still looking at something far away.

"Lizzie?" She looked up, as though Mary had awakened her from a trance. "What's going on?"

"I interviewed for a job at Luke's school. Teaching second grade. They offered it to me."

"Oh, Lizzie, that's wonderful. Congratulations." Mary's heart swelled with pride. Her daughter was so talented, and she wasn't at all surprised the school wanted her.

"I have to let them know next week whether I want to take it or not."

"And you're torn." All of a sudden, Lizzie's questions made perfect sense.

"I was hoping working here this week would help clarify things, but so far, all it's done is made me even more confused."

"How so?" Mary had some ideas what Lizzie meant, but she wanted to hear Lizzie work through them.

Lizzie was quiet for a moment. Mary turned her head and saw that it had started to snow. Tiny white flakes blew past the store window. She saw Pastor Miles hurry by, his hood pulled up over his head, hurrying toward shelter.

"I love being here. What you said about using the talents God has given you? That made sense to me."

"You always wanted to be a teacher." Even as a little girl, Lizzie had loved playing school, and whenever anyone asked what she wanted to be when she grew up, she'd always said a teacher.

"And those two years I taught before Emma was born were some of the most interesting, challenging, amazing years of my life."

Mary nodded. Lizzie had majored in early childhood education, and she had taken a job at an inner-city school in Boston after she and Chad got married. She had loved it, but when she got pregnant, she had quit and they had moved out to the suburbs to raise their family.

"But you're not sure you're ready," Mary said. Lizzie smiled.

"This week was supposed to be a test for me. And, well, you've seen how it has gone so far. I'm just not sure I can leave when my family still needs me so much."

A hundred thoughts ran through Mary's head—
encouragement, affirmation, reminders that children had
suffered through worse than having to find their own clothes
in the morning. But instead, she prayed for the right words
and then simply said, "You'll know when you're ready."

"So does that mean I should take the job, or that I
shouldn't?"

Mary reached out and scratched Gus on the head. "It
means you need to do what's right for you and your family,
and only you can know that."

"I was hoping for something a little more clear-cut."

"I know." Mary had eaten all she could finish of her
sandwich, and she held out a tiny piece of the leftover turkey
to Gus. The little cat gobbled it greedily. "But I know you'll
make the right decision."

They sat in silence for a few moments, and Mary watched
the snowflakes drift past the window. The only sound was the
faint crackle of the fire in the fireplace. Suddenly, there was
no place she wanted to be more than home, warm inside the
house, with her family.

Mary looked around the shop. There was no one here,
and there probably wouldn't be for the rest of the snowy
afternoon. She stood up and flipped the sign on the door to
Shut.

"What are you doing?"

"One thing I've learned about having a job and having a
family is that balance is important. And as much as I love this
shop, I love my grandchildren more, and I don't get to see
them enough."

Lizzie cocked an eyebrow.

"What's the point of owning your own business if you can't close early to spend a snowy afternoon at home with your grandchildren?"

Lizzie's face broke out into a smile. "What do you think, Gus?" She patted the cat, and he purred. "I'll take that as a yes. That sounds like a great idea."

Mary couldn't agree more.

# TWELVE

---❖---

Mary spent a happy afternoon playing Clue with Luke and baking peanut butter cookies with Emma, and by the time the dinner dishes were washed and the kids were in bed, there were several inches of snow on the ground. Henry called to make sure they were all tucked in safe and sound at the house, and Mary chatted with him as she finished cleaning up the kitchen, then said good-bye so Henry could go to bed. After she hung up, Mary stood at the sink and looked out the French doors. Snow covered the patio furniture and the deck, rising in soft piles as snowflakes fell softly through the quiet night.

Lizzie and Chad were curled up in front of the television with a movie, and Betty was on the phone with her son Evan, who was helping her sort through her financial records. Now would be a good time for Mary to work on her new frozen hot-chocolate ice-cream recipe.

She set a pot on the stove and pulled the milk out of the fridge. One of the photos Betty had taped to the front of the fridge hung askew, and Mary straightened it and closed the door. The whole fridge was covered with pictures and photo cards and graduation announcements for their families, and it made Mary happy every time she saw it.

Mary poured the milk into the pan, and as that heated, she pulled out a frozen chocolate bar and grated it onto a plate, opened a bag of miniature marshmallows, pulled out a container of heavy cream, and beat three egg yolks with her standing mixer. She envisioned a smooth chocolate base studded with marshmallows and ribbons of something approximating whipped cream. It would take some doing to keep the whipped cream from dissolving into the base, but she was determined to find a way. When she had all her ingredients ready, she turned back to the milk heating on the stove and stirred it slowly.

Mary's mind drifted back over the long day. The afternoon with the kids had been a wonderful time, but before that, the day had gone in several unexpected directions, and try as she might, Mary was having a hard time making sense of it. What was Taylor really up to? Would she really have gone to such lengths to steal her own computer? Why hadn't she told Mary about Max, or about using the donor list? She needed to find out more about Max and follow up on what was going on with Maureen, who was definitely not home sick in bed.

And then there was—

Mary stirred the milk and then set down her spoon. She was making herself crazy trying to keep it all in her head. She went to her purse and pulled out the list she'd made on the back of the envelope.

First, she made a list of everyone she knew of whose money had been taken: Betty, Eleanor, Cynthia Jones, Lincoln King, Madeline Dinsdale, Tabitha Krause...

Mary should check on Tabitha, she realized. Even though Dawn took good care of her, it had to be frightening to find

out you'd been a victim of a crime. Mary needed to find time
to check in and make sure she was handling it okay.

Mary then turned to her list of suspects. Taylor was at
the top of the list, and Mary added in what Eleanor had told
her. *Used list of museum donors to solicit money for her dance
company. Family belongs to yacht club, has access to a marine
radio.* Taylor looked suspicious, but Mary still had questions.
It still didn't make sense she would set up the whole ruse to
steal her own work computer.

*Waiter. Named Max.* She tapped her pen against the
counter. That was all she knew about him so far. She'd have
to focus more on finding out about him.

*Maureen Rowe. Husband is a marine biologist, has boat,*
Mary wrote. *Good chance he has access to a marine radio.
Grant running out soon. Maureen possibly about to lose job
at the museum.* It wasn't looking good for Maureen. She
had a solid motive—she needed money—as well as the
opportunity, according to the video, and if she was about
to be let go, there was a good chance she didn't have a lot of
loyalty to the museum right now. Mary thought about
her visit to the Rowe house today. Maureen hadn't been
unfriendly, not really, but she obviously had not wanted to
talk to Mary. *Called in sick both days since the theft but out
and about with kids.*

Mary gave the milk another stir. It was starting to foam
up around the edges.

*Evelyn Anders.* Mary's visit to Evelyn's studio had raised as
many questions as it had answered. *Husband designed banking
software,* Mary wrote. She needed to find out more about
that. Maybe she could ask Megan if she knew anything about

the software he designed, and she would try to find a way to talk to him herself.

The milk continued to bubble up, and Mary took the pan off the stove and slowly poured half the milk into the eggs in one long stream, then poured the mixture back into the pan to cool down.

"What flavor is this?" Betty came into the kitchen wearing a pair of relaxed cotton pants and a chunky wool sweater that had belonged to her husband, Edward. It was as dressed down as Betty ever got, and Mary was glad to see she was going to relax for the rest of the night. She helped herself to a few shreds of the grated chocolate Mary had left in a pile on the counter. Her eyes widened, and she coughed and then took down a glass and filled it with water.

"Careful. That's unsweetened chocolate," Mary said, stirring the custard base.

"Now you tell me."

"I'm trying to make a frozen hot-chocolate flavor." Mary dipped her finger into the hot custard and tasted it. So far so good. "It remains to be seen whether I'll be successful."

"It sounds good to me." Betty drained her glass and set it on the counter. "Is this the list you started last night?" She looked down at the envelope Mary had written on. She studied it silently for a few minutes and then looked up at Mary. "Wow. You've had a busy day."

"I did spend a good part of it running around town."

"So who did it?"

Mary laughed. "I sure wish I knew. It could be any of them at this point." She turned off the burner under the custard and kept stirring. "Or it could be someone else I haven't even considered yet."

Betty picked up the envelope and studied it again. "I'd forgotten about Taylor calling about her dance company."

"You got a call from her?"

"I think she called pretty much everyone who supports the museum. I have to admit it was a pretty smart idea. Most people who support the museum like supporting the arts in general."

"Eleanor didn't see it that way."

Betty snorted. "Eleanor wouldn't give Taylor O'Connor a glass of water if she had just walked through the desert."

"Oh?" Mary tipped the plate of shavings into the hot custard and stirred. "Why's that?"

"When Eleanor said she wanted to talk to you, I was afraid this was what was going to happen." Betty grabbed a marshmallow from the open bag and popped it into her mouth. She chewed, then nodded approvingly. "She has this grudge against the O'Connors. Richard got into a fight with Walter O'Connor years ago over something trivial at the club. It was about who got which boat slip or something ridiculous like that." Betty shrugged. Richard had been Eleanor's husband, who had passed away some years ago. "Richard and Walter never got past it, and Eleanor has never gotten over it."

"Really?" Well, that shed a whole new light over the exchange she'd had with Eleanor this afternoon. No wonder Eleanor had been so set on painting Taylor as the villain. "So I shouldn't take what she said too seriously?"

"I'm just saying to consider the source," Betty said. "I'm sure she didn't tell you anything untrue, but she no doubt made up her mind about the guilty party long before she ever heard any of the facts."

Mary considered this. It didn't change the fact that Taylor had used the museum's donor list to solicit money for her own dance company. Betty had confirmed that had happened. But it did mean she needed to look at just the facts and filter out the commentary that had accompanied them.

"Eleanor said something about Taylor going to a dance studio for lessons regularly."

Betty nodded. "Taylor mentioned it when she told me about her dance company. She goes to that dance school in that old barn out by the shopping center. She takes classes just about every morning before work."

"Goodness. That's a lot of dancing."

"She's very dedicated."

"But her father doesn't support her dancing, right? That's why she's interning at the museum?"

"That's one thing Eleanor and Walter agree on. They both think she should be doing something more productive with her time." Betty shrugged. "I don't see what they have against dancing. It's an art form just like anything else."

"So did you give Taylor money when she asked for it?"

"I did."

"I never knew you were such a fan of dance."

"I've always liked dance."

Mary smiled and wondered how much of Betty's newfound enthusiasm for dance had to do with Eleanor's disdain for it, but she didn't dare ask.

"So, did you find out anything else in your travels?" Betty changed the subject deftly. She took another marshmallow, and Mary swatted her hand away.

"Nothing real. I stopped in at Evelyn's—"

Mary's cell phone rang, and she pulled it out of her purse, which was hanging in the entryway.

"Hey, Mrs. Fisher."

"Hi, Megan."

"Can you come over?"

"Right now?" It was after nine o'clock. Mary looked out the window over the sink. The snow was piling up, and it was still coming down. "I'm not sure it's safe for me to be driving right now."

Mary turned back to the kitchen and saw that Betty was watching, waiting. She walked back into the kitchen and set her hand on the counter.

"Huh." Mary heard some clicks on Megan's end of the line.

"What's going on?"

"I think it's best if I show you. Can you come in the morning?"

Mary had read that it was supposed to stop snowing sometime tonight. The plows would come by in the early morning, and the streets should be cleared for driving reasonably early. She was planning to open the shop tomorrow anyway; she might as well get started on her day a little early.

"Sure. I'll try to be there by eight. Will that work?"

"Perfect. See you then."

"Wait," she said, trying to catch Megan before she hung up. "Can you tell me anything about what's going on?"

"It's too hard to explain over the phone. For now, let's just say I found something."

# THIRTEEN

◆—◆◆◆—◆

The next morning, Mary was at Megan's house a few minutes before eight. The snow had ended about midnight, and the plows and salt spreaders had been through regularly so the streets were clear, but she still drove slowly in case there was ice on the road. She loved how the snow blanketed the lawns in perfect sheets and collected on the naked tree branches. It transformed her block into a foreign, beautiful landscape, and she tried to appreciate it while it lasted. Today was supposed to be warmer than yesterday, and the snow had already started to melt in places where the sun hit it.

She parked on the street in front of Megan's house. Megan's younger sister Kathryn was shoveling the walkway to the house, and she had already cleared the driveway, so Mary had a clear path to the door.

"Hello, Kathryn." Mary waved, and Kathryn looked up, waved, and then kept shoveling.

Mary rang the doorbell, and a moment later, Megan yanked the door open and gestured for Mary to come inside. Today, she was wearing a pair of tight jeans the color of a summer tomato, a T-shirt with a picture of Pac-Man, and the same hoodie she'd had on yesterday. Mary wiped her feet carefully on the doormat and stepped inside.

"Hi, Mary," Megan's mother, Angela, called from the kitchen. She was wiping what looked like yogurt off Joy, the youngest Lee daughter, who was seated in a high chair next to the oak dining table. "Megan is very excited to see you."

Megan was already halfway up the stairs.

"I'm excited to see what she found," Mary said. "How are you doing?"

"Oh, you know." Angela finished wiping off the baby and tossed her rag into the sink, where it hit a spoon and knocked it onto the floor. "The kids have a week off school. So..."

Mary nodded. She remembered those days well. For the kids, it was a week's vacation, but for moms, it was a different story.

"The snow is supposed to melt, so maybe they'll at least be able to get out of the house this afternoon," Mary said.

"I sure hope so," Angela said as the baby began to whine. "You can go on up."

Mary nodded and followed Megan up the stairs. She wondered how Angela felt about her daughter, who was still in high school, doing IT work for companies in town, but Mary realized that if Lizzie had shown such enthusiasm and skill for something like that, Mary would have been ridiculously proud.

Mary followed Megan up the stairs and into a room covered with posters of bands Mary had never heard of. Megan had a desk set up in a corner of the room, with a large color monitor and computer tower as well as two open laptops and a stack of backup drives at the edge of the desk. There were spare keyboards and mouse parts scattered on the bookshelf next to the desk, as well as some bits and pieces Mary couldn't identify but suspected belonged inside a computer.

Megan gestured for Mary to sit down on the desk chair and pulled a plastic storage bin over and sat on it next to her. She pushed the thick frames of her glasses up and set her fingers on the keyboard. "I was able to access the glass museum's server remotely," Megan said, typing something on the keyboard. A box popped up on the screen.

"And a server is..." Mary didn't want to sound ignorant, but she wanted to understand what Megan was showing her.

"A server is a computer," Megan said, and she clicked on an icon in the box. Mary opened her mouth and closed it again, trying to figure out how to answer. Megan sat back, looked at Mary, and sighed. "When a group of computers is linked together to share resources and information, that's called a network. In most offices, the computers are all on a network, so you can share files and printers and such." Mary nodded. It made sense so far. "The server is the computer where all the network data is stored. It's sort of the main computer on the network."

Megan looked at Mary, and she nodded again to show she understood. It really was amazing that children today grew up just knowing things like this.

"Since I set up the network for the glass museum, I can access their server remotely. It's in Mrs. Livingston's office next to her desktop."

Mary assumed her desktop must be the computer that sat on her desk.

"That's amazing. You can see what's on her computer from your bedroom?" Mary watched as Megan clicked on a folder on her desktop and navigated through several subfolders until she finally got to the one she wanted. Then she got an uneasy feeling. "Does Virginia know you can do that?"

"Oh yeah. It's all standard. That way, if she calls me with a question, I can answer it from here and don't have to keep running over there. It saves me time and her money. I do that for all the businesses I work for. Now here are the server logs." Megan pulled up a window with a black background covered with white text. There were lines and lines of what looked like gibberish to Mary. "You can see here"—Megan touched the screen, pointing to a line of text a third of the way down the page—"that the database with the financial records was downloaded from the server Friday afternoon."

She looked up at Mary triumphantly. Mary squinted at the screen, trying to make sense of what Megan was saying.

She could see that Megan was waiting for a response, so she finally ventured an answer. "So what does that mean, exactly?"

"Seems like a pretty amazing coincidence, right? The secret file with valuable information is downloaded onto the laptop, and then the next day, oops, the thing goes missing?"

It did seem like an extraordinary coincidence. If what Megan was saying was correct, it proved that this wasn't some crime of opportunity. This was planned out. And that was consistent with Mary's theory that the faux distress call had been arranged precisely to provide the opportunity to steal the computer.

"Is there any way to know who downloaded it?"

"The user was logged in to the network as Taylor O'Connor. There's no way to know for sure that it was her, but that's where I'd start looking."

"But the laptop was password protected, right? So no one but Taylor would have been able to get onto the system."

"Theoretically." Megan blew out a breath. "But honestly, most people choose passwords that are easy to guess, such as a pet's name or a kid's name. She have kids?"

"No."

"Dog, then. Makes it totally easy to hack in."

Mary thought about that. It was a fair point, she realized. She could probably be more careful about choosing a more unique password.

Megan leaned forward again and started clicking on different windows on the screen. Mary thought about what this meant. Taylor—or someone logged in as Taylor—had taken the information, which was then used to steal money from the museum's donors, just one day before the laptop went missing. That had to be more than coincidence. And it did confirm that the laptop had the donors' bank account information on it. It didn't prove beyond a shadow of a doubt the laptop was stolen to get access to that information so the thief could clean out the bank accounts, but it did make Mary feel even more certain she needed to chase down that missing laptop. If only there was a way to track a computer's location....

"Megan?" The girl was now leaning over the keyboard, typing what looked like an instant message of some sort. "Did you say yesterday that a MAC address could tell you a computer's location?"

Megan nodded without looking up from the screen. Her fingers were flying across the keyboard.

"So can't we just use that to see where the computer is now?"

"No can do." Megan kept typing. "I've got the MAC address from when the laptop was on the museum's network, but we have to wait for it to access the Internet signal in a new location before we can get that info. That may have already happened, but I don't know that yet. I'm trying to find out."

"How do you go about finding where it accessed the Internet signal last?"

"You have to get the phone company to give you that information."

"Oh." Mary felt her body deflate. "How do we do that?"

Megan finished whatever she was typing, skimmed it over, and then hit a button to send her message. A moment later, a response showed up, and Megan smiled.

"As we've been sitting here, I've been chatting with a buddy of mine."

"A buddy?"

"One of my IT friends." Megan waved her hand dismissively. "I asked on a forum if anyone had any connections at the phone company, and my buddy says he has a friend."

"So what does that mean, exactly?"

"It means it's going to take some time, but I should be able to figure out where that laptop is."

"Who is this buddy of yours, exactly?"

"Stryper23. He's cool."

"His name is Stryper23?"

"That's not his real name, obviously. That's just his screen name."

"So what's his real name?"

Megan shrugged. "We don't use real names. But I've been talking to him for years. He's a good dude. He'll find us what we need."

Mary wasn't certain she understood what was going on, but she nodded. "I appreciate your help."

"No worries," Megan said, typing on the keyboard again. "Just wait. We'll get that laptop back soon." She kept typing and then hit Enter and sent her message. "I'll focus on this today. It won't be long now."

# FOURTEEN

———◆◆———

Before she headed to the shop, Mary had a phone call to make and a place she wanted to stop. She climbed into her car, blasted the heater, and called Tabitha Krause. She'd been meaning to stop by and see her old friend, and hey, Tabitha had been at the party Saturday night as well. Maybe she'd seen something Mary had missed.

Dawn answered and said Tabitha would be thrilled to see Mary. They set up a time for Mary to stop by that afternoon.

Then Mary tucked her phone in her purse and pulled away from the curb. She drove out to the old barn behind the shopping center where Creative Movement Dance Studio was housed. Last night before bed, Mary had used the information Betty had given her and found the studio's Web site online. The only class listed for the morning was an interpretive dance class, scheduled at eight. Mary pulled into the parking lot a little before nine, hoping to catch Taylor on her way out.

A few young women trickled out, and then, just as she was about to lose hope, Mary saw Taylor walk out of the studio, wearing warm-up pants and a fleece jacket.

Mary hopped out of her car and met Taylor on the path that led to the parking lot.

"Hello, Taylor."

"Oh, hey, Mrs. Fisher." Taylor smiled at her and tried to move to the side to get around her.

"Do you have a second? I wanted to ask you a couple of questions."

"Actually, I need to get to work—"

"I understand, but if you have just a minute, I'd be so grateful." This wasn't exactly an ideal place to have a conversation, here in the snowy parking lot, but it would do.

Taylor stopped and gave her a quizzical look, then hitched her bag up on her shoulder. "Okay. What's up?"

"I've been trying to track down that laptop."

"Any luck?"

"None so far. But Virginia let me take a look at the security-camera footage from that evening."

"Oh." Taylor's fingers curled tighter around the strap of her bag. "Okay..."

"I noticed something odd in the footage. It seems that when you went back to the office early in the evening, one of the waiters went with you."

"Oh. Yeah." A flush started to creep up her cheeks, and she seemed to be struggling for words. "I guess he did."

"Can you tell me about that? When I talked to you before, you didn't mention that fact."

Taylor's fingers were curled so tightly around the strap that her knuckles were turning white. Then she seemed to make a decision. She set down her bag and let out a breath.

"I didn't mean for him to come back with me."

Mary nodded, encouraging her to go on.

"As I told you before, I'm trying to start a dance company here in Ivy Bay, and I was talking to that waiter about it. His name is Max. He seemed really interested, so I said I would go into the office and get him some information out of my purse. Well, he came back with me, and even though we're not really supposed to bring people back there, I figured it would be okay just this once. He seemed nice, and it felt like we really had a connection."

"Did you see him notice your computer?"

She shook her head.

"Did you see him do anything strange?"

"No. All he really did was look around. He saw the picture of my dog and asked me about him, and that was about it."

Mary had noticed the framed photo on Taylor's desk when she'd been in the office. Mary remembered Megan's comment that everyone's computer password is their kid's or their pet's name. Did Max suspect that when he was eyeing the laptop?

"Was your password by any chance your dog's name?"

Taylor's cheeks burned. "Yeah."

"Okay." That meant that Max had no doubt been able to get in. "And then what happened?"

"Then I got out the flyer I had in my purse that explained about the dance company, and we went back out to the party."

"Can you think of anything else that he might have noticed or done while you guys were back there?"

Taylor shook her head.

"Did he leave any way for you to get in contact with him?"

Taylor hesitated, and then she sighed. "Okay, totally honest here. We exchanged numbers, but when I called him, it was the number of a quilting shop in Hyannis."

"He gave you a false number?" So it hadn't been Max she was texting that day at the museum.

"Apparently. It was—" She shook her head. "I thought we had a real connection, so . . . well, I was surprised. And kind of embarrassed, to be honest."

"And he hasn't called you?"

"No."

Mary felt bad for the girl. It couldn't be pleasant to be rejected like that. Still, though, she should have told Mary the truth. And that didn't explain away the database being downloaded onto her laptop.

"I found out something else strange when I was looking into the missing laptop," Mary said. "It seems you downloaded the file with the museum's donors' financial information onto your laptop the day before it went missing. Does that sound familiar?"

"What?" She cocked her head, and her mouth dropped open. "No. I don't know anything about that."

She seemed to be genuinely confused, but at this point, Mary wasn't sure what to believe.

"So you didn't download that file onto your laptop?"

"No way. I wouldn't touch that file. I don't even have access to it."

"Megan says the database program was downloaded onto your laptop Friday afternoon." Mary watched her carefully, but her eyes were wide, and she was shaking her head, just barely. "If you didn't do it, do you have any idea who did?"

"I really don't, Mrs. Fisher. But if that file was on the stolen laptop..." The full import of what Mary had said was washing over Taylor. "That's bad."

"Yes, Taylor. It's very bad."

"I swear I had nothing to do with that. With any of it."

Mary desperately wanted to believe her.

# FIFTEEN

◆◆◆

M ain Street was bustling. Mary steered her car slowly
down the road and saw that Jimmy Shepard was shoveling the sidewalk in front of his store, and Steve Althorpe
was just vanishing inside the doors of Ivy Bay Bank & Trust.
A group of teenagers walked down the street holding Sweet
Susan's butter-yellow-colored coffee cups. The lights of
Mary's shop weren't on yet, but it looked like Susan Crosby
had cleared the sidewalk for her. They often helped each
other out with tasks like this. Mary would need to stop in
and thank her.

Lizzie had agreed to open the shop and bring in Gus,
since Mary wasn't sure how long she would be at Megan's, but
there was still a half hour before the store was set to open, so
Mary didn't take the lights being off as a bad sign. Lizzie was
probably on her way now.

Since she had a little time, Mary decided to keep driving
and make one more stop before she went into the shop. She
drove down to the corner of Meeting House Road and turned
left. She passed Cape Cod Togs and Little Neck Pharmacy,
then turned left onto Liberty Road. Toward the end, next
door to a storefront labeled Beansprouts Day Care, was a

small brick building. The name Charter House Caterers was carved into a wooden sign hung above a large plate-glass window. The lights were on inside, and a woman was shoveling snow from the sidewalk in front of the door, so Mary parked and picked her way across the slushy sidewalk toward the building.

"Excuse me," Mary said to the woman clearing the sidewalk in front of the shop. In the front window, there was a dining table covered with a fine white tablecloth and set with elaborate blue-and-white china, deep-blue linen napkins, white taper candles, and a centerpiece of peach stargazers. It was beautiful, and if it was intended to show off what a nice dinner Charter House Caterers could provide, it did the trick. "Are you with Charter House?"

The woman stopped shoveling and straightened up. "Sure am." She had gray hair pulled back into a long ponytail underneath a red knit hat, and she wore jeans and snow boots.

"I'm Mary Fisher." Mary stuck out her hand, and the woman adjusted the shovel in her hands and shook it reluctantly. "I'm trying to get in contact with a waiter who worked at a party your company catered Saturday night."

"Oh yeah. The glass museum, right? You called yesterday?" The woman's face was red from the exertion of shoveling, and she seemed grateful for the chance to catch her breath.

"I did. I know it's a strange request, but it's important that I speak with him."

"Well, I don't have any idea where he is, but if you talk to him, tell him he's welcome to drop off his uniform anytime because he won't work for us again." The woman had a thick New England accent that told Mary she was a local.

"Oh? Why not?"

"He didn't show up to the brunch we booked him for Sunday morning. Not even so much as a phone call. Left us in the lurch bad. Now he won't pick up when we call. But I want that uniform back."

She went back to shoveling. The blade scraped across the sidewalk with a metallic grating sound, and then snow flew off the blade and onto a pile in front of the abandoned storefront next door.

Mary tried to choose her words carefully. "I will tell him if I get in touch with him, but that's the thing. I'm looking for a way to get in touch with him. If you could give me his contact information, I'd gladly pass on the message."

The woman studied Mary. Another shovelful of snow flew toward the pile.

Mary decided to change her tack. "The party at the museum was lovely. I can't even imagine how much work it takes to put on an event like that. Eleanor Blakely tells me you always do a nice job, and after Saturday, I believe it."

"Eleanor told you that, huh?" The woman laughed. She stopped and studied Mary again.

"She spoke very highly of your services."

"Eleanor's been a loyal customer for years. We do a good job for her." She sent another shovel of snow toward the pile. "She sent you here?"

"Yes. I'm anxious to get in touch with Max, and she thought you might be able to help."

The woman leaned on her shovel and considered. "I can give you the phone number he gave us, but he doesn't seem to be answering it." She stopped scraping and banged the shovel against a patch of ice on the sidewalk.

"Did he fill out an application when he applied for the job?"

"Sure did." The woman stood up and leaned her weight against the handle of the shovel. She sized Mary up. "I'm not supposed to give that information out, but Eleanor's been good to us. And I'd really like to get that uniform back. Those things aren't cheap, and his was brand-new."

"Thank you so much. I appreciate it."

"Be right back." The woman rested the shovel against the side of the building and disappeared inside the shop, and a few minutes later, she came back out with a photocopy of the information sheet that Max had filled out—Mary scanned the document—just last week. It was just one sheet and listed his name, address, contact information, work history, and references. "Careful with this. Like I said, I could get in trouble if it got out I gave you this. Tell Eleanor how much we would like to work with her again soon."

"I will. Thanks so much for your help."

"Sure."

Mary walked back to her car, careful to stay on the parts of the sidewalk that had been shoveled or sanded, and drove back to Main Street. There was a spot right under the elm tree in front of her shop, and she pulled in and was pleased to see that the lights were on inside the store.

There. Lizzie was really stepping up. All Mary had to do was show her she trusted her, and Lizzie had risen to the occasion.

Mary opened the door to the shop. "Oh." She froze, her hand on the door.

Emma and Luke were jumping on the upholstered chairs by the fireplace at the back of the store, and a Christian rock song was blasting over the store's stereo system.

"Hi, Grandma!" Luke called, and he tossed one of Mary's sea-green pillows into the air. It landed on the hearth behind him.

"Goodness." Mary finally mustered the wherewithal to step inside the shop and let the door fall closed behind her. She dropped her purse and coat on the floor behind the counter. Gus's tail was sticking out from behind the counter, where he was huddling with a fearful look in his eye. Lizzie was nowhere to be seen.

Emma stopped bouncing on Mary's good chair. "Mom went to get stamps at the post office."

"And she left *us* in charge!" Luke hadn't stopped jumping, but a swift kick from his sister meant he got the message.

Mary quickly walked to the room in the back of the store and shut off the music.

"Hey!" Luke protested.

"Don't be mad, Grandma." Emma, much more sensitive than her younger brother, rushed to pick up the pillow Luke had thrown. "We just wanted to have a little fun."

"How long has your mother been gone?"

"I don't know. Ten minutes?" Emma shrugged, but her eyes were still pleading for Mary to forgive them. "Luke noticed your sound system, and we thought it was dumb that you never used it. So we decided to help you out and play some good music, and then, well, I guess we just got a little carried away."

"Indeed." Mary motioned for Luke to get off the chair, and he hopped down.

"It's not like there were any customers or anything." Emma ran her fingers through her now-messy hair and tried to straighten it.

"Well, except that one dude who popped his head in and then left," Luke said, laughing. He blew out his cheeks and made his fingers into circles to represent glasses. It sounded like Ian Howland had stopped by for the next book in the thriller series she'd gotten him hooked on. She'd need to apologize to him later.

The bell over the door dinged, and Mary turned to see Lizzie walk in.

"Oh, hey, you made it," Lizzie said, smiling as she shrugged off her coat. "How did your meeting with Megan go?" She set her purse down on the counter and walked toward them all, holding her coat in her hands.

"It went fine." Mary tried to decide what to do. Here Lizzie was, clearly with no idea anything was wrong. Mary felt like a jerk pointing it out to her...and yet, she couldn't honestly believe this was acceptable, could she? To run off to do errands and leave her children in charge of the store? "I was surprised to see Emma and Luke here."

Emma and Luke looked at each other.

"Oh yeah, sorry about that. I called to ask you if it was okay, but you didn't answer your phone." Lizzie hung her coat up, moved over to the beverage station, and helped herself to a cup of coffee. "You guys go finish straightening the children's nook, like I asked you to," she said to the kids, and they quickly moved to the other side of the store. Emma pulled a book off the shelf and plopped down into the pedestal bathtub, and Luke immediately grabbed a stack of picture books and started building a tower with them.

Lizzie turned back to Mary and gestured toward the chairs. Mary sank down into one of them gratefully. "Chad isn't feeling well, and he asked if I could bring the kids in with me. I wasn't sure what you'd think, but in the end, I decided you're always talking about how you want to see your grandkids more, so I'd give it a shot. I wasn't sure what else to do." Lizzie lowered herself into the other chair.

"I'm sorry Chad isn't feeling well," Mary said weakly, trying to figure out where to start.

"It's just a head cold. But you know how men are. They get a sniffle and think they're dying."

"The kids couldn't stay home with him?"

Lizzie wrapped her hands around her coffee cup and watched Mary for a moment. "I'm sorry. I didn't realize it would be a problem." Her tone made it clear she was hurt, and Mary felt bad, and yet...

"I try to make this store feel like an oasis for my customers," Mary said. "I want it to be the kind of place a person can come and get away from everything and escape into a book...."

Lizzie opened her mouth and then closed it again.

"And I understand the need to run errands, but that's what your lunch hour is for. That's when Rebecca does all of her running around."

Lizzie looked at Mary, her eyes wide, as if she couldn't believe what Mary was saying.

"I'm sorry, Mom," she finally said. "I really didn't think it would be a problem. That girl Ashley is always here, and you don't seem to mind that, so I thought it would be okay to bring *your own grandchildren* in for a little while."

Mary cringed. Lizzie was being unfair, but how did Mary respond in love? And she did have a point, but Ashley was a huge help at the store; she never jumped on the furniture, and she was never left in charge of the shop. Mary didn't see how she could explain any of that without further hurting Lizzie. Probably best to just let it go.

"Let's just get this place straightened up." Mary pushed herself to her feet and retrieved the aqua-blue pillow from where it was wedged under the end of a bookshelf.

"Don't do that. If you have a problem with something, let's talk about it."

"I think it's probably best if we just move on." She fluffed the pillow by squishing it between her hands. "I'm glad you're here."

"No, Mom, you always do this. You're obviously upset, but you won't talk about it. You just, like, shut down, and I don't understand why, and I don't understand what I did wrong. And it's not fair to do that."

Mary took a deep breath. This is what she'd been afraid of. Lizzie tended to quickly escalate a small misunderstanding into hysterics. She'd done it since she was a teenager, and, frankly, right now, Mary didn't have the energy to deal with it.

"I don't really want this to be a big thing, so I'd rather not do this right now."

"*Do what?* Talk to me like an adult? Explain why you're upset with me? Work through a problem instead of just ignoring it, hoping it will go away?"

Mary noticed Emma and Luke were now staring at the two of them, their mouths open. Mary knew from experience Lizzie would only get more upset the longer they drew this out.

"Maybe now would be a good time to take your lunch break."

Lizzie stared at Mary, her mouth open, as though she were working out what to do. Then, slowly, so slowly Mary was almost afraid of what she was about to do, Lizzie set her coffee cup down and pushed herself to her feet. Without a word, she shook her head and walked over to the children's nook. "Come on, guys. Time to go. Get your coats."

Luke and Emma obeyed without any fuss, and a few minutes later, Mary was left alone in the quiet store. She felt as though she were about to cry.

# SIXTEEN

◆◆◆

What had just happened? Lizzie had just gotten mad at her, but as she played it back in her mind, Mary couldn't understand how things had escalated that quickly. Should she have responded differently?

But how could Lizzie not see that leaving the kids to run wild in the store was a bad idea? If Lizzie couldn't admit she'd done something wrong, how could they honestly expect to accomplish anything by talking about it? The Bible said to watch your words and hold your tongue. It was better not to talk this through while Lizzie was so upset and risk saying the wrong thing.

Still, Mary felt like a pile of rocks had settled in the pit of her stomach. She cleaned up the stack of books Luke had left on the floor, straightened the children's nook, and then finished putting the reading area back in order. Finally, she made herself a cup of coffee and settled on a stool behind the counter. The caffeine wouldn't help her stomach, but all of a sudden, all Mary felt like doing was curling up in bed and disappearing under the covers, and this would help keep her awake.

The first thing she did was call Ian Howland and leave a message on his answering machine that the coast was clear and he could come get his book anytime. Then she stared at her computer screen for a long time, replaying the scene with Lizzie in her mind. It didn't make her feel any better. Finally, she shook her head and told herself to focus. Working on finding the missing laptop would help keep her mind off the fight with Lizzie.

She pulled out the copy of Max's application for the catering job. Best to start at the top. She jiggled the mouse to wake up her computer, took a long gulp of her coffee, and typed the name Max Harrington into the search bar on her browser.

A few sites popped up. There was a news article about a Maxwell Harrington in Louisiana who had won a Powerball jackpot. The picture showed him posing in front of a new sports car, a smug look on his face. This guy was several decades older and about a hundred pounds heavier than the man Mary was looking for, so she clicked back to the search results. There were scores for a high school tennis player in Rhode Island. Rhode Island wasn't far away, but that kid was too young to be the Max she was looking for.

She came up empty searching for his name, so she moved on to the next space on the application. Phone number. Max had listed a Cape Cod phone number, and Mary dialed it, trying to figure out what she would say while it rang. It went straight to a generic voice-mail message that didn't identify the phone's owner, just as the woman had promised.

There wasn't anything suspicious about that, Mary thought. Not on its own, anyway.

She moved on to the address he had listed on his application, on a Sycamore Lane in Dennis. A quick search online revealed that no such address existed. Mary expanded her search and included the neighboring towns, but did not come up with any Sycamore Lanes. Well, that was suspicious.

Mary gulped down some more coffee and moved on to the employment history Max had listed on his application. Just as she was reading about his first job as a lifeguard, the bell over the door tinkled and a UPS delivery man came into the shop, wheeling a cart loaded down with three boxes of books.

"My goodness." Mary gestured for him to stack the boxes by the door, and she came around the counter to take a look. "These are all for me?"

"Yes, indeed." The delivery man scooted the cart out from under the boxes and tapped the one on top. "Are you restocking the whole store at once?"

"I didn't think I ordered this many books." Mary knelt down and read the label on the side of the box. This box contained the entire order for the high school she'd asked Lizzie to place. So what was in the other boxes? She moved onto the next box and saw that it contained the exact same order. Strange. And then she scanned the label on the third box. It held the same thing.

"There are three of the same order?" Mary straightened up.

"I don't know. I just deliver the boxes." He gave Mary a jaunty wave and headed back out into the cold.

Mary used a box cutter to slice open the tape on the top box and unpacked the books. Yes, it was the full order. She moved that box aside and opened the next. It had the exact same books inside.

Oh dear. Had Lizzie placed the same order three times? Mary prayed not. The profit margin on books was quite small, and with the expedited shipping...If they had three times as many books as she would be able to sell, Mary was going to lose money on this order, for sure. Even if she packed these books up and returned them right now, she'd still have to pay for the shipping and that would erase the small profit she'd make on selling the ones she actually needed.

She'd have to ask Lizzie what happened. Mary sighed. She was not looking forward to that conversation, especially on the heels of what had just happened.

She shook her head. She'd worry about that later. She would focus on Max for now. She turned back to his application.

The first job he had listed was as a lifeguard at one of the beaches on the south shore. He'd done that for a few summers and then gotten a job in the dining hall at a small private college in Boston. He'd worked there, according to this sheet, until May of last year. Mary did some quick calculations in her head. It seemed like Max had been a sophomore in May. But then, according to his application, he had taken a job at a restaurant in Cape Cod. The most recent job he had listed was as a waiter at a seafood restaurant in Barnstable called Atmosphere. He had started in May and worked there until December, according to the application.

Which meant that, if the information on this application was correct, Max hadn't gone back to school. Either he had graduated early, or he had dropped out for some reason. But then, if he had lied about his address and maybe his phone number, who was to say any of the rest of this information was true? Mary would need to find out more.

She started by looking up the restaurant named Atmosphere online. She found an article in the *Barnstable Baysider* that said Atmosphere had closed for good over the holidays.

Well, that didn't mean anything, Mary decided. The timing actually worked out. If Max had worked there until it closed, then the dates he listed on his application made sense. Unfortunately, since it was closed, it made it more difficult to verify that he had actually worked there.

Mary wrapped her hands around her mug, savoring the warmth, and read back over the article. The owner of Atmosphere was named Tristan Ball, it said. He had started out working for Sam Townsend, of Sam's Seafood, as a fry cook and had opened his own restaurant ten years ago.

That was interesting. Sam's Seafood was known as a dive, where they served baskets of fried food on picnic tables, but it served some of the best seafood around. It was nothing like this restaurant, which the photos in the article showed to be more upscale. The place was nice enough, with white tablecloths and framed watercolors of seascapes on the walls, but it lacked the character that so many of the more popular restaurants had. Still, Mary was sad to see any small business close. But maybe Tristan Ball would be able to tell Mary something about Max Harrington. Mary pulled out the phone book she kept behind the counter and searched the white pages for Tristan Ball. She found his name easily, took a sip of her now-tepid coffee, and dialed the number.

"Hello?"

"Hi, may I speak with Tristan, please?" Mary asked.

"Speaking." The man had a soft, almost gentle voice.

"Hi, Tristan. My name is Mary Fisher, and I am looking for a reference for a former employee of yours." Mary explained she was looking for information about Max Harrington and that he had referenced his work at Atmosphere on a recent job application.

"Max? I'm afraid I don't know anyone by that name."

"Oh. Well, I guess he must have—"

"Wait a minute. Harrington, you said? There was a Harrington kid who worked here, though. What was his first name...?" Mary heard some papers rustling. "Jonathan? I think that was it. Jonathan Harrington."

"The young man I'm thinking about was quite tall, with short blond hair?"

"Yep, that's him." Well, that was interesting, Mary thought. He was now going by a different name. Add that to the list of things he'd lied about.

"His application says he worked there from May through December of last year, when your restaurant closed. Is that right?"

"I'm afraid not." He sighed. "He was let go in October."

"Let go in October? Can I ask what for?"

"For stealing."

# SEVENTEEN

◆◆◆

"Stealing?" Mary repeated. Max Harrington—no, Jonathan Harrington, she reminded herself—had been fired for stealing?

"What happened?"

He hesitated. "I'm not really comfortable saying more. But if you're thinking of hiring him, I'll just say I have some reservations."

"Thank you for your honesty. I appreciate it." Mary liked Tristan. He was honest but didn't want to disparage Max. She appreciated that. "Can I ask you what kind of employee he was while he worked for you?"

Tristan was quiet just a beat too long. "The customers loved him," he finally said. "He was good-looking, and he could be very charming. We had some regulars, a group of older women who came in all the time for lunch. They always wanted to sit at one of Max's tables, and he had them eating out of the palm of his hand. But..."

Mary waited.

"He was unreliable," Tristan finally said. "He missed shifts sometimes, got in late, that sort of thing. He's not a bad kid, though," he quickly added. "I think there were some problems at home he was dealing with."

"Do you know what sort of problems?"

"Not really. I just got the sense that things weren't really right there, somehow."

Mary nodded while she thought. "Do you know where he lived?"

"I'm afraid not."

"Do you have any idea what sort of job he took after he was let go?"

"No, ma'am."

Mary was sure there was more he could tell her, but she couldn't think of what else to ask. "Thank you so much for talking to me."

"Sure thing. And hey, I'm starting up a small fish fry out by the beach in Centerville this summer. If you're ever in the area, you should come check it out."

"I will," Mary said. Her mouth was watering just thinking about fried fish. She hung up and took a sip of her now-cold coffee. She grimaced and pushed the mug away.

Well, that was interesting. There appeared to be several things Max hadn't been honest about on his application, and several things she still needed to verify. But did that make him capable of arranging such a large hoax? Why go to all that trouble? She thought through her list of suspects and realized he had the most tenuous connection to the museum; he might be the only one who would need such a big distraction to get away with the theft.

She looked back down at the application and pulled up the Web site of the college he'd attended. She clicked around, looking for a number for the dining hall. The site was covered with photos of students lounging on lawns under brilliant autumn foliage and walking past ivy-drenched walls. Eventually, she found her way to a page of information about facilities and was scanning through it when the bell over the door dinged.

Mary looked up, ready to greet her customer, and she was only a little disappointed to see that it was Evelyn Anders.

"Hey, there, Mary." She was bright and chipper as a California day. "I brought those paperweights, just like you asked."

That wasn't quite how it had happened, but Mary nodded and looked at Evelyn, looking for the paperweights. Her hands were empty, and she was peeling off her coat and digging into her purse.

"Albert is bringing them in. He's just looking for a place to park first. But since I was coming here anyway, I wanted to show you this."

Evelyn pulled a small package of tissue paper out of her purse, then set it on the counter and pulled back the paper to reveal a glass ladybug. "Now I know you specifically asked for the book paperweights, but I wanted to make sure you saw this too. I have a bunch of them, and I think they'd look just perfect in the store."

"Well, now, that is nice." Evelyn had done a nice job on the little bug, but Mary wasn't exactly running an art gallery here. "But I think I'd prefer to start with just the book paperweights and see how that goes. I can always add to my inventory later, right?"

Evelyn nodded, still good-natured, and began to wrap the bug back up. "No problem. I think you're going to see that they're big sellers, and I have no doubt you'll be back for more."

Mary did hope so, but mostly she just admired Evelyn's persistence. Mary supposed now that Evelyn was retired, she was finding her identity in being an artist and was doing her best to make that a reality. Mary could understand that. If she didn't have her bookshop, she would lose a piece of herself.

The door opened again, and a tall man came in carrying a long, flat box. "Special delivery," he said, smiling at Mary. He closed the door and set the box on the counter, then held his hand out to Mary. "Albert Anders. Nice to meet you."

Mary couldn't believe her luck. Here was the man she'd needed to talk to, in her store. Taking on this inventory was already proving worthwhile, even if she didn't sell a single piece. Albert was a tall man, solid, with a receding hairline. He wore a new down parka from a brand favored by hikers and outdoor enthusiasts, but somehow it seemed clear that he wasn't really either. He had a firm handshake, and something about him felt warm and cheerful.

"Thank you so much for taking a chance on Evelyn," he said as he took the lid off the box and pulled out a paperweight wrapped in tissue paper. "She's so talented. I just know these things are going to sell like hotcakes."

"They are nice," Mary said, taking the unwrapped paperweight he handed to her. It really was pretty. The clear glass was shaped like a book, and it felt solid and heavy. "I'm planning to put them in a basket and set them right about here," she said, gesturing toward an area next to the register.

"That'll look nice." Albert finished unwrapping the pieces and set them gently on the counter. Then he turned, crouched down, and held out his hand toward Gus, who was curled up in front of the radiator. "Nice kitty."

Gus eyed him, and then, when Albert rubbed his fingers together, pushed himself up and walked over.

"Yes, I think it will." Mary watched as Gus rubbed his cheek against Albert's hand. "Thanks so much for bringing them in," Mary said to Evelyn. "With the weather so bad, I wasn't sure if you would make it or not."

"That's why he's here." Evelyn jabbed her thumb at Albert. "It's not just because he's so good-looking. It's also because I'm terrified to drive in snow."

Mary supposed she hadn't gotten a lot of experience driving in snow in California. They would both have to get used to it now.

"At your service, milady." Albert straightened.

"I'm so glad you're here, because I actually was hoping to ask you a few questions, and this saves me the phone call," Mary said, trying to keep her voice as neutral as possible. "Evelyn tells me you used to be in software development."

"Oh yes." Gus now rubbed against Albert's leg. "Thirty-five years. Just retired a few years back."

"You must have seen a lot of change in your field in that time," Mary said.

Albert laughed. "You can say that again. When I was in grad school, a computer would have taken up this entire shop, and all it could do was some basic computations." He pulled his cell phone out of his pocket and tossed it on the counter. It was the newest model of a very popular line of smartphones, Mary couldn't help but notice. "These days, this tiny little computer can do everything except your laundry, and you carry it around in your pocket." He laughed good-naturedly.

"Now, I think Evelyn said something about you specifically doing banking software?"

"Yes, indeed. Evelyn likes to say I took a boring job and focused on the most boring aspect of it I could find"—he nudged Evelyn gently with his elbow, and she laughed and shoved his arm away—"but I found it fascinating. There's so much at stake, and the integrity of your program really matters. There are so many layers of security built into each interface, and—"

"Oh boy. When he starts talking about interfaces, that's my cue to step away." Evelyn gestured toward the bookshelves. "I'll be browsing."

"Since when have you needed an excuse to start shopping?" Albert laughed. Evelyn shook her head and wandered off into the stacks. The two seemed to enjoy a good relationship, joking back and forth.

"Anyway, yes, I spent a good part of my career working on banking software," Albert said, turning back to Mary. "Evelyn mentioned that you'd had some friends who had their accounts hacked."

"Yes, although I'm not sure if they were hacked, exactly. I think it's more likely someone used their bank account numbers to go into their banks and transfer money out."

"That seems more likely to me," Albert said. "Account hacking does happen, but as I mentioned earlier, there are so many layers of security it is extremely difficult."

COVER STORY ∽ 197

Mary nodded. "If you were going to steal money from a bank account, how would you do it?"

She watched his reaction carefully, but he simply laughed.

"I would find a different way to make money. Everything is traceable these days, and life in prison doesn't sound fun to me." Gus was still rubbing against his legs, so he bent down and scooped up the little cat.

"I feel the same way. But I am curious."

"The best way to steal money remotely would be exactly what you mentioned: a bank transfer." Gus laid back in Albert's arms, and Albert scratched the cat's belly. "Most banking software these days is airtight, if I do say so myself. If you tried to hack it, you'd get caught right away. You'd need to go through more traditional channels. I'd set up a couple of offshore accounts, and I'd use the bank account information and routing numbers—Would I have those?" He looked at Mary, who nodded her approval. "And then I would transfer the money into one account, then another, masking my footsteps. Then I'd have at it."

What he said seemed to make sense, but more important, the way he said it seemed…*genuine*. It was the only word that came to mind. If he was covering up for something his wife had done, or something they had done together, he was a very good liar. And he was so good with Gus, and the little cat was clearly in heaven. Mary knew better than to assume her cat was a barometer of criminal activity, but Mary did have a hard time thinking badly of anyone who treated him so well.

"That appears to be what the thief had done in this case," Mary acknowledged.

Albert shook his head. "I'm really sorry to hear it. It's horrible."

"You weren't affected, were you?" Mary leaned forward. "The common thread in the thefts appears to be donors to the glass museum. I know Evelyn was at the fund-raiser..."

"We always use credit cards for any transactions that don't involve cash. You have more protection in case something goes wrong," Albert said, rubbing Gus's ears.

Mary nodded. That was a lesson they'd all learned this week. Though the people affected were going to get their money back, it had shaken them all.

"I found a few things." Evelyn reappeared and set four hardcover books on the counter.

"I had no doubt you would," Albert said, laughing.

Evelyn hit his arm playfully. "Hey, you can't complain about me reading. Reading is good for you. And with weather like this, I'm going to need something to keep me busy." She gestured to the window, where the layer of snow on the branches was thinning.

"I'm not complaining. Just remarking." Albert bent over and set Gus down gently, then straightened up and pulled his wallet out of his back pocket. "What's the damage?"

Mary rang up the books and told him the total, and Albert made a big show of sighing and rolling his eyes while Evelyn laughed. Mary handed Evelyn the bag of books.

"Let me know if you have any more questions, Mary," Albert said as they walked to the door. "I'm happy to help however I can."

Mary waved and watched through the front window as they picked their way down the sidewalk. They seemed very happy together. And Albert seemed so...unassuming. Helpful. If he was hiding something, would he have been so open about his work? And Mary couldn't think of a motive for them. If Evelyn was trying to get herself taken seriously as a glass artist, why steal from the people in town known to support glassmaking? And even if they had wanted to steal money from the museum's donors, why would they have gone to such great lengths to create the distress-call ruse? Albert seemed to know exactly how to work the system, and going to all that trouble would only create opportunities for things to go wrong. Plus, the Anderses seemed to have plenty of money. She supposed appearances could be deceiving, and greed often drove even the wealthiest people to want more, but still...it didn't add up.

But then, Mary had seen Evelyn walking down that hallway and come out talking with Maureen during the time the laptop had been stolen. And Evelyn had denied she'd talked to Maureen.

As much as she wanted to, Mary couldn't scratch Evelyn Anders off her list yet.

The store was quiet, so Mary turned back to her computer to search for more information about Max Harrington.

The bell over the door dinged again. Lizzie was back, this time without the kids.

"Hi, there," Mary said, perhaps too enthusiastically.

"Hey." Lizzie tucked her purse behind the counter and peeled off her coat. "I left the kids back at the house."

"Lizzie, I'm sorry. I didn't mean—"

"It's okay. I understand." But the hunch of her shoulders and the tight line of her mouth made it clear that even if she did understand, she wasn't happy about it. "Do you want to take your lunch now? I think I can deal with the crowd while you're gone."

Mary didn't want to believe that her daughter was trying to get out of spending time in the same room as her, but that's sure how it felt.

"Lizzie, we need to talk about what happened earlier."

"Why start now?" Lizzie took her coat to the back room of the shop and disappeared inside. Mary waited for her to come back out, but she didn't.

Mary got the message. Lizzie was still mad. Well, Mary was too upset to feel hungry, but maybe it wouldn't be the worst thing if she went out and gave Lizzie a little more time to cool down.

"I think I will take my lunch now, after all," she called.

"Cool." Lizzie didn't come out to say good-bye, so Mary grabbed her coat from the spot on the floor where it had fallen that morning and slipped it on.

"Bye," she called, but Lizzie didn't answer.

*Please, Lord*, Mary prayed as she stepped out the door, *help us to set things right.*

# EIGHTEEN

◆◆

Mary's heart ached as she walked down Main Street. The soles of her shoes crunched on the rock salt scattered across the sidewalk. Much of the snow was gone, but the wind was cold, and Mary pulled her scarf tighter around her neck and shoved her hands deep in her pockets. She replayed the earlier conversation with Lizzie over and over in her mind.

Lizzie had been irresponsible all week. She hadn't treated her time at Mary's bookshop like a job. No real employer would let her show up late and bring her kids in to work and turn away clients, as Lizzie had done this week. Lizzie had unrealistic expectations if she thought she could get away with that, and it was better she find out now than when she'd accepted the job at the elementary school and a classroom full of children were depending on her.

Lizzie obviously didn't see it that way. As she walked, Mary thought through all the things she wanted to say to Lizzie, all the reasons that Lizzie clearly wasn't ready to go back to work. But no matter how many times she went through it in her head, no matter how sure she was that she was right, it didn't make her feel any better.

That wasn't what Lizzie seemed to be upset about this morning, not really. Something else had set her off. Not for the first time, Mary wished she could understand what her daughter was thinking. Lizzie had always taken after John— headstrong, independent, passionate—whereas Mary had always been more rational. John and Lizzie had always had a bond Mary hadn't quite seemed to share, and they understood each other without even having to speak. Mary felt a pang as she wished that John were here to explain things to her now.

No matter. She would try to talk to Lizzie tonight. Maybe with some time alone, Lizzie would cool down and start to see things rationally.

Mary turned left on Meeting House Road, and a moment later, she stepped inside the county clerk's office.

"Hi, Bea." Mary shut the door firmly behind her. Bea Winslow peeked up from behind the counter.

"Hi, Mary," she called. Mary moved forward and saw that Bea was looking at an online auction site. "Megan told me you called yesterday. Was she able to help?"

Had it only been yesterday Megan had come by the shop? So much had happened in that time Mary found it hard to believe.

"Yes, she's great."

"She is, isn't she? She's a smart one." Bea gave her a sly smile. "Takes after her grandmother that way."

"Absolutely," Mary said, laughing along with Bea. "But today, I'm here to look at some records."

"Have at it." Bea gestured around at the bookcases and piles of paper that covered every surface in the room. Mary knew it was only worse downstairs, where the really old records were kept.

Mary looked around and tried to figure out where to start. She was looking for information on Max or Jonathan or Whatever Harrington. He was so young she doubted he'd been married, so there likely wasn't a marriage certificate on file. She knew he was alive, so there would be no death record, and she had no idea if he'd been born locally or not. She didn't even really know where to start, and she could spend all day riffling through old binders of documents.

"I think I'll start with the computer," Mary said. Bea nodded. Megan had built a searchable database program that allowed her to look for all sorts of pertinent records in one place.

Mary sat down at the computer and shook the mouse to wake the screen up. She pulled up the familiar program and tapped her fingers on the keyboard. Might as well start at the beginning, she decided. She searched for birth records for a Max Harrington in Barnstable County but found no one with that name. She tried again with Maxwell, but got no results. She searched again, this time leaving off the first name, and got a Jonathan Maxwell Harrington who had been born around the right time.

So he was going by his middle name. But Tristan had called him Jonathan. Did he use both? Or had he recently started using Max?

Next, she searched for marriage records, using all the permutations of the name she had, but she came up with nothing. She searched through the court's records and found nothing. She was starting to worry there was nothing to find on Jonathan Maxwell Harrington, but she did a search in the real-estate database anyway. She typed in the name Harrington and waited while the ancient computer searched the homemade database for records all over Barnstable County. She watched the little hourglass turn over and over again. Forget the glass museum. They should hold a fundraiser to get money to buy a new computer for this place. Finally, the computer returned her results.

And when she saw what her search turned up, she felt her stomach drop.

Mary stared at the computer screen, trying to make sense of what she was looking at. It looked like—she leaned closer to the screen—it looked like a Peter Harrington owned a house on 17 Meadowspring Drive in Dennis. There was no guarantee he was related to Max, Mary reminded herself. But looking at the rest of the entry, there was little doubt in her mind.

The records showed a lien on the property for several years of unpaid property taxes, as well as a lien for a mortgage, as well as a judgment lien against the property. But then there was something else.

"Bea, could you come take a look at this?" Mary called. Bea nodded and got up. She was surprisingly nimble, and she made it to Mary's side quickly. Mary pointed at the line of information on the screen. "What does this mean?"

Bea adjusted her glasses and peered at the screen. She murmured under her breath. "This right here means he hasn't paid his taxes," Bea said. Mary nodded. Bea moved her finger down to the next line of text. "And this shows that he wasn't paying his mortgage either. The bank and the state don't take too kindly to that, that's for sure. He must have been in dire trouble. And this..."—she pointed at the notice of the judgment lien—"this means that the bank had started the foreclosure process. But then..." She ran her finger down to the next line of text. She let out a long, slow breath. "Well, this is interesting."

"Does it say what I think it does?" Mary was almost afraid to breathe, scared that Bea was going to see something different in these numbers than she did. Because if it said what she thought it did—

"It almost looks like the loan was paid off. The taxes too."

Mary pointed to the date listed on the screen. "And look at this."

Bea let out a low whistle. "It was paid off yesterday."

Mary nodded. That was what she had seen as well. After years of back property taxes and a mortgage in default, Peter Harrington had somehow managed to make a payment large enough to pay back everything he owed—and he had done it all yesterday.

"Looks like Peter Harrington suddenly came into a ton of cash," Bea said. She straightened up. "Who is this guy?"

"I'm not sure." Mary shook her head. "But I'm going to find out."

# NINETEEN

---◆◆◆---

Mary made her way back to her shop and poked her head in the door. Lizzie was busy talking to a woman Mary didn't recognize about a book in the local history section. She pantomimed that she was going to drive somewhere, and Lizzie nodded and turned back to her customer.

It wasn't the warmest reception, but it could have been worse, Mary thought as she climbed into her car. She pulled up the directions Bea had printed off for her and set out down Route 6A toward Dennis. Twenty minutes later, she drove into a newer development with large houses and searched for 17 Meadowspring. This development was pretty nice, actually. The houses were set back from the road and shaded by arching trees, and it didn't have the big-box feel that Evelyn's neighborhood had.

She pulled up in front of number seventeen. It was a large, square white house set back down a long driveway. A split-rail fence ran around the edges of the property. At the end of the driveway was a Realtor's For Sale sign with a small notice at the top that said Short Sale. The Harringtons must have been trying to sell the house at a loss before the bank could foreclose, and they must not have had a chance to take down the sign yet since their windfall. Well, that gave her an opportunity.

She turned into the driveway and parked her car next to a dinged-up Audi and a BMW with splotches of rust on the side panel. On the back windshield of the Audi was a bumper sticker advertising what looked like some elite college.

Mary carefully made her way to the door and rang the doorbell. A few minutes later, a heavyset woman in fleece pants and a cable-knit sweater answered the door.

"Hi," Mary said uncertainly. "My name is Mary Fisher. I noticed the For Sale sign, and this is such a beautiful house I wondered if it would be possible for me to take a look."

The woman sized Mary up. "I'm afraid we're not selling, after all," she finally said.

"Oh, that's too bad. It's such a gorgeous property, and I just love this neighborhood. I would so love to take a look around..." It was all true, Mary thought. It really was a beautiful home.

Mary let her voice trail off. Even though the house had just been paid off, the taxes on a property like this must be very high, and as Mary knew, the family could ill afford them. Even if they had suddenly come into enough money to pay off what they owed, it didn't mean they could afford to keep paying the costs going forward. Mary watched as the woman seemed to be thinking it through, and finally, she stepped back and gestured for Mary to come inside.

"Come on in." She held out her hand. "I'm Helene. Pete, we've got company," she called over her shoulder.

Mary heard a man grunt from a room somewhere inside the house and the tinny ringing that said a television was on.

"Oh, this is beautiful." Mary gazed up at the entryway ceiling, which soared above the second story and framed an open oak staircase. Windows high above, eye-level with the second floor, let in muted winter sunlight. "This room gets so much light."

The woman nodded and led Mary into a dining room to the left of the entryway. It had high ceilings, a brass chandelier, and oxblood walls, and the oval-shaped table looked like it had seen many family meals.

"It's gorgeous," Mary said.

"Thank you." The woman seemed confused, but she was friendly enough, considering a total stranger had just shown up at her door and demanded a tour. "So, the house is just over four thousand square feet, and there's a storage space over the garage that could be winterized and done up, if you needed more space." She eyed Mary, as if wondering what a woman her age could possibly need with all that space. "The kitchen is this way." She led Mary into a large, bright kitchen with cherry cabinets and a granite-topped island. Mary could see a pantry the size of her first apartment off to the right. It must cost a fortune to keep this place going, especially in the winter. Just heating all these rooms would be more than most people could afford.

Mary ran her hand over the smooth granite. "This is beautiful. How long have you owned it?"

"We bought it new ten years ago. Back then, Pete was—" She faltered and seemed to be searching for the right words. "Well, things were different then."

"I can see why you bought it."

"We've always loved it," the woman said. "It sits on an acre, and as you can see"—she gestured to sliding-glass doors behind her—"there's a three-season sunroom here."

"And this must be the living room." Mary walked past a smaller dining table and poked her head in the room where the television was blaring. A man in a leather recliner looked up at Mary. The television was playing some home-improvement show. Both Pete and his wife were home on a Wednesday afternoon. That, coupled with their financial problems, most likely meant one of them had lost a job, Mary thought.

"Pete, this is Mary Fisher. She's interested in the house."

"Shoulda come by a week ago."

Helene's eyes widened, and she quickly took Mary's arm and steered her back into the entryway.

"What happened a week ago? Oh no, did you already get an offer on the house?" She was trying to draw Helene out, but she wasn't biting.

"No, it's"—Helene shook her head—"it's kind of complicated. We could still be interested in selling at the right price." She quickly led Mary into what looked like a library, with walls lined with dark bookshelves and a cheerful fireplace.

"This is just stunning." Mary actually could imagine curling up here with a good mystery on a stormy night. It was a great room, though the shelves seemed to be mostly filled with magazines and knickknacks. "Can I ask why you're selling?"

Helene looked away, toward the living room, and Mary couldn't see her face. "It's too big for us, now that the kids are grown."

"Oh, how many children do you have? I have a son and a daughter. I understand what you mean about the house being too big. When my children left home, it just felt like John and I were rattling around in that house."

"We've got two boys." She held on to the back of a wing-back chair, as if holding herself up.

"Do they live nearby? It's so nice when the kids can come to visit."

Helene hesitated. Mary pretended not to notice and walked toward the fireplace in the middle of the far wall and looked at the photographs in silver frames scattered across the mantel.

"Yes," she finally said. "Jonathan lives over in Barnstable. And Jake, our oldest, he lives out in Plymouth."

"That's so nice." Mary zeroed in on a picture of Max—Jonathan—in a cap and gown in front of a brick building with an oxidized copper cupola that somehow looked vaguely familiar. "My daughter lives in Melrose, and it's so close I know I shouldn't complain, but I don't see her enough." She bent in and studied the picture. Max looked younger, there, and a bit thinner, but it was definitely him. "Wait a minute; is this one of your boys?"

"That's Jonathan. That's his high school graduation."

"You know, he looks kind of familiar." Mary lifted up the frame and studied it, as if trying to place his face, but really she was watching Helene's reaction. She was gripping the chair harder, and she was biting her bottom lip. "Does he ever do catering? He looks exactly like a waiter I met at a party on Saturday night."

Helene's face had gone white, and she opened her mouth and closed it again. She seemed to be struggling to come up with how to respond.

"I know that's him. We chatted for quite a while." That part wasn't exactly true, but it was close, and Mary thought the white lie was justified in this case. "And in fact, I wanted to get in touch with him. I was there when they were cleaning up, and I think he might have accidentally left with something of mine. What a crazy coincidence that he's your son."

Helene froze. All the warmth was gone from her eyes. "Who did you say you were?"

"I'm Mary Fisher. I own a little bookstore on Main Street in Ivy Bay." She set the frame back on the mantel gently. "I would really love to get in touch with your son. Could I get his phone number?"

"I think it's time for you to leave."

"Oh, but I haven't even seen the upstairs. How many bedrooms did you say you had?"

"I said it's time for you to leave. Pete!"

Mary heard the recliner foot rest slam down.

"Could I leave my information for you to pass on to him, then?" Mary tried to pretend everything was normal, that she wasn't being thrown out of the house, but inside her mind was spinning. They knew something. Why else would Helene be reacting this way?

"Get out." Pete appeared in the doorway, his bulky frame blocking the light from the entryway. He was tall and solid, and he looked imposing, as she was sure he knew.

"Well, I guess it's time for me to get going," Mary said brightly, as if it were her idea. "Thank you so much for the tour. I'll be in touch if I decide to make an offer on the house."

Neither Pete nor Helene said a word, but Pete moved out of the doorway so Mary could pass by. She opened the front door and turned back to them to wave, and saw that they were both glaring at her. She stepped outside and walked quickly to her car.

It didn't prove anything, she knew. There were lots of reasons a mother would not want some stranger getting in touch with her son. But they knew something. They had to.

Mary knew what her next step had to be, but she had no idea how to go about it. How could she track down Jonathan?

# TWENTY

———◆◆◆———

Mary was still puzzling over her visit to the Harringtons when she pulled up in front of Tabitha Krause's house. Tabitha lived in one of the oldest neighborhoods in Ivy Bay, and Mary usually loved looking at the beautiful old homes, but today, she was too distracted to do much dreaming. She stepped out of her car and walked up the path someone—no doubt Dawn—had shoveled off this morning. She grabbed the heavy knocker and banged it against the door.

A moment later, Dawn pulled open the door. "Well, hello, Mary. Thank you so much for coming."

"Is now still a good time?"

"It's perfect. Tabitha just got up from a nap." She stepped back so Mary could enter and held out her arms for Mary's coat.

It smelled like cinnamon and chocolate in the house, as though someone had been baking. Mary took a deep breath. It smelled wonderful.

"Why don't you come on in and have a seat in the parlor? I'll go get Tabitha," Dawn said.

"Thanks. I know where it is."

Dawn hung Mary's coat on a hanger and put it in the coat closet in the entryway. Then she started up the intricately carved staircase, her footsteps muffled by the crimson runner that ran up the middle of the steps. Mary had always loved this house. When they were children and their mother would bring them to see Tabitha, Betty had always felt this place was cold, but Mary loved the dark wood and the oil paintings of long-dead ancestors that adorned the walls. It made her feel like she was visiting an old English castle.

Dawn disappeared down a hallway at the top of the stairs, and Mary found her way to the parlor. The high-ceilinged room was lovely, with rich velvet draperies, a thick Persian rug, and beautiful Queen Anne furniture. Mary sat down on a love seat and looked around the familiar room. There was an intricately carved upright piano in the corner that Mary had loved to play as a child, though she'd never been very good. Looking back now, she was sure her little performances had been torture for all the adults present, but Tabitha and her parents had always clapped politely.

"Hello, Mary."

Mary looked up to see Tabitha shuffling toward her. Mary stood and wrapped her in a hug. The normally reserved Tabitha held on a few moments longer than Mary had anticipated, and then she pulled back and settled down on a chair opposite Mary. "Dawn is going to bring us some coffee. And, Dawn, is there any chance we could get some of those cookies you're making as well?"

"Of course." Dawn made sure Tabitha was settled comfortably and then disappeared into the kitchen.

"Dawn's church is doing a bake sale for that injured boater. So it's good all around—they raise money, and I get to sample."

"That's certainly nice of her." Mary shifted in the chair. "It sounds like a lot of people are having a rough time right now. I was so sorry to hear that you'd been affected by the bank thief as well."

"Yes, it's terrible, isn't it? All this technology is supposed to make things easier, and here it just means someone can go in and steal my money without even setting foot in a bank. Used to be, you'd at least have to show up with a gun and a mask and a bag marked with a dollar sign to rob a bank."

Mary saw that Tabitha was smiling, and there was a twinkle in her eye, so Mary laughed. "Yes, it does seem strange that someone could be halfway around the world and make off with someone else's life savings, doesn't it?"

"Amelia has been helping me sort through it all." Mary was thankful Tabitha's granddaughter lived in town and was able to help. "And Steve Althorpe says I'll get it all back, but I don't know. It's scary. You just don't know what's safe these days."

Dawn walked into the room carrying a tray with two mugs of coffee and a plate of cookies. "I'll be right back with the milk and sugar," she said as she set it down and then turned and walked back into the kitchen.

"Now, Betty said something about this money stuff being linked to the glass museum?" Tabitha took a cookie from the tray and set it on a napkin Dawn had left, and Mary gladly did the same. It felt like ages since she'd eaten.

216 C SECRETS of MARY'S BOOKSHOP

"I'm almost positive it is." Mary explained how the fake distress call had been a ruse to distract everyone so no one would notice a laptop disappearing, and how she'd seen the security footage and had been chasing down clues but so far had nothing but theories.

"So who is on your list of suspects?" Tabitha bit into a cookie and held her hand under her chin to catch the crumbs.

Mary hesitated. She had a strong feeling Max the waiter was involved in this somehow, but she hadn't really ruled anyone else out yet. She didn't want to cast aspersions on anyone, but Tabitha seemed to always know what was going on in town. Maybe she could tell her something she'd missed about one of her suspects.

Mary told Tabitha about Taylor, whom Tabitha waved off as not brainy enough to plan and carry out such a massive plot, and Max the waiter, whom Tabitha had noticed. She joked that if she were a few years younger, she might have flirted with him herself.

"Who else you got?"

Mary hesitated. "Well, do you know this new glass artist in town? Evelyn Anders?"

Dawn was starting to walk away after delivering the milk and sugar, but at the mention of Evelyn's name, she froze.

Tabitha nodded. "I remember meeting her that night. Blonde, tan, flashing money around, kind of tacky?"

Mary tried to keep her face neutral. "She was wearing a long blue dress."

"That's her. I don't know. She didn't seem like the type to me. And she seems to have plenty of money. She seemed to want to be accepted as an artist more than anything to me."

"That's what she appeared like to me as well." Mary watched out of the corner of her eye as Dawn turned toward the door out of the corner of her eye. "Dawn, did you run into her that night as well?"

"Oh, I don't..." Dawn moved toward the kitchen door. "I need to get that next batch of cookies out of the oven."

"Dawn?" Tabitha turned around in her chair and eyed her. "Did you see something?"

Dawn looked like a deer caught in the headlights.

"It's okay," Tabitha said. "Whatever you saw, I'll make sure no one bothers you about it..."

"It's not that," Dawn said. She sighed and stepped closer. "It's just that I promised I wouldn't say anything."

"Did you see someone steal the laptop?" Tabitha asked, eyebrows arched.

"No, Tabitha. Nothing like that."

Mary patted the cushion of the love seat, and slowly Dawn lowered herself down next to her.

"If you saw something that night, please tell us." Tabitha toyed with the napkin in her lap. "If there's anything that can help get that money back, we need to know."

"That's the thing. It won't help you get the money back. But I know that Evelyn didn't have anything to do with taking it."

A hundred questions ran through Mary's mind, but she simply sat in silence, waiting for Dawn to go on.

"I went out to the car to get a sweater for Tabitha," Dawn finally said. Tabitha nodded, slightly, confirming that that had happened. "I went out the front door and around to the side of the building, where we had parked, and I saw two women by the side door, the one that leads out from the hallway off the main gallery."

"Which two women?" Tabitha asked.

"Evelyn Anders and Maureen Rowe. Evelyn was crying. I went up, thinking maybe she needed help, but she said she didn't, she was fine, just upset."

"What was she upset about?" Mary reached for another cookie and bit into it. The sugar rush was exactly what she needed.

"Apparently, she was there trying to get attention for her art. She wanted to meet glass collectors, and she thought the fund-raiser would be a good place to rub elbows with people of similar interests. But when she approached Mason Willoughby, he had less than nice things to say about her work."

"Oh no." Mary had seen how proud she was of the pieces she'd made. She could imagine how hurt she must have been to hear Mason, not exactly known for his tact, say something disparaging about her artwork.

"She was upset, so she went outside to regain her composure."

"That's horrible." Tabitha set down her mug decisively.

"Maureen was there, comforting her. I gave her a tissue, and she cleaned herself up and tried to recover. She asked us both not to say anything. She didn't want it to get around that she was an unstable artist or anything like that. So then I gave her a hug, came back around to the front door, and went back inside."

"Do you know what time this all took place?" Mary asked.

"I don't know. Seven thirty or so? It was not too long after Chief McArthur came in talking about that distress call."

"So, pretty much exactly at the time the computer was taken," Mary said.

"Evelyn didn't have anything in her hands, and there was nowhere to hide a laptop under that dress, I promise you."

"She must have been freezing, standing out there in that light dress," Tabitha said.

"Well…" Dawn hesitated. "I hope you don't mind this, but I sort of let her borrow your sweater for a few minutes, Tabitha. I knew I probably shouldn't, but she looked so pitiful, and I—"

Tabitha smiled. "You did the right thing, Dawn." She was quiet for a moment, probably reviewing the events in her mind. "Evelyn came back in a few minutes after that, if I remember correctly. I saw her come back inside the gallery with Maureen, though I didn't know they'd been outside," Tabitha said.

Mary nodded, running through different scenarios in her mind. If Evelyn had been embarrassed about breaking down, that could explain why she had denied talking with Maureen that night. She didn't want anyone to talk to Maureen and find out that Mason hadn't liked her work. It was plausible, and, beyond that, it felt right to Mary. She hadn't believed Evelyn guilty, and this seemed to clear her. But if she wasn't responsible, who was?

"Thank you, Dawn," Tabitha said, and Dawn nodded and stood, then walked back to the kitchen.

"I guess I can cross Evelyn off my list," Mary said.

"I suppose so." Tabitha bit into a cookie. "So who does that leave you with?"

"Maureen. We know she was outside with Evelyn when Dawn saw her, but we don't know why she went outside in the first place. She went down the hallway several minutes before Evelyn. She might have had time to take the laptop and stash it somewhere before Evelyn came out. And I plan to look into that waiter more."

"*Hmm.*" Tabitha bit into a cookie. "What about Eleanor? She has access to a marine radio."

Mary laughed. "Eleanor's account was hacked. I doubt even she would go to such great lengths to throw us off her trail."

Tabitha set the cookie down on her plate. "How about Thomas?"

"Eleanor's grandson?" Mary shook her head. "He was talking to me the whole time during the window of opportunity when the laptop was stolen."

"Well, that's too bad. He would have made a great suspect. He's bright enough to have arranged the whole plot and lazy enough to have seen it as a quick way to make a buck. Plus, he has that boat Eleanor gave him. And I saw him during the party with pink cheeks and a runny nose."

"What do you mean?"

"What happens when you go outside in the cold February air, Mary Fisher?"

All right, the cold often did make her nose run, and it often brought color to her cheeks, but so did heat, or embarrassment, or any number of things. Maybe Thomas had a cold. Maybe he'd been upset. Maybe he'd been outside to get some air, or to make a phone call, or...

Okay, she saw what Tabitha was getting at, but that didn't mean anything. You could make a good case against Thomas, Mary agreed, but you could do the same for anyone on her list, really, and Thomas had an ironclad alibi.

"Well, I don't think I saw anyone else acting strangely," Tabitha said. "I wish I could be of more help."

"You've been very helpful," Mary said. "You notice a lot," she added.

"It's because of my invisibility cloak."

Mary set down her mug gently and tried to figure out how to answer. Tabitha must be getting tired. Should she call Dawn?

"I blend in, is what I'm saying. When you're as old as I am, no one notices you," Tabitha said. "Because I need help getting around, they all assume I'm a doddering old fool, and they don't notice me watching them and listening to everything they say."

Mary recognized the truth in this. She'd experienced it herself, and she was a full generation younger than Tabitha. People often wrote off women of a certain age as not worth paying attention to. Well, that was their mistake, since this woman of a certain age was getting closer to solving this mystery every minute.

"If you ever need a partner in crime, so to speak, let me know. I'm good at being the fly on the wall. You be the brains; I'll be the beauty."

Mary laughed heartily and pushed herself up slowly. "Thanks so much for your help." She stepped around the coffee table and helped Tabitha to her feet, then wrapped her in a hug.

"I hope you find that thief soon."

"I'll do my best."

"Essy would be proud."

Mary smiled as she walked back to her car. She hoped Tabitha was right, that Mary's mother, Esther—Essy to her best friend—would be proud. They'd always had such a good relationship, talking, praying, and laughing together, even as Mary grew up and had kids of her own. They'd always been able to talk about anything. A heaviness settled over Mary as she remembered the fight with Lizzie that morning and the tension still between them. She needed to make it right.

She tried to think through what she would say when she walked back into the store. "I'm sorry" would be first, but what then? Mary still didn't totally understand what the fight had really been about. She puzzled over it as she walked back to her car.

Dawn had given her a bag of the fresh-baked chocolate-chip cookies to take to her grandchildren, and she set that gently on the passenger seat and started the engine. Mary's eyes lingered on the bag.

What had Tabitha said about those cookies? Dawn's church was holding a bake sale for that boater injured during Saturday night's rescue efforts. Why was that sounding so familiar?

She thought back through everything that had happened in the past few days, trying to nudge whatever memory was hiding back there. There was something she was missing...

*Oh my.*

She remembered now. Mary pulled out her cell phone and made a quick phone call. When she heard that her suspicion had been correct, Mary hung up, both relieved and deflated. And then she leaned back against the back of the seat, closed her eyes, and started to pray.

# TWENTY-ONE

Half an hour later, Mary was walking through the lobby of Cape Cod General Hospital, scanning the signs for directions to the correct room. Finally, she gave up, went to the information desk, and was directed to the fourth floor.

She poked her head into the room just as Johanna Montgomery walked out.

"Good to see you, Mary," Johanna said. And then, in a lower voice, she said, "It's good of you to come. I think she's glad to have someone to talk to."

"Oh good," Mary said and waved as Johanna headed down the hall.

In the room, Maureen smiled at Mary and gestured to the empty chair next to hers on the far side of her husband's hospital bed. James was asleep. The lights were off, and aside from the hazy winter sunshine coming in through the window, the only light in the room was a small reading lamp over Maureen's chair.

"Hi, Mary," she said quietly.

Mary held out the bouquet of flowers she'd brought. Looking at the cookies Dawn had given her, Mary had realized that her prayer group had been praying for a JR, who was still recovering after an accident, and remembered seeing the cover story of the *Ivy Bay Bugle* about the injured boater, and the pieces had all fallen into place.

"I'm so sorry to barge in like this. I hope I'm not disturbing you."

"Not at all." She gave Mary a grateful smile. "It's too quiet in here anyway. Johanna wanted to do a follow-up story for the *Bugle*, so I left the kids with my mom so we'd have some peace to talk. But this is the first time I've had some time to myself to just think since the accident. And, well, I guess I can understand why everyone tells you to keep busy."

"I remember that feeling." Mary had sat by John's bedside for weeks on end as he fought the cancer that had eventually taken his life. Everyone assumed they would be interrupting and hesitated to stop by, but Mary was so grateful for the company most of the time.

"I just now heard." Mary kept her voice low to avoid waking James, who seemed to be resting peacefully. There was the low hum of machines, and Mary heard some nurses talking down the hall, but the room was quiet. "How is he?"

"He's doing better." Maureen placed a bookmark in her page and set the book on the compact table next to her chair.

"When I stopped by on Tuesday, I had no idea.... You must have thought I was so rude. I'm sorry for that."

"It's okay. I figured you didn't know what was going on. And I'm sorry I was so impatient. I was flustered. I"—she shook her head—"I'd just gotten a call that he'd taken a turn for the worse, and the nurses wanted me to come right away."

"Oh my goodness. Is he—"

"He's going to be fine."

Mary felt herself breathe an actual sigh of relief.

"It happened Saturday night, while he was out looking for the missing boaters?"

Maureen nodded. "When I heard about the boaters, I hurried outside the museum to call James. He has a boat for his work, and I knew he would want to help."

"It's amazing to think that on a freezing February night, people would rush out onto the water to help strangers."

"Boaters look out for one another. And, well, that's the kind of guy James is." She stretched her legs out in front of her and leaned back. "On our first date, he pulled off the road to help a kid whose bike tire had gone flat. I was all dressed up and decked out, and there he was in the dirt with some kid like he had nowhere better to be. It's what made me fall in love with him."

"So you went outside to call him during the party, and he rushed out to the water."

"Yep. He dropped the kids at my mom's, and then he went out on his boat. His boat isn't big, and it's not meant for rough water, so he was staying close to the shore. He was getting tired and was about to come in when he saw something floating in the water." Maureen pulled her legs back and watched her sleeping husband. Mary saw his chest rise and fall gently. "He thought it could be a body, so he bent down to grab it, and he fell in. He swam around back to climb back in, but a big wave hit, and he was knocked into the propeller."

Mary already knew this, but she still couldn't help an involuntary intake of breath.

"It cut his leg up pretty badly. For a while, it looked like he might lose it, but it looks like it's going to heal up in time."

"I'm so glad."

A nurse poked her head into the room, saw that James was sleeping, made a notation on a clipboard, and walked out of the room.

"Yeah." Maureen moved her head gently up and down against the back of the chair. "Me too."

Mary considered her next question carefully. "When did you find out about the accident?"

"Oh, I don't know. One, two in the morning?"

"Dawn Santiago said she saw you outside the glass museum the night of the party, around seven thirty?"

"I don't really know what time it was, but yeah, like I said, I went outside to call James as soon as I heard. And then I ended up talking to Evelyn Anders for a bit. Do you know her?"

"I do."

"She's sweet." Maureen's voice was low and soothing in the hushed room. "She was upset because of something someone had said to her, so we chatted for a bit. Then Dawn came up, and we went back inside."

The story checked out, and so did the timing. That meant she could officially cross both Maureen and Evelyn off her list of suspects.

"I'm sorry you have to deal with this on top of..." Mary cleared her throat. "Well, I've heard the museum is having some financial trouble. I'm sorry this happened on top of that."

Maureen didn't say anything for a minute. "I'm not going to pretend I'm not worried. And I don't really have any vacation days to spare, so I've been calling in sick. I know

Virginia knows I'm not really sick, and we'll see if she says anything about it. But this whole thing with James kind of puts everything in perspective. I might lose my job, but things could be a lot worse. God was looking out for us that night, for sure."

"I suppose that's true." Mary hoped she would have that kind of faith if she were ever in a situation like Maureen's. "When you left that night, you had a tote bag with you...."

Maureen's cheeks flushed. "The caterers were throwing away some pastries, and I knew the kids would love them."

"Ah, yes. I could never resist the lure of the free pastries myself."

Maureen nodded, her eyes resting on her husband's sleeping form.

"Maureen, I need to get going. But can I do one thing before I leave?"

Maureen hesitated. "Sure."

"Can I pray with you?"

A smile crossed Maureen's face, and together, they bowed their heads.

# TWENTY-TWO

◆◆

When Mary made it back to the shop, Lizzie was busy with a customer. The three boxes of books were still stacked where Mary had left them.

"Lizzie," Mary said as the customer left, "is there any chance you might have placed that order more than once yesterday?"

Lizzie glanced over at the boxes, shaking her head, but then she knelt down and examined them. "No way."

"No way?"

"I thought the order didn't go through, so I tried it again. And then it looked like that didn't go through, so I tried it one more time. I didn't realize I was placing the same order three times." Lizzie's face was white, and she was still shaking her head. Then she started mumbling under her breath, and suddenly she stood up, stormed to the back room, grabbed her coat, and went out the door. "I'm taking a break," she called over her shoulder on her way out.

Mary watched her go, uncertain what to do. She watched as Lizzie walked to the corner, crossed Meeting House Road, and kept walking, vanishing out of sight.

Mary kept watching for a few minutes, hoping she'd come back. Lizzie was upset. She was no doubt embarrassed too. But she couldn't just walk out like that, not if this were a real job. Slowly, sadly, Mary turned and shelved the books in the top box. She tucked the other two boxes behind the counter. She'd decide what to do about them later.

Fifteen minutes later, Lizzie came back, her eyes red, and vanished into the back room. She eventually came out but avoided Mary for the rest of the afternoon. By the time the sky had darkened and it was closing time, Lizzie had successfully thwarted every attempt Mary made to talk about what had happened.

Mary went through the motions of closing up the shop, but her heart was heavy. She scooted Gus into his carrier and flipped the sign on the door to Shut, and they walked to the car in silence.

Dinner was tense. Chad was still feeling under the weather, the kids were stir-crazy from being cooped up all day, and Lizzie snapped at them more than was probably necessary. After dinner, the kids and Chad retreated upstairs and Betty vanished into her room, no doubt glad to give Mary and Lizzie a wide berth.

When the kitchen was clean, Mary walked into the living room and found Lizzie curled up on the couch, reading one of Betty's interior-design magazines. Mary sat down at the other end of the couch. Lizzie kept reading.

"Lizzie?" Mary adjusted a velvet pillow behind her back and tried to find a comfortable position.

Lizzie lowered the magazine. "If we're going to do this, Mom, let's do it for real. That means no shutting the conversation down when I say something you don't want to hear."

Mary didn't know what to say. But Lizzie seemed open to talking in a way she hadn't earlier, so she nodded. She gave up trying to get comfortable and pulled the pillow out from behind her, settling it on her lap.

"I'm sorry I brought the kids to the shop today. I didn't realize it would be a problem. And I'm sorry about the mix-up with the order. I'll pay for the difference. I've messed up this week. I'm sure you'll be glad when Rebecca comes back and can fix all the things I did wrong."

Mary grasped the fringe on the corner of the pillow and twisted it around her finger.

"But maybe you wouldn't need an employee if you actually spent any time in your shop. You get after me for taking a long lunch or coming in late, but then you disappear for hours at a time. It's a little ridiculous. You're so busy running all over town it makes me wonder whether you actually like running the bookstore so much, or whether you just like the idea of it."

Mary let those words settle in, and she didn't say anything for a minute. *Lord, give me the right words to say*, she prayed. Mary's first response was shock. How could...What was Lizzie—

Then, she felt her defenses rising. Sure, she hadn't been at the store too much in the past few days. That was because she was working on finding out who stole thousands of dollars from her friends and her sister! How could Lizzie say that Mary should have been in the store instead? Plus, she owned the store. It was her prerogative to come and go as she pleased.

But Mary remembered her promise to not simply react when she heard something she didn't like. She didn't want to think about it, but was there some truth to what Lizzie was saying?

The truth was, Mary loved running her bookshop. Sure, some days, she needed to run errands during the hours the store was open, and sure, she was often working on a mystery that took her out of the shop for stretches at a time. But that didn't change the fact she genuinely enjoyed what she did.

But was that really what Lizzie was getting at?

Mary pulled at the fringe. She thought back to their conversations earlier in the week. Lizzie had been wrestling with whether to go back to work and how that would affect her other responsibilities. And now, she was pointing out that Mary, too, struggled to juggle her work and the other parts of her life. She'd missed her prayer group this week, for instance, and she wasn't getting to see her grandkids as much as she wanted to, not to mention leaving the shop to investigate the mystery, as Lizzie had pointed out.

"I can see how you could ask that question," Mary acknowledged. Lizzie's shoulders relaxed. "I do love my shop. I love working there."

Lizzie was picking at a stray thread on the piping of the couch, but she seemed to be listening.

"But I also love that running the shop means I have the flexibility to arrange my schedule the way I want to."

Lizzie pulled on the thread.

"I'm sorry I didn't make it clear to you that I'd be in and out. Rebecca and I have been working together for so long I forget that it's probably not a traditional arrangement. I should have been clearer about my expectations to you in the beginning. Next time, I'll know to do that."

Mary heard Luke cry out upstairs, but heavy footsteps rushed into the bedroom where he was staying. Chad had it under control.

"Part of what I love about my job is how I'm able to shape it around my life. But that's not true of every job."

Lizzie was still pulling at the thread, but she was nodding, staring at something far away.

"Are you thinking about that teaching job?"

Lizzie didn't say anything for a moment, and then she sighed.

"Partly, yes." She tugged at the thread one more time, and then she let it go. "I'm sorry I got so frustrated earlier. But yes, I was surprised by how much you are gone. I thought we were going to be spending the week together in the shop, and that's not really how it is."

Mary felt her stomach twist. "Oh, Lizzie, I'm—"

Lizzie held up her hand. "It's okay. I don't know what I was thinking, really, but it wasn't reality. I guess in my head, I think of this as a hobby of yours, something you do for fun. I forget it's actually your business and your job. And that means someone has to be there during business hours. And sometimes, that's not you."

Mary wanted to say more, but it looked like Lizzie had more to say, so she stayed quiet.

"Owning your own business gives you that flexibility. If I took the job at the school, I wouldn't have that same freedom. I guess that's what I'm wrestling with now. What if one of the kids got sick and had to stay home? Or what if they were on break and Chad got sick, like today? I can't just leave a classroom of second graders because my own children need me."

"You would have sick days," Mary said quietly.

Lizzie nodded. "Yes, and I suppose I would be off when the kids were out of school too. But that's not really the issue, is it? It's more about things like who will help them get dressed in the morning if I'm rushing to get out the door too? Who will pack lunches? Will we end up eating more takeout because I'm too busy to cook? Will our lives become too crazy? Is it worth it?"

"That's something only you can answer, honey." Mary was glad Lizzie seemed to have cooled off, and she wasn't sure whether to risk making her upset again. "I bet, though, that if you do decide to take it, they will all rise to the challenge. Luke will learn to get himself ready if he has to. Chad is a good father, and I would guess he will pitch in to take over some of the things you handle now."

Lizzie kept staring off into space, considering.

"But there will be trade-offs, for sure. Your life will be busier. It will be fuller too, but you will have less flexibility. And you're the only one who can decide if that's best for you and your family."

"I don't know what to do," Lizzie said quietly.

"Then do the one thing you always know how to do." Mary scooted closer to Lizzie and reached for her. Lizzie let Mary take her hands, and she bowed her head. "Let's pray."

"Lord, thank You for this amazing opportunity Lizzie has been offered," Mary prayed. "Please give her wisdom as she thinks about whether to take this job or not. Please guide her, and please give her peace about her decision. In Your name, we pray. Amen."

"Thanks, Mom," Lizzie said, and she pulled Mary into a hug. Mary held on to her daughter as long as she could, but then Lizzie pulled away. She smiled shyly, then got up and walked into the kitchen to get herself a drink.

"So what were you planning on doing the rest of the evening?" Lizzie asked from the kitchen, more to break the silence than anything else, Mary guessed.

Mary had managed to cross a couple of suspects off her list, but her suspicions about Jonathan had grown, and Mary was starting to think there was something she was missing. She walked into the kitchen. "I was thinking I would look at the surveillance video from the party the other night again."

"Can I watch it too?" Lizzie had filled a glass with water and took a sip.

"Sure." Mary thought there were probably more interesting things for Lizzie to do on her vacation, but she was thrilled Lizzie could stand to be in the same room with her again, and she was glad to have an excuse to spend time with her daughter. She retrieved her laptop and set it on the table, and she pulled the envelope and a pen from her purse. She settled in at the table, Lizzie in the seat next to her.

They watched the video on double time until just before seven fifteen, when the call had been made. Then Mary slowed down the video and found the suspects in the room. Max was moving around the room handing out drinks. Taylor was chatting with Betty.

So neither of them could have made the call. That meant none of her remaining suspects had set the plan in motion.

She paused the video and scanned the room, looking to see if she could find anyone notable missing. There was Eleanor and Virginia. Maureen was by the door, and Evelyn was chatting with Mason Willoughby. But where was—

That was strange. She backed the video up. There he was, at 7:05, helping Eleanor move a stack of brochures about the museum to the table at the front of the room. Then he moved toward the front door of the gallery.

When they had viewed the tape the first time, Mary and Betty had been so focused on who was going in and out of the hallway at the far side of the room, where the laptop was, that they hadn't taken much notice of who was going in and out of the door between the gallery and the lobby. Dozens of people went in and out of that doorway in the time frame they'd been interested in, including, Mary now saw, Dawn Santiago, who she knew had gone outside to retrieve a sweater for Tabitha, and...Thomas Blakely.

At 7:07, Thomas stood by the door, looked around the room, and slipped out. Mary noted the time on her envelope.

"Who's that?" Lizzie asked.

"Thomas Blakely."

"Eleanor's grandson?"

Mary nodded, her eyes glued to the screen. At 7:19, he slipped back into the room, and just moments later, Eleanor had stopped him and introduced him to Mary. They continued to chat until Chief McArthur stormed in. Then he stood next to Mary for the next ten minutes or so—the exact time frame when the laptop had been stolen. There he was, a shocked look on his face, asking Mary if he should go out and help in the rescue.

What had he told her? His parents had a boat, and he could use that?

Mary thought back over the things she'd learned this week, and something snagged in her memory. Thomas's parents no doubt had a boat, but Tabitha had said that Thomas had one of his own. Eleanor had given it to him. Why wouldn't he have mentioned his own boat?

It wasn't proof of anything. There were dozens of reasons he could have mentioned his parents' boat but not his own. Maybe something was wrong with his boat. It was possible his was put up for the winter, but theirs was more accessible. He could have simply misspoken in the heat of the moment. But still, it did seem odd.

"But it couldn't have been him," Mary murmured. True, he had left the gallery, and, if Tabitha could be believed, the museum, at the right time to make the call, but that didn't mean anything. There were dozens of reasons he could have stepped outside, and there he was, right there on the recording, definitely *not* stealing a laptop at the time the laptop disappeared. She glanced down at the timeline Mary had noted on the envelope. Thomas couldn't have taken the laptop, but he *could* have made the distress call.

But it didn't make sense. Why would he—

And then something Lizzie had said earlier in the week came back to her. Luke and his little friend Aiden had tag-teamed her to get the cookies they weren't supposed to take. Aiden had distracted her while Luke stole the cookies.

Thomas could have made the call, setting up someone else to steal the laptop.

It was suddenly obvious to Mary that it was entirely plausible. In fact, Eleanor had suggested it, back when she'd been trying to convince Mary to have Taylor arrested, but Mary had written the whole conversation off and hadn't thought to consider that Eleanor might have an excellent point.

"What did you just figure out?" Lizzie said.

"Who says I just figured something out?"

"The look on your face."

Mary smiled, then explained her suspicion. "But who was Thomas working with?" Mary stared at the frozen screen.

"Who's left on your suspect list?"

Mary looked down. Jonathan and Taylor. Both had motives. Both had the opportunity. Neither one, as far as she knew, had any connection to Thomas Blakely. She would need to look into that, for sure.

Yes, she decided. First thing tomorrow morning, she would find out exactly what connection, if any, Taylor and Jonathan each had to Thomas Blakely.

# TWENTY-THREE

————◆◆◆————

Mary bolted upright in bed. Her phone was ringing. She grabbed for it in the still-dark room, bumping into the glass of water she kept on her bedside table and knocking over a stack of paperbacks.

She fumbled with the buttons on her phone. Her heart beat wildly. A phone call in the middle of the night was never good. At least Lizzie and her family were here and safe under her roof. She said a quick prayer for Jack and his family and held the phone up to her ear. "Hello?"

"Mrs. Fisher. I got it."

It took a moment for Mary's mind to catch up. "Megan?"

"Yeah. I got the location of the laptop."

"Just now? How did you get that in the middle of the night?"

"It's almost seven." Megan laughed.

Mary's eyes flew to the clock on her bedside table. Megan was right. It was later than she'd thought. There was light creeping around the edges of her curtains. Mary had been so deeply asleep it only felt like the middle of the night. She pushed herself up.

"How did you find it?"

Megan sighed. "When you go on the Internet, you use an Internet service that someone is paying for, right? If it's at home, you pay for it as part of your phone bill, usually; at a library or café, you can access a wireless signal that the library or café is paying for, right?"

"Okay." Mary's uncaffeinated mind was moving slowly, but she was following so far.

"The phone company knows which MAC addresses have accessed that Internet signal. So my friend Stryper got access to the phone company's records, and he found that the laptop's MAC address had accessed a wireless signal at a place right around here since it was stolen."

"Meaning?" Sometimes Mary felt like Megan was speaking in riddles.

"Meaning we know of a wireless signal the thief used in the past few days. And that wireless signal is tied to a physical address, where the phone company sends the Internet bill."

Mary's heart skipped a beat. "You're saying you have the address where the thief is?"

"Was. The signal hasn't been accessed since yesterday afternoon, so there's no telling if our man is still there, but I can give you the address. Do you have a pen?"

"Hang on." Mary got a pen out of her purse and reached for the nearest piece of paper she could find—the back page of one of the paperbacks on her bedside table. "Got it."

"Okay. The last place the computer was logged on to the Internet was at this address: 124 Maplewood Lane, #2, in Barnstable."

Mary scribbled the address down. "I can't thank you enough."

"Let me know how it goes. I hope you catch this guy."

"Thanks." Mary tossed back the covers and stepped onto the soft carpet. "I plan to."

———

Mary was ready within minutes. She went downstairs and found Lizzie and Luke were already making pancakes together, and Mary told Lizzie the situation. Lizzie volunteered to open the store, and Mary gratefully accepted. She had a feeling things were going to work out just fine with Lizzie in the shop today. She buttered a bagel and tucked it into her purse. Then, before she left, she knocked on Betty's door to let her sister know what her plan was. To Mary's surprise, Betty was just slipping on her coat.

"I heard you tell Lizzie you knew where the computer is. I'm coming with you to get it."

"Betty, I don't think—"

But Betty was already hoisting her purse up on her shoulder. "Let's go get my money back."

Mary knew it wasn't that simple; they weren't going to just recover stacks of cash. In fact, if Mary's suspicions were correct, much of the money had already gone toward paying off the Harringtons' mortgage. But she also knew it would be pointless to fight against her older sister.

"Let's go, then," Mary said, and together they walked out to the car.

It was warmer today, and the sun was shining brilliantly. It felt nice after so much cold. Betty punched the address into her phone's mapping software, set it on the dashboard, and then settled behind the steering wheel. Betty drove, because Mary wanted to call Chief McArthur and update him on what she'd learned as they drove. He wasn't in yet, but Mary left a message on his voice mail telling him she had some new leads on the missing laptop and that he should call her.

Fifteen minutes later, they pulled into an apartment complex out by the highway, behind a shopping center, and drove along the rutted pavement until they found 124 Maplewood Lane. The paint was peeling on the door, and the stairs that led to the second floor were starting to rust.

"This is it," Mary said dubiously.

"Let's go, then." Betty grabbed her purse and stepped out, and Mary followed her up the stairs that snaked up the side of the building and shook with each step. They stopped on the landing on the second floor; in front of them was a door, its black paint turning up in the corners, and a high window. She knocked on the door and waited.

She didn't hear anything moving inside the apartment.

"Are you sure this is the right one?" Betty leaned back to check the number on the front of the building. Mary knocked again. Beneath them, in the parking lot, a woman was buttoning her coat and straining against the wind as she walked across the parking lot, but there was no noise from inside.

"Doesn't look like anyone's home," Betty said. Mary agreed, but then noticed envelopes sticking out of the mailbox. She opened the lid and took out a stack. There were a handful of catalogs for nice clothing stores, a few bills— addressed to Jonathan Harrington, Mary noted—and a letter from a bank. Mary studied the envelope from the bank. She recognized the name. This was the name of the bank that had held the mortgage on Peter Harrington's house.

Betty moved to the other side of the landing, stood on her tiptoes, and peeked in the window.

"Mary, come look at this."

Mary moved over and looked into what looked like the living room of the apartment. It was difficult to tell, though, because the room was completely empty. No furniture, no lamps, nothing on the walls. Just...empty.

"Is this where he lives?" Betty asked.

"I assumed so." Mary took in the empty room, looking for something, anything, to explain why Max's apartment was completely empty.

"Looks like he moved out."

Mary stepped back from the window, trying to make sense of it. At this point, all signs pointed to Max Harrington as the one who had stolen the computer. Had he taken off, just like that? Megan had said that the last time the Internet had been accessed here had been Wednesday afternoon, and it was Thursday morning now. Had he cleaned out his apartment and left in that time?

Actually, it made sense. Yesterday afternoon, Mary had talked to Max's mother; she could have called him and warned him that Mary had been asking after him. That might have spooked him into vacating. But if so, where had he gone?

Mary shook her head. She had thought they were so close. Now, she wasn't sure where to look. She would check with the leasing office, but she strongly suspected that Max hadn't left a forwarding address. What should she do now?

She looked down, and her eye caught on the envelope on the top of the stack in her hands. In the top left corner, there was a familiar logo. Where had she seen that logo before...?

And then it hit her. She knew how to find Jonathan Harrington.

# TWENTY-FOUR

⬥◆⬥

"Tell me what you know about Thomas Blakely," Mary said as Betty drove back toward Ivy Bay.

"Thomas?" Betty tapped her fingers on the steering wheel. "I thought we were looking for the waiter."

"I think they're connected." Mary told her how she now knew Thomas and Max had been working together. They had gone to boarding school together. The logo she'd seen on the alumni mailing from Meryton Academy in Max's mailbox was one she'd seen before—on the back window of his parents' car, for one, but also on Thomas's graduation announcement Betty had hanging in a magnetic frame on the fridge in their home. A quick call to the school had confirmed that Thomas and Max had been roommates their junior and senior years.

"So maybe they went to boarding school together. How does that mean they are responsible for stealing the laptop?"

"Trust me on this one. I think I'm on to something. What do you know about Thomas?"

"Well, I know he's been... troubled, I suppose you might say."

"Troubled?"

"Typical rich-kid problems. Father who works too much and buys expensive toys to make up for it; mother who puts too much pressure on her children; too much money and not enough supervision. That kind of thing."

Mary knew that Betty and Edward had tried hard to raise their son differently, even though Evan enjoyed some of the same advantages as Eleanor's children. They had put a lot of value on hard work and living modestly, and Evan was proof that their approach had been effective.

"He started acting out while he was at boarding school. He was suspended once or twice, I believe, but for some reason, the school always gave him a second chance." Betty rubbed her thumb across her fingertips to indicate money was actually the reason the school had taken him back.

"Do you know what he was suspended for?"

Betty shook her head. "I don't know many of the details. Eleanor didn't talk much about it, for obvious reasons. But I think I heard something about cheating once, and there might have been something about a theft? It was something small, like an old cell phone, and he had a good story about thinking it was his, so they couldn't prove he'd done it on purpose, I don't think."

"Wow. Not an auspicious start."

"I suppose everyone does dumb things when they're young." Betty turned on her blinker and turned right onto the main road. "Then he went off to Yale, just like his father and *his* father and basically every man in that family. He was studying computer science, and Eleanor was so proud of him. But then, earlier this year, right after Christmas, he dropped out."

"Dropped out, or was kicked out?"

"Unclear. All I know is that he was suddenly taking a break, and he moved back home. Only his parents wouldn't let him stay there, so he moved in with Eleanor."

"That says something, doesn't it? His own parents wouldn't let him move home?"

"Oh, I don't know. Like I said, that family has lots of problems. I don't know if they were mad or just disappointed or if they had something else entirely going on. All I know is that Eleanor took him in and made him work. That's why he was at the fund-raiser. She said if he was going to stay with her, he had to help her."

Mary mulled this all over as the scenery flew past the car windows. The roads and walkways were cleared for now, but patches of snow still clung to yards and covered open fields. If Thomas had been helping Eleanor with the party planning, could he have been to the museum and scoped out the computers before the party? That would have given him time to set up a plan to take the laptop during the party.

"Did Eleanor give Thomas a boat?"

Betty rolled her eyes. "Oh yes. As a graduation gift. You can imagine what we all thought of that. She even pays for him to keep it at the club. She spoils that boy. Always has. He was her first grandson, and she could never say no to him."

Mary mulled this over. She'd known about the boat, but she hadn't realized Eleanor paid for him to keep the boat at the club. That couldn't be cheap. It wasn't enough to explain why he would have stolen the laptop, but it did help show what kind of person he truly was—spoiled and entitled.

"Why didn't you tell me any of this about Thomas?"

"I didn't know Thomas was even under consideration. He wasn't on your list of suspects, last I checked. And if I remember correctly, he was talking to *you* in the video during the window of time the laptop was taken."

"I hadn't thought to think of him until I remembered how Luke stole the cookies."

"Huh?"

Mary explained the scenario as she thought it had happened. Max was desperate. His family had hit hard times and was about to lose their home. He had to drop out of college and was working to help out, but it wasn't enough. He connected with his old pal from high school—or maybe they'd been in touch the whole time. Mary wasn't sure, but she did know Thomas was no longer in college and suddenly found himself with time on his hands and in need of a way to change his situation. So they concocted a plan.

Thomas scoped out the museum and realized what its most valuable assets were—its donors' information. But the computers were in the office, in full view of Virginia's desk; to get access to those records, he'd have to do it while no one was in the office paying attention to the museum's computers. And somehow they'd come up with a plan to steal the laptop by creating a distraction during the party. Thomas had grown up around boats and had both the knowledge and the equipment to make the call; not only that, but he had known that making such a call would leave not only the glass decanter but also the back office unguarded. And Max would be able to talk his way into a job and gain access to the office. The plan worked as they'd hoped, and Max had stolen the laptop when he went down the hallway to reload the glasses.

"It sounds so far-fetched," Betty said as she turned onto Meeting House Road and followed it to where it looped around the pond and the Emerson gristmill in the oldest section of town. The water in the small pond was crusted with a thin layer of ice, and it sparkled in a thousand places, reflecting the winter sunlight. "Two prep-school kids making off with so much cash."

"But you're starting to believe it too, aren't you?"

Betty let out a long breath as she slowed the car and parked it in front of Eleanor's house. "I'm starting to think you might be on to something." She turned the key, and the car went silent.

Mary climbed out of her car, pulled her jacket tighter around her, and walked toward the front door. Eleanor lived in a large gray Federal-style house just across from the pond, on one of the most prominent locations in town. The house had been built by Isaac Emerson, a miller who built up a great fortune by charging his neighbors to use the gristmill, and it had stayed in the family ever since. It was a beautiful home, elegant and gracious, but Mary still felt trepidation as they knocked on the front door.

"Oh." Eleanor's eyes widened when she saw Mary and Betty on her porch. She kept the door pulled most of the way closed. "Well."

"Hi, Eleanor." Betty pushed the door open and stepped inside, and Mary was grateful her bossy older sister was here. "We have a couple of questions we'd like to ask Thomas. Is he here?"

"Well, why don't you come right on in?" Eleanor said, trying to regain control of the situation, but Betty was already heading up the stairs.

"He's not here," Eleanor called, but Betty didn't stop. The old stairs creaked and groaned with each step she took, but soon Eleanor and Mary trailed Betty down the wide-planked hallway. They passed a mahogany side table and a Federal-style convex mirror set above an old steamer trunk. Mary knew many of the antiques were original to the house and that Eleanor took great pride in keeping them polished and preserved. Betty finally stopped in front of a closed door, and she knocked gently.

"Like I said, he's not there," Eleanor called weakly, and Betty nodded and pushed the door open.

It was clear that he hadn't been there for a while, in fact. As they stepped into the room, Mary saw that the bed was neatly made, and there was a stack of mail piled on it. Most of the clothes in the closet were gone, and there was a cup of coffee on the bedside table with spots of mold growing on the top.

"When was the last time you saw him, Eleanor?" Betty asked.

"Why don't we go downstairs? We can talk there," Eleanor said, her voice weak. Betty and Eleanor stood still, watching each other, and then finally, Betty gave in.

"Okay, let's go downstairs," Betty agreed.

Mary followed Betty and Eleanor back down the stairs and into the formal living room. Eleanor gestured toward a love seat upholstered in an intricate tapestry design, and Mary and Betty sat there. It was stiff and hard and the seat was low to the ground, but Eleanor had set a couple of thin pillows on the cushion, and Mary adjusted them behind her while Eleanor settled into a high-backed chair. There were photographs in polished sterling-silver frames on the end tables and lined up along the mantel.

"Eleanor," Mary said gently, "do you have any idea where Thomas might be?"

"No." Eleanor looked down at her hands.

"When was the last time you saw him?" Mary continued.

Eleanor didn't say anything for a moment. Finally, she answered, "Sunday morning. He packed a bag and said he was going to visit a friend."

"And you haven't seen him since?"

She shook her head.

"Do you know what friend he was planning to visit or where?"

"He's not at his parents' place. And he's not answering his phone." Eleanor's voice cracked on the last word.

"You know why we're here, don't you?" Mary may have her differences with Eleanor, but she was a grandmother, and she knew what it was like to love your grandchild, to want to believe the best of them, no matter what.

"I was hoping it was all just a misunderstanding," Eleanor said quietly. "But I had begun to suspect..."

She let her voice trail off, as though she couldn't let herself voice the words.

"How long has Thomas been living here?" Mary asked gently.

"When he got kicked out of school, I said he could stay here, but there were conditions. One of the conditions was that he had to help me with the fund-raiser and whatever else I might need, and another was that his trust was frozen. I was sick about it. I didn't want to cut him off, but the tough-love thing didn't seem to be working, and I wasn't sure what else to do."

"Is there any chance he was able to get that account unfrozen?" Betty asked.

A young man used to spending money however he pleased no doubt didn't take kindly to suddenly seeing his funding cut off.

Eleanor shook her head. "I checked on that. But, then, when the money started disappearing from people's accounts, I..." She took a deep breath and sat up straighter.

"Was that the only thing that made you suspicious?" Betty asked. "Or was there more?"

Eleanor pressed her lips together. "Thomas had been to the museum with me the week before the party. He had even helped Taylor with something that wasn't working right on her computer Friday afternoon."

Mary's mind raced. Thomas had had access to the laptop itself, and therefore to the computer network. Mary could see it all in her head. Thomas, a computer-science major, offering to help her with some computer glitch. Poking around on the network. Could he have downloaded the database from the server then? Maybe he was interrupted, knew he had to come back and get that database? And then he schemed with Max to come up with a plan to get access to it for Saturday night?

"You always want to believe the best about your family, don't you?" Eleanor said quietly.

Mary's heart ached for Eleanor. She knew how hard this must be for her. "You do," Mary agreed, thinking back to her tumultuous week with her daughter.

"Do you know anything about a Max or Jonathan Harrington?" Betty asked. She was trying to change the topic, to shift it off of Thomas, and Eleanor seemed grateful.

"The name sounds vaguely familiar, but I don't know who that is."

"We think he may be a friend of Thomas's from boarding school who was working as a waiter at the party." Mary watched Eleanor's face carefully, but she didn't betray anything.

"I don't know." Eleanor shook her head. "Do you think they're together somewhere?"

"I think there's a good possibility," Mary said. She couldn't stand to see Eleanor's sad expression, and she turned to look at the collection of small-framed photos on the end table next to her. "He didn't say anything about where he was going?"

"No."

"Did he have any favorite places to hang out? Any place he'd always dreamed of visiting?" Betty asked.

"I suppose he could have gone back to stay with a friend at Yale," Eleanor said carefully.

It was a possibility, but Mary didn't think so. She knew the laptop had been in the area as recently as yesterday afternoon. They could have left town since then, though. Mary prayed she hadn't missed her window of opportunity.

Mary glanced at the yellowed photos of Eleanor's family— photos of Eleanor and Betty's husband, Edward, as children; a picture of her own children gathered around some long-gone Christmas tree; grandchildren sitting on a picnic table eating watermelon. Her eyes roamed across the photos, searching for something, anything to rest her eyes on.

And then she saw it. A photo of Thomas perched on the bow of a gleaming white boat. He was squinting into the sun, his khaki shorts slung low on his hips, his skin tanned and smooth. He looked happy.

Mary's pulse started racing. "I have an idea where Thomas is."

# TWENTY-FIVE

— ◆◆◆ —

Mary raced out to the car, with Betty and Eleanor trailing close behind. Mary stopped at the passenger door and waited while Eleanor picked her way across the icy street. Then, as Betty went around to the driver's side, Eleanor stared at Mary. Without a word, Mary moved to the back passenger door, and Eleanor climbed gracefully into the front seat.

Goodness. If Thomas had been willing to stand up to someone like Eleanor, there was no telling what he would do.

"Why would he be on his boat in February?" Betty asked as she drove toward the Highbourne Club. "Is that even possible?"

"Sure it's possible." Eleanor adjusted the strap of her seat belt. "Stupid, but possible."

"But there are other boats out." Mary felt like she was shouting to be heard from the backseat. "When I was at the club the other day, I saw them."

"Yes. Well." Eleanor adjusted in her seat. "Some people do enjoy winter sailing. And at Highbourne, they'll take care of a lot of the more mundane details for you."

"Mundane details like..."

"They'll hoist and haul your boat out of the water for you, as well as winterize it. They drain the pipes and check it before they store it. All the things that make it...well, irritating to deal with boating in the winter."

"Ah." It must be nice. "So it would be feasible for Thomas and Jonathan to have gotten the boat out last night."

"Oh, sure. But"—Eleanor seemed to have to strain to make herself say the words—"if they did that, they probably would have taken off already."

Mary hadn't even thought about that possibility. Could they have sailed away, escaped to Canada—probably no farther than that, not yet—and succeeded in their plan?

"Let's not jump to conclusions," Betty said and turned off the main road and onto a side road that ran toward the water. "We knew the laptop was used at Jonathan's apartment yesterday afternoon. Even if they got the boat out last night, they wouldn't have headed out in the dark, right?" Betty turned to Eleanor, who nodded glumly.

"I sure hope they didn't."

"Even if they really are at the boat, which is still a guess at this point, they probably stayed somewhere last night and got the boat out this morning," Betty continued. "So there's a chance they're still there."

"Why don't we just call the club and ask if they got Thomas's boat out for him?" Mary asked.

"They won't tell us." Eleanor craned her neck to look for the club around the curve in the road.

"They won't tell his own grandmother whether he's using the boat slip you pay for?"

"The club is very"—Eleanor coughed—"discreet."

"Discreet." Mary rolled the word around on her tongue, trying to make sense of it.

"Lots of things happen there that people don't necessarily want to get back to their families, the cops, or whatever," Betty translated. "The staff there is paid not to notice most of what goes on around them."

Goodness. It had seemed like such a nice place when Mary had gone there for lunch. She'd had no idea it had such a seedy underbelly.

"We'll be there in just a minute, anyway," Eleanor said, and directed Betty to the valet parking near the front entrance. The two women in front climbed out of the car and headed toward the door, but Mary was still sitting in the backseat. That was it? They just handed this stranger the car keys and went inside? Mary shook her head. She wasn't used to this.

She pushed the car door open just as Eleanor turned back to yell, "Come on, Mary!"

Mary trailed Eleanor and Betty as they walked through the lobby. Several people said hello to Eleanor, and she smiled and waved as if this were just a perfectly normal day at the club. They threaded their way through the seating area by the back door, waving and smiling, and finally stepped out onto the docks at the back of the building. She blinked against the bright sun, which sparkled off the bay, as she followed Eleanor down the dock. She turned left at a T and followed the dock where it branched off over the water.

And then, suddenly, Eleanor stopped. Mary looked up and saw what she was looking at. There, in a boat slip halfway down the dock, was a sailboat with the words *Lazy Days* on the side.

"That's it," Eleanor said. "That's his boat."

For a moment, they all stood, frozen, on the dock. Finally, Mary reached down and pulled her cell phone out of her purse.

"What are you doing?" Betty asked.

"Calling Chief McArthur."

"Oh, Mary..." Eleanor looked at her, pleading in her eyes. "Do we need to bring the police in? We don't know for sure—"

"Ivy Bay Police," the voice on Mary's phone answered.

Mary asked to be put through to the police chief, and a moment later, she explained where she was and what was happening.

"Stay right where you are, Mary. I'll have someone out there in a few minutes to board that boat. Under no circumstances should you get on that boat yourself."

"Got it. We'll be here," Mary said. She hung up and then turned to Betty and Eleanor. "He says to wait here. They're sending someone to check it out."

Betty nodded, but Eleanor bit her lip, turned her face away, and then started off down the dock toward the boat.

"Eleanor!" Betty called, but she kept walking.

Mary looked at Betty and then back at Eleanor, and then started after her. "Eleanor, wait." Mary caught up with her and reached out her hand, touching Eleanor's shoulder. "Stop. Chief McArthur wants us to wait."

Eleanor whipped around, and Mary saw tears streaming down her cheeks. "If you think I'm going to stand idly by and wait for the police to come arrest my grandson, then you're out of your mind." She shrugged Mary's hand off her shoulder and started walking again.

For a moment, Mary stood stunned. She tried to imagine what she would do if the police were coming for Luke. She would want justice to be done, and yet—

And yet she loved that child so much she wasn't sure what she wouldn't do to protect him. It didn't matter if he had hurt her, or stolen from her, as Thomas had from Eleanor—her love was strong enough to forgive just about anything. She'd want to help him, no matter what.

Mary took off down the dock and reached Eleanor just as she got to the boat. Eleanor was already climbing over the low railing and stepping onto the deck.

"Thomas!" Eleanor called.

Mary climbed carefully on board after her. Betty trailed behind. "You stay on the dock, Betty. We'll be right back."

"Thomas, I know you're in here," Eleanor called.

The cockpit at the rear of the boat was empty, but a set of small steps led down into a small living area, and Mary heard a bang from inside. Eleanor scrambled down the steps, and Mary followed just behind her. They stepped into a low living area, with a galley kitchen on the far end. Thomas and Jonathan were standing next to a foldout table, half-eaten sandwiches in front of them. A sleek silver laptop lay at the end of the table.

"Grandma, what are you doing here?" Thomas said, his voice high and tight.

"A better question is, what are *you* doing here?" Somehow, even in this tense situation, with tears streaming down her cheeks, Eleanor still managed to be intimidating. She crossed her arms over her chest and narrowed her eyes at her grandson.

Thomas studied her, trying to gauge how much she knew. "It's such a nice day, we were thinking of going for a sail," he ventured.

"I'm not an idiot. Don't lie to me," Eleanor said.

Mary stepped forward and moved toward the laptop as casually as she could.

"The police are on their way, Thomas. You only have a few minutes to convince me that this situation is very, very different than how it looks," Eleanor said.

Jonathan lunged for the laptop. Mary grabbed for it too, but he was closer, and Mary's fingers grazed the smooth surface as he tucked it under his arm and barreled toward the steps. The laptop safe in his care, Jonathan hesitated, watching Thomas for instructions. Mary heard Betty step onto the boat, and her heart sank. She prayed Betty would at least have the good sense to stay off it.

"Liar." Thomas stood still, defiant. "You would never call the cops on me."

Eleanor brushed a hand against her cheek and wiped away a tear. "You're right. I didn't call the police. But Mary did."

Mary watched as a look of pure hatred washed over Thomas's face. "It's a victimless crime," he said defiantly. "The bank refunds all the money, anyway. No one gets hurt."

Eleanor, for once in her life, seemed speechless.

The sound of sirens rang out.

"Toss it," Thomas called, and Jonathan ran up the stairs. Mary followed him.

"Watch it," Betty said as he pushed past her, and she, too, lunged after him as he headed toward the side of the deck.

"How many old ladies are after you, Thomas?" Jonathan yelled, and despite the situation, Mary felt the urge to laugh. She grabbed the back of his sweater, but Jonathan was stronger than she was, and a moment later, she watched as the laptop toppled over the side of the boat and sank into Cap Cod Bay.

"It doesn't matter," Mary said. "We have all the evidence to prove that you two stole the laptop and used it to rob several people."

Jonathan was heading back into the galley, dragging Mary, who still clung to his sweater, with him. The sirens grew louder.

"We gotta get out of here, bro," he called, ducking his head inside, and Mary saw that Thomas was already nudging Eleanor out of the way as he moved toward the stairs. Mary tried to hold Jonathan back as he turned and scrambled across the cockpit toward the dock.

Jonathan cursed as the sirens stopped. The police were at the club. Jonathan mumbled under his breath and untied the ropes that anchored the boat to the dock. Then he moved toward the steering wheel in the cockpit at the rear of the boat. Mary clung to his sweater the whole time. Betty reached for Jonathan as well, and together, the two sisters tried to yank him back toward the dock, but then Mary heard the sound of the motor kick on.

"What's going on?" Betty asked, and Mary shook her head, though she had a very bad feeling. Chief McArthur burst out of the back doors of the club, coming toward them.

"Don't you dare! Thomas Alexander Blakely!" She heard Eleanor shouting from inside the boat, but Jonathan was already backing the boat away from the dock.

Chief McArthur, followed by two deputies, raced down the dock toward them.

Mary wasn't sure what to do. Should she try to jump? She eyed the distance between the boat and the dock and realized she'd never make it. Should she try to wrest the steering wheel away from Jonathan and steer back into the dock? She didn't have the slightest idea how to drive this boat or how she'd tear Jonathan away. But she couldn't just stay here.

"Mary?" Betty said, clinging to the railing at the stern of the boat, her eyes wide. Mary saw that Betty was trembling.

"Mary!" Chief McArthur called, but whatever he said next was swallowed by the wind.

"Come on, Betty." She grabbed for her sister's hand. She wanted to get Betty inside, off the deck, toward relative safety. If someone fell over the side into the icy water, their chances were not good.

"Where are we going?" Betty asked weakly, but she grabbed Mary's hand.

"I don't know." All Mary could tell was that they were not obeying the marina's no-wake rule as they raced toward open water. "I don't think they know. I think Jonathan just panicked." She put her arm around Betty, navigated around the boom, and steered her inside. "But Chief McArthur saw. He'll send help."

Down in the living quarters, Mary found Eleanor sitting on a bench, crying, while Thomas yanked open drawers and rummaged through them, cursing under his breath. Betty sat down at the table. And then the engine sputtered.

"What the—"

"Thomas?" Eleanor looked up at him through tears.

Jonathan started the motor again, and it ran for a moment and then sputtered again. The boat shook.

"When did they put the boat in the water?" Eleanor asked, her eyes now wide.

"This morning." Thomas's face was suddenly white. "The guys from the club were getting it set up for us, and we came on to grab lunch. They were going to come back and finish hooking everything up."

The engine revved, but the motor was struggling.

"Hooking everything up?" Eleanor's voice was like steel. "You had it winterized in the fall, right?" Thomas nodded. "And they hadn't finished 'hooking everything up' when we pulled away from the dock?"

Thomas nodded and grasped the counter behind him to hold himself up.

"Dear Lord," Eleanor said, jumping up. She scrambled up the stairs and wrenched the steering wheel from Jonathan. Thomas ran up behind her. Mary started to follow, but then she spotted it, in one of the open drawers. A marine radio—perhaps the one Thomas had used to make the fake distress call in the first place.

"You idiot!" Eleanor was screaming at Jonathan, and a moment later, the engine went dead.

Mary didn't know what was wrong, but she could feel that something was definitely happening to the boat, as it started to list to the right. She grasped the radio and tried to remember what Lieutenant Peters had told her about how it worked.

She turned the dials and found what she hoped was channel sixteen. "Help," she cried, as the boat lurched again to the side. *Oh, Lord, please don't let us swamp*, she prayed. "Help!"

Wait, no, that wasn't right.

"Mayday, Mayday, Mayday," she said and then let go of the button and waited. There was nothing but silence. She tried it again. Again, she waited, and there was no response. Her heart started to sink. But then the radio crackled to life.

"Roger Mayday. This is the United States Coast Guard. What is your location?" a man at the other end of the radio said.

"Thank you!" Tears stung her eyes. "This is Mary Fisher. We're in a boat on the water just outside the Highbourne Club. We've been kidnapped, and there's something wrong with the boat. Please send help, quickly!"

"Roger. Mary Fisher, please switch to channel one four for instructions."

Mary stared at the radio, trying to remember what Lieutenant Peters had shown her. She tried it and then tried again, and a moment later, she was talking to the coast guard again.

"Mary Fisher, we're sending help. Can you tell us anything about your location?"

Mary stood on the bottom step and poked her head out onto the deck. "We're moving east, away from Ivy Bay. I can see the lighthouse a little ways ahead of us." Mary gasped as she saw that the boat sat much lower in the water than it had a few minutes ago. Something was definitely wrong.

"So you see land to the starboard side?"

Mary had to think for a minute, but finally, she agreed that yes, she did.

There was a thud below them. Then Thomas cursed, and the boat listed farther to the right. "What was that?" Betty's eyes were wide, and she was trembling more.

"I think the boat is sinking," Mary said into the radio. Carrying the radio, she started up the steps to the cockpit. She looked back at Betty, who had her eyes closed and was mumbling something under her breath. She was praying. Mary added her prayers as she rushed up the steps.

"I've got it," Thomas was yelling, knocking Eleanor's hands away from the steering wheel. Jonathan stood by, his face white, as the boat continued to list. "If you would just *back off,* I could fix this." He struggled to regain control of the wheel as Eleanor reached for it.

"Thomas Alexander Blakely, you will listen to me right now," Eleanor said in a voice so chilling, so commanding even Mary stopped in place. "I have been sailing decades longer than you have. If any of us are going to get out of this alive, you will hand the controls to me right now."

Thomas looked from Eleanor to Jonathan, who nodded, his face white. Then, slowly, he released the controls, and Eleanor grabbed them. Mary felt a surge of affection for Eleanor. She was in charge here, that was clear, and Mary could not be more thankful.

"The engine is off," Mary said into the radio.

"Roger."

Thomas and Jonathan turned to Mary, their mouths open, and Mary lifted her chin. They had clearly underestimated this bunch of old ladies.

"Grandma, we're fine," Thomas was saying. He scrambled up into the bit of higher deck and started untying the boat's main sail. "We'll just use wind power."

"Clearly, you should have spent more time learning about your own boat." Eleanor's mouth was set in a thin line. "Do you know what happens when the club winterizes a boat?"

Thomas shook his head, but he was only half listening, working on freeing the sail.

"They flush the hoses with antifreeze and disconnect them. So if the man from the club had not yet hooked the hoses back up"—Thomas stopped what he was doing and listened—"then the hose that is supposed to be funneling water to the engine has been funneling gallons of seawater directly into the engine compartment instead. Every second the motor was running was bringing more water in to sink this thing."

Thomas looked down at his feet like a little boy who'd just been scolded.

"You'd better keep working on that sail, boy, and steer us back toward land quickly," Eleanor said.

Mary had been so thankful for the clear, warm day earlier, but now she wished for large gusts of wind.

"It's hard to say how much water is on board, but judging by how quickly we're going down in the water, I'd say there's not much chance we can bail it out quickly enough." Eleanor moved up to where Thomas stood and helped him let out the boom, searching for the wind. "Our only hope is catching a few big gusts."

Mary prayed like she'd never prayed before and kept her eyes on the water around the boat.

And then, off to the left, there was a boat. Mary could just make out the orange side of the small skiff she'd seen in the Ivy Bay Marina.

Something below them groaned, and there was a metallic clang as the boat sank lower into the freezing water. Mary headed downstairs and told Betty to come up to a higher level.

"Is it bad?" Betty asked, but her eyes showed she already knew the truth. Water was starting to collect on the floor of the cabin.

"The coast guard is almost here," Mary said, helping her sister up. She gathered the life jackets she'd seen under the bench by the table, helped Betty climb up to the deck level, and prayed as the coast guard boat inched closer. She handed out life jackets, and even Jonathan and Thomas took them without a word. Off in the distance, she saw other boats on the horizon, racing toward their injured craft. There must be at least half a dozen boats on their way to help. Mary's distress call had brought in the cavalry.

Something underneath them collapsed, and they were only a few feet above the water level now. Despite the warm day, the wind out on the open water was bitterly cold. Mary had never been more thankful for the good people of Ivy Bay, who had once again dropped everything to rescue a troubled boat.

The coast guard boat was the first to arrive, and Mary and Eleanor helped Betty scamper across the slick deck and into the waiting arms of Lieutenant Peters. Eleanor went next, and she settled gracefully onto the rescue boat. She adjusted the orange life preserver around her neck and sat back like there was no place she'd rather be. Mary may not ever come to enjoy being around Eleanor, but she sure was thankful for her today.

By that time, the Ivy Bay police boat had arrived, and the deputies boarded the sinking ship and cuffed Thomas and Jonathan before loading them onto the police boat.

A deputy held out his hand to help Mary come too, but Mary shook her head. Just behind the police boat, the *Misty Horizon* was idling. When the police boat moved out of the way, Henry quickly steered his clunky boat as close as he could get and held out his arms. Mary fell into them gratefully, and Henry rushed back to the controls and moved his boat away from the sinking ship.

Mary followed him into the control room and stood next to him. Henry scooted over and made room on the bench. Then he pulled a heavy parka out from a storage area under the steering wheel and handed it to her. She slipped it on and sighed. Suddenly, Mary felt as if she had no strength left in her body.

"You came."

"Of course I came. As did just about every boater in town."

Mary looked around and saw that Henry was right. Boats were arriving from every direction, racing toward the craft, which now had most of its cabin below sea level.

Henry's radio crackled to life, and Mary heard Lieutenant Peters announce that the boaters were safe and no more help was needed.

"I was finishing getting my boat cleaned up when I heard the distress call come in. I was able to get out quickly, so even though the other boats were faster, I got here as soon as I could."

"You were still at the marina?" Mary looked at the small digital clock on Henry's dashboard and realized that it wasn't even noon yet. This day had already felt like a lifetime, and it was still morning.

"I was, and when I heard it was Mary Fisher calling for help, I couldn't believe it. I got out here as soon as I could."

"Thank you." She sagged against his warm body, and he took one hand off the steering wheel and wrapped his arm around her.

Up ahead, Mary could see the Highbourne Club, but the coast guard boat and the police boat raced past it, back toward the spit of land that stuck out into the bay. They were headed for the Ivy Bay Marina. Henry's boat was bigger and heavier than the other two boats, built more for sturdiness than for speed, and the others would get in before they did. That was okay with Mary. Henry had gotten there quickly when he needed to, and now she didn't mind resting here with him. She already felt safe, and even with the craziness of what had just happened still playing through her mind, she kind of enjoyed being here out on the water with him.

"So are you going to explain what you were doing out there on a sailboat in February?"

Mary turned her head so she could look back. Just the masts of Thomas's boat were visible now, the whole deck and cabin submerged. It was hard to imagine she'd been standing there only moments before.

"I will later," Mary promised. "But for now, let's just say we caught the thieves."

Henry laughed. "Of course you did, Mary." He shook his head. "You always do."

Mary watched as the tall, proud mast sank lower and lower into the bay, until there were mere inches left. And then, in the blink of an eye, it slipped under the water. Just like that, the boat was gone, traveling toward its final destination on the bottom of Cape Cod Bay. If you didn't know any better, you'd never know it had been there at all.

"What are you thinking?" Henry asked as Mary turned her head and looked forward again. They were edging around the spit of land, and up ahead, Mary could see the masts of the boats in the Ivy Bay Marina.

A thousand thoughts ran through her head. She thought about how she'd put Betty in danger, and Eleanor as well. She thought about how she couldn't wait to hug her daughter and her grandchildren, and how much she was looking forward to going back to being a bookseller. She thought about how God had protected them out on that bay, how He protected her again and again from the messes she managed to get herself into.

"I'm thinking how much I have to be grateful for."

"Amen to that," Henry said and pulled her closer.

As they entered the marina, Mary could see Eleanor and Betty huddled on the dock, reflective Mylar blankets around their shoulders. A little way down from them, Jonathan and Thomas were being shoved into a police car. Behind them, the windows on the Harbor View restaurant gleamed in the bright midday sun; beyond the marina, she could see the glass museum and the rooftops of the houses and the spire of Grace Church rising straight and proud into the air. She lifted her eyes heavenward.

Yes, she had a lot to be grateful for, indeed.

# TWENTY-SIX

——— ◆◆◆ ———

It was late afternoon before Mary was released from the police station. She, Betty, and Eleanor had repeated their story several times. Mary made a statement, and finally, Chief McArthur released them. Betty and Eleanor headed home to change into warm, dry clothes and to rest, but Mary decided to go to the bookstore.

The bell over the door dinged as she stepped inside, and Lizzie waved. She was just leading three teenage boys to the counter, each one holding a copy of *The Adventures of Sherlock Holmes.*

Mary went into the back room and hung up her jacket while Lizzie was ringing the boys up. Then, after they left, she made herself a cup of coffee and settled down on the stool next to Lizzie. The noise woke up Gus, who yawned, stretched, and hopped up on Mary's lap. She stroked his fur gently and sipped her coffee.

"Rough day?" Lizzie asked as she sat down on the other stool.

"You could say that." She rubbed the soft fur under Gus's chin, and he purred and stretched his neck up to the ceiling.

"Aunt Betty called and filled me in on the whole story. I'm glad you're okay."

"When did she do that?" Part of her wished Betty had left it to Mary to share the story, but another part of her was grateful she didn't have to figure out a way to broach the subject herself.

"While you were giving your statement to the police." Lizzie reached out and scratched Gus behind the ears. "What in the world possessed you to get on that boat, Mom?"

"Eleanor."

"Ah."

"She got on first. I had to go after her."

"Of course you had to." Lizzie's voice dripped with sarcasm. "I'm glad you called for help when you did."

"Me too," Mary said. "How were things here?"

"Just fine, actually. I think I'm finally starting to get the hang of it." Lizzie laughed. She and the rest of the family were heading home the day after tomorrow. "Just in time."

"I really appreciate all your help this week." Mary took another sip of her coffee and savored the warmth as it went down. Out there on the boat this morning, she thought she'd never be warm again.

Lizzie snorted. "I think we both know I wasn't much help."

"Of course you were." Gus nuzzled her hand to remind her to keep petting him, and she stroked his back absently. "If you hadn't been here, I wouldn't have been able to go out and solve the mystery. I never would have been able to catch up with Thomas and Jonathan today."

"Is that supposed to make me feel better? Without me, you wouldn't have been out on the bay on a sinking ship with a couple of thieves?"

"It was supposed to make you feel better, yes, but when you say it like that, I can see how it didn't." Mary wrapped her hands around her cup. "I'm glad you were here this week, Elizabeth. I know I don't always do the best job showing it, but I love spending time with you, and I couldn't be more proud of you."

Lizzie didn't say anything for a moment. Then, slowly, a shy smile broke through.

"Thanks, Mom. Same here." She petted Gus gently. "And this store really is amazing. I can't believe what you've done. A whole second career."

Lizzie went quiet again, and Mary had a feeling she knew what Lizzie was thinking about. She tried to phrase her next words carefully. "Have you thought any more about the job?"

A pained look crossed her face, and Mary wondered if she should have avoided the subject, but then Lizzie spoke.

"I'm going to tell them no. As much as I want the job, I'm not ready." She bit her lip and looked down at the counter like she couldn't look Mary in the eye. "I guess I'm not as good at balancing everything as you always were."

"Oh, honey." Mary didn't know what to say. Is that what Lizzie really thought? Mary had always felt like she was doing some crazed juggling act, that some ball was always falling, that it was always all about to land on the ground. She had loved her life, but it wasn't necessarily exactly what she wanted for her daughter. How had she managed to convey that she wanted Lizzie to be just like her? "I'm glad you're making the right decision for your family. If you still want to teach, there is plenty of time for that later. The most important thing is that you do what's best for you and for your children, no matter what that is."

Gus poked his nose toward Lizzie. She sniffed, and he moved off of Mary and stepped gingerly into her lap.

"Really?" Lizzie rubbed her hand along Gus's soft head. "You don't think I'm taking the easy way out?"

Mary laughed. "I've spent time with those kids this week. Staying home to focus on them is *not* easy."

Lizzie laughed a little too. "No, it's not," she agreed.

"Those kids are very lucky," Mary said softly, "to have a mother who loves them so much."

"They're the best thing in my world." Lizzie sighed as Gus snuggled in, rubbing his head against her arm. "And I'm pretty lucky when it comes to mothers too. Thanks for putting up with me this week."

"I didn't put up with you. I've loved having you here, and I'm so thankful for your help in the shop."

Mary looked around her little shop, taking in the warm coral walls, the cheerful fire dancing in the fieldstone hearth, the inviting reading chairs, the cozy children's nook. She couldn't be prouder of the life she'd built here. Stepping inside the store made her feel full in a way very few things in life ever had.

But then she looked back at her daughter. She was so beautiful, so precious, and Mary had loved watching her grow into a strong, confident, caring mother herself. Looking at her now, Mary knew that nothing in this shop—nothing in the world—could ever compare to the fullness in her heart when she saw her daughter.

She only had one more precious day with Lizzie and her family before they packed up and headed home. Mary looked around the empty shop one more time. Then she thought about Emma and Luke, the way they flew at her when she came in the door, their soft squishy hugs and their sweet little voices that said the funniest things.

And then she got up, flipped the little sign on the door to Shut, and started straightening the books on the front table.

"We're closing early today."

Lizzie looked up, her eyebrow cocked. "But those kids might be coming in for their books for class."

"They can come back tomorrow. Today, I'm going to spend every last moment I can with the people I love more than anything in this world."

"Who's that?"

Lizzie was holding back a smile, and Mary laughed and gestured for her to get up and help her.

"Sorry, Gus. We're closing early today." Lizzie set the cat gently on the floor, and he protested loudly but then went to his spot by the radiator and settled back down.

"I am going to miss this place. It's been great working here."

"I'm sure you'll have plenty of other opportunities, if you ever want to come back. I have an in with the owner." Mary laughed.

She knew Lizzie wouldn't likely ever come back to work with her again, and maybe that was for the best. But today, she couldn't wait to get home and enjoy the most precious thing in her life. She held the door open as Lizzie stepped out, and together, they headed home.

# ABOUT THE AUTHOR

Elizabeth Adams lives in New York City with her husband. When she's not writing, she spends her time playing with their rambunctious daughter, cleaning up after two devious cats, and trying to find time to read mysteries.

# A CONVERSATION WITH ELIZABETH ADAMS

————◆◆◆————

**Q:** *You live in the northeast, like Mary, and this book is set in winter. How do you spend the cold winters?*

**A:** I shiver. I long for spring. My husband, who is from Michigan and is much better at dealing with the cold, bought me a giant puffy parka that looks like a sleeping bag. It looks ridiculous, but I love that coat. It gets me through the winters.

**Q:** *Do you have any favorite winter activities?*

**A:** When it's cold out, I try to stay inside as much as possible. I'm not one of those people who can't wait to strap on a pair of skis or grab a sled. I go out to run, but that's not because I love being out in the cold, it's because I have to get exercise. Is it fair to call reading an activity? I hope so, even though it's not particularly active, because that's my first choice in the winter (well, and the summer...).

**Q:** *What's your favorite recipe or something you're "famous" for making?*

**A:** I think it's fair to say I'm not famous for making anything. But I do like to make homemade pizza on nights when I can't think of anything else. I use my bread maker to make dough for the crust, and then top it with whatever's in the fridge. Often that's tomatoes and mozzarella, with basil from the garden. Sometimes I'll cut up and stir-fry onions with green and red peppers and top with blue cheese. On nights when the cupboard is particularly bare, I've been known to top the crust with chopped kale, white beans, and parmesan. Trust me, it's better than it sounds. I always add a drizzle of good olive oil and some sea salt. You really can't go wrong. It's almost as easy as ordering a pizza and way healthier (and generally more delicious).

**Q:** *Eleanor is proud of Ivy Bay's glass museum. What parts of where you live are you most proud?*

**A:** I live in a gritty part of Brooklyn, where car repair shops and manufacturing warehouses are as common as houses. But our little block is an oasis, lined with beautiful homes and arching trees. Neighbors say hi to each other and look out for one another. We have planting parties in the spring, where we get together to beautify the street, and we have a big block party every fall. I'm proud of how my neighbors have come together and made this block something we can all be proud of.

**Q:** *If you could vacation anywhere in the world, where would you go?*

**A:** Oh goodness. This is difficult. How long do I have? What's my budget? If I have just a few days to get away and relax, I would probably go to Cape Cod. But there are so many places in the world I haven't seen yet. There are a lot of places in Europe I still want to see—Italy, Germany, and Switzerland, to start. But I love South and Central

America too, and I'd love to make it to Africa or India someday. I don't know. This is too hard. Next question.

Q: *When you visit quaint little towns like Ivy Bay, what are your first stops?*
A: I usually find out where the locals eat and go there for a meal. Touristy places are fine, but for a taste of what life is really like in a new place, that's the best bet—and it often has the best food!

Q: *Do you know anyone like Henry in your life?*
A: I guess I have to say my husband here, right? Luckily, it's true. My husband Wayne is the most caring, trustworthy guy I know. He would drop everything to help a stranger, and he always makes me laugh. I'm glad I snagged him.

# MARY'S HOT CHOCOLATE

On a blustery winter day, Mary loves nothing more than to curl up with a book and a cup of hot cocoa. Here's how she makes it. This recipe serves four.

*¼ cup powdered unsweetened cocoa*
*¼ cup sugar*
*pinch salt*
*4 cups whole milk*
*½ teaspoon vanilla*
*whipped cream or marshmallows to top (if desired)*

Blend the dry ingredients with about a half-cup of milk over very low heat in a small saucepan, stirring until smooth. Stir in the rest of the milk, beating with a wire whisk. Heat the mixture over medium-low heat, stirring occasionally, until hot. Add the vanilla, stir, and pour evenly into four mugs. Top with whipped cream or marshmallows.

# FROM THE GUIDEPOSTS ARCHIVES

*And God saw every thing that he had made, and, behold, it was very good....*—Genesis 1:31 (KJV)

After seven months of motherhood I was fed up. The cycle of diapers, dishes and chasing a crawling child seemed tedious and often unimportant. How I yearned for an *important* job to do—one where I could make decisions that mattered and lunch with people who went places and did things. Instead, I lunched with a child who usually spilled his food.

Then I found the weed. I nearly missed it, hidden behind the grapefruit tree. It wasn't very big—fifty like it would have hardly filled my palm. And yet, how perfect! A royal purple center surrounded by seven of the tiniest white petals, each as carefully designed and executed as a prize-winning rose.

God hadn't seemed to care, making that weed, whether anybody else thought it was important or not, or even whether anybody saw it or not. The important thing was to make it as perfectly as possible. Somehow, seeing it nestled in the grass behind the tree, I sensed that just making it had given its Creator joy.

Few of us are engaged in what the world calls "important" work. But God's idea of importance is so different from the world's. A tiny hidden weed receives the same loving, careful attention as a universe.

*Lord, give us Your perspective on life. Show us the true meaning of "importance."*—Patricia Houck Sprinkle

# A NOTE FROM THE EDITORS

———◆▸◆◂◆———

We hope you enjoy Secrets of Mary's Bookshop, created by the Books and Inspirational Media Division of Guideposts, a nonprofit organization. In all of our books, magazines and outreach efforts, we aim to deliver inspiration and encouragement, help you grow in your faith, and celebrate God's love in every aspect of your daily life.

Thank you for making a difference with your purchase of this book, which helps fund our many outreach programs to the military, prisons, hospitals, nursing homes and schools. To learn more, visit GuidepostsFoundation.org.

We also maintain many useful and uplifting online resources. Visit Guideposts.org to read true stories of hope and inspiration, access OurPrayer network, sign up for free newsletters, download free e-books, join our Facebook community, and follow our stimulating blogs.

To learn about other Guideposts publications, including the best-selling devotional *Daily Guideposts*, go to ShopGuideposts.org, call (800) 932-2145 or write to Guideposts, PO Box 5815, Harlan, Iowa 51593.